For George Mann and Ian Whates

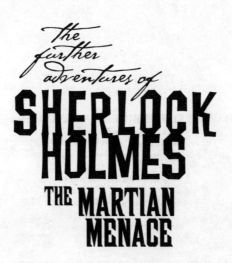

the
further
adventures of
# SHERLOCK HOLMES
## THE MARTIAN MENACE

ERIC BROWN

TITAN BOOKS

THE FURTHER ADVENTURES OF SHERLOCK HOLMES:
THE MARTIAN MENACE
Print edition ISBN: 9781789092950
E-book edition ISBN: 9781789092967

Published by Titan Books
A division of Titan Publishing Group Ltd
144 Southwark Street, London SE1 0UP

First Titan edition: February 2020
10 9 8 7 6 5 4 3 2 1

A CIP catalogue record for this title is available from the British Library.

Printed and bound by CPI Group (UK) Ltd, Croydon CR0 4YY

What did you think of this book? We love to hear from our readers.
Please email us at: readerfeedback@titanemail.com,
or write to Reader Feedback at the above address.

To receive advance information, news, competitions, and exclusive offers
online, please sign up for the Titan newsletter on our website:
**www.titanbooks.com**

# *Prologue*

*The Tragic Affair of the Martian Ambassador*

In the spring of 1910, Sherlock Holmes was involved in a singular investigation that was to have far-reaching consequences for my friend, for myself, and for the world at large – though little did I realise this at the time.

Shortly after the second Martian invasion, Holmes decided that the quiet life of beekeeping at his Sussex cottage was not for him. He elected to curtail his retirement, return to London, and resume his vocation as a consulting detective. Interesting developments, to say the least, were occurring in the capital, and Holmes told me that he wished to be in the thick of it.

On the morning in question I was reading *The Times* and Holmes was poring over his recently acquired *Encyclopaedia Martiannica*. At one point I set aside the paper and glanced across at my friend, who had taken a break from his studies and was stuffing his pipe.

"What are you reading about now?" I enquired.

He flicked a negligent hand at the open encyclopaedia. "An entry on the biology of the Martian race," he said. "Did you know, Watson, that Martians are not asexual, as first supposed, but hermaphroditic, and sprout their young in sacs attached to their integument?"

"I must admit my ignorance in that area," I said.

"And were you aware, moreover, that they did not partake of human blood during the first invasion in '94, as described in one or two of the more sensational newspapers at the time? They might have laid waste to vast swathes of our planet, and killed tens of thousands into the bargain, but they were not blood-drinkers. Hullo, and what's this?" he said, interrupted by a commotion in the street.

I glanced through the window in time to see an electrical car swerve to avoid an obstruction in the road, blaring its horn as it did so. The saloon had fetched up on the pavement and a noisy crowd had gathered and was remonstrating – not with the driver, I hasten to add, but at the cause of the vehicle's sudden veering from the highway.

"My word," I said.

Planted in the very centre of the road, solid and immovable, was a gunmetal grey girder pocked with rivets the size of saucers – the leg of a Martian tripod.

These were the vehicles that had wrought such havoc around the world in 1894, until common terrestrial viruses had proved the invaders' undoing. Little did we know back then, as we celebrated our unlikely salvation, that a second wave of Martian spaceships would make its way across the gulf of space six years later, this armada bearing more peaceable extraterrestrials inoculated against Earth's microscopic defenders.

Holmes joined me at the window as a hatch swung open in the underbelly of the tripod's domed cabin. What emerged from within, descending on an elevator plate, was the squat, tentacled form of a Martian.

I might mention here that I have been taxed as to how to refer to the Martians in this account. As Holmes had mentioned, they were hermaphroditic, and by rights perhaps I should call a singular Martian 'it'; however, it seems demeaning to refer to them in this way, so I shall employ the terms 'he', 'him' and 'his' from now on.

As the alien descended, a knot of curious citizens watched his progress. Although the Martians occupied our planet in their hundreds of thousands, it was not every day that one of their number was seen, as it were, in the flesh. Their singular three-legged transportation devices might have ubiquitously prowled the capital from Richmond to East Ham, and from Barnet to Croydon, but the creatures themselves showed a distinct inclination towards privacy.

A police constable was soon on the scene, and this worthy met the Martian at ground level and escorted him through the rapidly parting crowd.

Holmes rubbed his hands together in delight. "Why, I do believe, Watson, that the Martian is making a beeline towards 221B."

Indeed, the alien was hauling his bulk up the steps towards our front door.

Presently Mrs Hudson, appearing unaccustomedly agitated, burst into the room. "Mr Holmes!" she cried. "Would you credit it, but there's one of those horrible Martian creatures downstairs, and it says it wants to see you promptly!"

My friend smiled. "Then if you would kindly show the fellow up, Mrs Hudson."

"And have it leave its dreadful slime all over my new carpets?"

"I will personally pay for their cleaning," he said.

With an indrawn breath, Mrs Hudson withdrew.

Evidently our extraterrestrial visitor, for all its many tentacles – or perhaps because of them – found the ascent of the staircase something of a trial, for it was a good five minutes before Mrs Hudson flung open the door and stood aside as the Martian shuffled into the room.

We are all aware, from the many illustrations provided by our national dailies, of the appearance of the beings from the red planet. However prepared I might have been, the sight of the creature in such close proximity provoked in me the contradictory emotions of fascination and revulsion, for the Martian was truly a hideous specimen.

He stood just under five feet tall, his bulk consisting of a head and body combined in a way that bore no relation to any terrestrial creature, and this perhaps accounted for my revulsion. Set into the oily brown skin of his torso were two huge eyes, like jet-black jellyfish, and a quivering, V-shaped beak. Beneath this were two groups of eight tentacles, which the creature used as both arms and legs.

Holmes gestured the alien to a chaise longue, the only piece of furniture in the room able to contain his bulk.

The Martian sat down, arranging his limbs across the brocade in a manner at once businesslike yet prim. As we watched, the peculiar V-shaped mouth opened and closed. "Mr Holmes," he said in croaking English, "I am Grulvax-Xenxa-Goran, deputy ambassador to Great Britain, and I have come today to request your investigational services."

For a number of years, Holmes had been teaching himself the fundamentals of the notoriously complex Martian tongue – and now it was a temptation beyond his powers of resistance to reply to the deputy ambassador in his own language. My friend gave vent to a horrible series of eructations, which surely taxed the elasticity of his larynx.

The Martian flung several of his tentacles into the air and

replied excitedly, "But you have mastered our language as no other Earthling yet!"

"I take that as a compliment," Holmes said. "Now, as to the nature of the investigation in question?"

"I am afraid that must remain undisclosed," the creature said, "until you have agreed to accompany me to the ambassador's residence, where I will furnish you with the relevant details."

Holmes frowned, not enamoured of such a stipulation. His curiosity, however, was piqued. In an aside, he said to me, "This can be no little matter, Watson, if the ambassador himself requires our presence." To the Martian, he said, "Very well, Mr Grulvax-Xenxa-Goran. Shall we hasten to the embassy?"

"We will avail ourselves of my tripod," said the Martian.


To stride the boroughs of London as if on the shoulders of a giant!

We sat ensconced on a padded couch in the cockpit of the tripod and goggled in amazement at the city far below. Tiny cars beetled like trilobites along the busy streets, and in the skies air-cars buzzed about like insects. Pedestrians went about their everyday business as if oblivious of the tripod striding in their midst.

The journey was over all too soon. In due course we were deposited outside the Martian Embassy in Grosvenor Square and entered the building. The deputy ambassador ushered us into a lift and we ascended to the first floor, and thence into the sitting room of the ambassador's suite, where we paused beside a polished timber door.

Without further ado, Grulvax-Xenxa-Goran said, "I made the discovery this morning, Mr Holmes. Beyond the door is the ambassador's bedroom, and it is my habit to enter at eight, once he has risen, to apprise him of the day's agenda."

Holmes fixed the deputy with an eagle eye. "And this morning?"

"This morning I found the ambassador stabbed to death in his bed. I immediately locked the door and posted a guard."

Grulvax-Xenxa-Goran opened the door and stood aside, and Holmes and I entered.

We were in a bedchamber dominated by a large double bed, upon which reposed the bulk of the Martian ambassador. I did not require a doctorate in Martian medicine to ascertain that the ambassador was quite dead.

"Stabbed," Holmes opined, "by a sharp implement just below the mouthpiece – the area in the Martian body where the major pulmonary organ is located."

After a brief search of the room, Holmes muttered, "But of the murder weapon there is no sign."

Grulvax-Xenxa-Goran shuffled back and forth at the foot of the bed, clearly in a state of agitation or grief. "Immediately after making the discovery," he said, "I contacted my superiors on Mars via our sub-space communicator and summoned an investigational team, though it will be a week before they arrive on Earth. The ambassador's life-mate will also be aboard the vessel, come to retrieve her partner's corpse for burial in the sands of our home planet."

I stood over the bed and gazed down at the dead Martian, gagging at the obnoxious stench of escaped bodily fluids. I withdrew a handkerchief and covered my mouth and nose.

Ichor, sulphurous yellow and viscid, had leaked from the wound in its torso and pooled on the sheets around its bulk. Its vast eyes were open, and stared blindly at the ceiling. Its V-shaped mouth likewise gaped, as if emitting a final painful cry.

Beside the bed was a small table upon which lay several envelopes, each one slit neatly open. Holmes examined their postmarks one by one and informed me that they had been delivered the day before.

He turned to Grulvax-Xenxa-Goran. "And you say the door was locked?"

"From the inside, by the ambassador," the Martian replied.

"Was he in the habit of locking his bedroom door?"

"The ambassador valued his privacy."

"I take it you had a spare key?" Holmes asked.

"That is so. And I fetched it when the ambassador failed to respond to my summons at eight."

"And the key, deputy ambassador – is it kept in a place from where others might easily take it?"

"It is kept in an unlocked drawer in the bureau," he replied, gesturing to the adjacent outer room with a quivering tentacle.

"How many members of staff would have access to the other room?"

"Just four: two of my own kind, and two of the humans who work at the embassy."

"If you would kindly summon them forthwith for questioning, I would be most grateful."

The Martian shuffled from the room, closing the door behind him.

Holmes crossed to the open window. "Hullo, what's this?"

He lifted the window further open and peered out. The drop to the gravelled forecourt below was in excess of thirty feet, with no convenient drainpipe, wisteria or the like to provide suitable access.

Holmes stood back and contemplated the wall below the windowsill.

I saw then what had attracted his attention – a gouge in the wallpaper four inches beneath the sill, and an abrasion on the paint of the woodwork itself.

"If the ambassador was in the habit of keeping his window open at night," Holmes said, "and an intruder armed with a grapple and rope... You catch my line of reasoning, Watson? Then again, there might be an entirely innocent explanation for the marks."

I examined the wall more closely, and when I turned from the window I saw Holmes cross to the bedside table, sort through the envelopes, then tuck something into his breast pocket, an expression of supreme satisfaction on his aquiline visage.

Before I could question him, however, the deputy ambassador returned.

"The staff are gathered and await you, Mr Holmes."

"And you have been in the employ of the embassy for how long?" Holmes asked.

We were seated at a table in a small room in the ambassador's suite, which Holmes had requisitioned for the purpose of conducting the interviews.

"Three years this May," replied the gentleman by the name of Herbert Wells, a sad-faced man of perhaps forty with expressive, melancholy eyes and a straggling moustache. In a singular recapitulation of the physical nature of his employers, Wells had short legs and a stocky, barrel-like torso.

"And your position at the embassy?"

"I work as a scientific liaison officer to the ambassador and his staff," he said in an odd, high-pitched voice. "I liaise between the Martian scientists and engineers who visit our world, and their opposite numbers on Earth."

"And you trained at…?"

"The Royal College of Science, under none other than the great Professor T.H. Huxley himself."

Holmes cleared his throat. "In your time working here, have you had reason to notice any hostility towards the ambassador?"

Wells hesitated. "The ambassador is… was… well liked, by both Martians and humans. I cannot imagine who might have done this."

"Are you aware of the political factions that exist among the Martians? We well know that there was political strife, not to say animosity, between certain nations before their arrival here."

"I know of certain political differences between the Martians, yes, but I was not aware that such differences existed between the ambassador and his staff, or any other Martians who had dealings with him on Earth."

"Very well. Now… we come to the business of what happened last night. Grulvax-Xenxa-Goran saw the ambassador at ten o'clock, at which time the ambassador repaired to his bedchamber and locked the door. Therefore he died at some time between ten o'clock last night and eight this morning. Where were you between these hours?"

"I have a room in the basement of the embassy, sir. I retired at nine, where I wrote for two hours before going to bed."

"You keep a diary?"

Wells smiled. "I write fiction," he said. "Though nothing of what I write finds favour with publishers' current tastes. Too fantastical," he finished.

Holmes murmured his condolences. "Perhaps what is needed in these fantastic times is a little more social-realism," he said. "And you rose at?"

"Seven-thirty, as usual. It was just after eight when Grulvax-

Xenxa-Goran summoned me with the alarming news."

Holmes regarded his long fingers, splayed on the tabletop before him, then looked up at Wells. "And I take it that you know where the spare key to the ambassador's bedchamber is kept?"

"Yes, sir. In the bureau in the outer room."

"To which you have access?"

Wells nodded. "Yes, sir."

"That will be all, Mr Wells. Will you be kind enough to send in Miss Cicely Fairfield?"


Wells opened the door to be met on the threshold by a vision of striking loveliness, a young woman I guessed to be barely eighteen, raven-haired and swarthy skinned, with a serious demeanour. Holmes watched the couple as they gripped each other's hands and uttered what might have been reassuring words, before Miss Fairfield smiled bravely and strode with exceptional deportment into the room. She wore a navy blue crinoline dress and a fitted bodice.

Holmes regarded her keenly, his gaze lingering on her bodice, and I noticed what might have been egg yolk adhering to the material. It appeared that she had partaken of a hasty breakfast that morning.

She seated herself at the table. "Mr Holmes, Dr Watson, it is an honour indeed to meet such illustrious upholders of the law. I have followed your exploits with considerable interest."

Holmes smiled. "In which case you will have no objections to aiding our enquiries?"

The slightest frown marred, for a second, the perfection of her forehead. "Of course not, Mr Holmes."

The interview that followed was the swiftest I have ever seen my friend conduct. It seemed barely two minutes from when Miss

Fairfield entered the room to the time she swept out.

"If you could inform me of the position you hold in the embassy, Miss Fairfield, and the duration you have been here?"

She regarded Holmes with a level gaze, her vast brown eyes unwavering. "I was employed as the private secretary to the late Martian ambassador, and I have held the position for a little over six months."

"And your duties entailed?"

"I organised the ambassador's itinerary, dealt with his correspondence, and arranged business meetings."

"Would you say that, over the months you have held the post, you have come to know the ambassador?"

She frowned as she contemplated the question. "I am not sure that one is able to come to *know*, with any certitude, the person of an extraterrestrial being."

"But did he seem, in your dealings with him, a fair employer?"

"I had no... complaints," she said hesitantly.

"And between the hours of ten last night and eight this morning, you were on the premises?"

"I have an apartment nearby, but last night I was working late. It was after midnight when I left my office and made my way home."

"And when was the last time you set eyes on the ambassador?"

"That would have been around seven, when I finished taking that day's dictation."

My friend then surprised me by saying, "Thank you, Miss Fairfield. That will be all, for now."

She inclined her fine head towards Holmes and myself. "Good day to you, gentlemen."

She was almost at the door when Holmes asked, "One more question, if I might?"

She turned. "Yes?"

"How long have you known the ambassador's scientific liaison officer, Mr Wells?"

"For a little short of six months," she replied.

"And how would you describe your relationship with him?"

Something very much like annoyance, or perhaps indignation, flared in her eyes. "Mr Wells and I are engaged to be married, Mr Holmes," she said defiantly, whereupon she turned and hurried from the room.

For the next hour we interviewed the two Martian staff members, attachés who liaised on matters of state with the British government. They could tell us little about the ambassador, other than that they held him in high regard and were terribly shocked by his death. When asked if he had enemies among the many Martians in London, each replied that the ambassador had been highly respected.

In due course Holmes dismissed the second attaché and turned to Grulvax-Xenxa-Goran. "I presume you have alerted Scotland Yard as to what has happened, and that your own medical authorities will deal with the ambassador's corpse?"

Grulvax-Xenxa-Goran waved a tentacle. "Inspector Lestrade is on his way as we speak," he said, "and the body will be removed just as soon as he's conducted his enquiries."

"And I wonder what old Lestrade will make of the sad affair?" Holmes said in an aside to me. "Come, Watson, we have learned as much as is to be learned here. We shall continue the investigation elsewhere."

"And where might that be?" I asked as we took our leave.

"We are heading for Madame Rochelle's," he said.

I echoed the name. "But isn't that…?" I began.

"Indeed it is, Watson. Madame Rochelle's is perhaps the most infamous brothel in all London."

"I'm not at all sure…" I began as we paced down a narrow alley off the Strand, glancing over my shoulder to ensure that we were not observed.

"Curb your fears, Watson. We have penetrated more insalubrious premises than this one in the course of our investigations. Aha… this must be it."

A dark recess gave access to a door, upon which Holmes rapped with his cane. A second later the door opened and a thin face peered out.

My friend whipped an unfamiliar, gold-bordered card from his pocket and showed it to the doorman. This had the effect of an open sesame, and we stepped inside.

"Where on earth did you come by the card?" I whispered as I followed Holmes down a darkened corridor.

"Where else, Watson, but in the ambassador's bedchamber."

"Ah! So that's why you were looking like the cat with the cream," I said.

Holmes paused and turned to me. "Your powers of observation, Watson, are as acute as ever."

I huffed at this. "And what else did you find in the bedchamber?"

My friend gave a short laugh. "I found nothing, Watson. That is, I did not find what I was looking for."

"And what might that have been?"

"The opener with which the ambassador had slit his private correspondence."

"The murder weapon!"

"A brilliant deduction. Now, I think through here…"

He opened a green baize door and instantly we were assailed by music – Debussy's *Nocturnes* – from one of the new-fangled Martian harmony-grams, along with the overwhelming reek of perfume and a scene to shock the most jaded of sensibilities.

Young ladies in various stages of *déshabillé* disported themselves around the room upon chesterfields and divans and were courted – shall we say? – by their suitors. Several among the clients were Martian, and it was a nauseating sight indeed to see the ivory limbs of the young ladies entwined with the writhing tentacles of their otherworldly patrons.

"I never even dreamed…" I began.

Holmes commented, "Some Martians find our women irresistible, Watson."

"What shocks me more, Holmes, is that some of the fairer sex succumb to their advances."

"Such is the tragedy of their circumstances," said Holmes.

A scantily clad woman of middle years advanced upon us, smiling. "Welcome, gentlemen. If I might take your coats…"

Holmes proffered his calling card. "If you would be kind enough to present this to Madame Rochelle."

Two minutes later we were ushered into a highly scented and sweltering boudoir. A buxom woman, whose wrinkled flesh spoke of advanced years, sat upon what appeared to be a throne beside a blazing fire.

"Mr Holmes hisself!" she declared in a Hackney shriek. "Never thought I'd see the great detective on my turf, so to speak. Are you sure I can't tempt you with one of my more beautiful girls, Mr Holmes?"

He maintained an admirable *élan*. "We are here to investigate a murder, Madame."

"A murder? Who's been murdered? I swear that none of my girls–"

"I understand that the Martian ambassador himself was a frequent visitor to your establishment?"

"'Was' is right, Mr Holmes. He stopped coming here a few months ago, and I right miss him, I do. The ambassador was a bit of a character, he was."

My friend considered her words and stroked his chin with a long forefinger. "Could you tell me if any of your ladies were in the habit of visiting the ambassador at the Martian Embassy?"

"What? You think I send my girls out into the city? I protect my girls, I do."

"I am sure you do, Madame Rochelle," said Holmes. "I wonder if you can recall whether, when the ambassador visited your establishment, he exhibited a preference for a certain type of lady?"

Madame Rochelle thought about that. "He liked 'em dark, Mr Holmes. No blondes for the ambassador. Dark and sultry was how he liked his wimmen."

In due course Holmes thanked Madame Rochelle, assured her once again that we did not care to avail ourselves of the pleasures of her establishment, and withdrew.

We escaped the cloying confines of Madame Rochelle's and once again breathed the refreshing spring air of the Strand. Holmes hurried over to a communications kiosk – yet another wonder for which we had to thank the Martians – on the corner of the Strand and Northumberland Avenue. "Excuse me one moment, Watson," he said, and entered the kiosk.

He emerged minutes later and explained. "I contacted Mr Wells and Miss Fairfield, and arranged to meet them, in secrecy, on Hampstead Heath at six." Without further ado he crossed the pavement and slipped into W.H. Smith's, emerging a minute later to hail a passing cab.

"And now?" I asked as we climbed aboard.

"To the Martian Embassy," he said, and seconds later we were hurtling through the streets of the capital towards Grosvenor Square.

A Martian underling showed us into the embassy and summoned the deputy ambassador.

Holmes asked if he might once again examine the ambassador's bedchamber, and Grulvax-Xenxa-Goran escorted us to the suite.

Holmes crossed to the bed while I remained on the threshold with the deputy, stopped in my tracks by the foul stench issuing from the corpse. Holmes, for his part, seemed not to notice the odour, for he had his back to me and appeared to be searching through the late ambassador's inert tentacles.

"Aha!" he said at last, and turned to us with an expression of triumph.

Grulvax-Xenxa-Goran shuffled past me. He gave vent to a series of oesophageal belches, then said, "Mr Holmes?"

"I am happy to inform you that the case is solved," he said. He stood beside the bed and gestured at the tangle of dead limbs. "My earlier examination of the corpse failed to locate the implement that caused the fatal injury for the very good reason that it was concealed beneath one of the ambassador's limbs."

Grulvax-Xenxa-Goran hurried across to the bed and I, gagging at the stench, joined them. I stared down at the tangle of tentacles and saw, protruding from beneath a pseudopod, a bloodstained letter opener.

The Martian spoke. "Are you saying, Mr Holmes, that…?"

My friend said, "My investigations led me, in due course, to an establishment at which the pleasures of the flesh might be indulged by those of little self-restraint. It is my painful duty to inform you that the ambassador was a frequent visitor to this establishment, where he developed a predilection for ladies of a certain type."

Before me, Grulvax-Xenxa-Goran appeared to slump. "I was aware of his weakness," he said, "and more than once attempted to reason with him, to no avail."

"It is my opinion," said Holmes, "that remorse overcame the ambassador, and in the throes of self-recrimination, and guilt at his unfaithfulness to his mate – at this very moment travelling through space towards Earth – he took his own life."

The deputy ambassador said, "A tragic affair, Mr Holmes."

Presently we took our leave, and as we hurried across the square towards the taxi rank I said doubtfully, "Suicide? But… how was it that you didn't find the letter opener when you first examined the corpse?"

My friend said nothing, but opened the rear door of the cab and slipped inside. "To Hampstead Heath," he told the driver.

We came to the crest of Parliament Hill and stood in silence, all London spread before us. The sun was setting, and a roseate light bathed the capital. I made out familiar landmarks, St Paul's and Nelson's Column, and the more recent addition to the city's skyline: the docking station at Battersea. Prominent across the city were the towering tripods, stilled now after the activity of the day, hooded and slightly sinister. Soon, when the sun went down, they would begin their curiously mournful and eerie ululations.

Holmes pointed. "Look, Watson, down by that oak. Mr Wells and Miss Fairfield, holding hands like the lovers they are. Shall we join them?"

We made our way down the incline and met the pair beneath the oak's spreading boughs. Both looked suspicious as we approached, Miss Fairfield's beautiful visage drawn and paler than usual.

Wells stepped forward. "You said you had news."

"Indeed," said Holmes. "The case is solved."

At this Wells frowned. "Solved?" he said, looking from Holmes to myself.

"It appears," I said, "that the weapon was concealed beneath the ambassador's limbs all along."

"But isn't it curious that you did not find the knife when you first examined the corpse?" Miss Fairfield asked.

"Not in the slightest," Holmes replied, "for the implement was not there when I made my initial examination."

"What?" I cried.

"Then how…?" Wells began.

"I purchased a letter opener from Smith's just one hour ago, and planted it upon entering the ambassador's bedchamber."

I stared aghast at my friend. "Do you know what you're saying, Holmes?" I expostulated. "Why… but that means the ambassador cannot have taken his own life!"

Holmes smiled, then turned to Mr Wells and Miss Fairfield. "That is correct, is it not? Perhaps one of you would care to explain?"

Miss Fairfield opened her mouth, shocked. "Why, I have no idea what you might mean."

"Come," said Holmes, "I am quite aware of the ambassador's… predilections, shall we say?"

At this, Miss Fairfield broke down. Wells embraced her, and it was a full minute before she regained her composure and looked Holmes squarely in the eye.

"A few months ago," she began, "shortly after my appointment as the ambassador's private secretary, he made his feelings known to me. I was revolted, of course, but with increasing insistence he proceeded to press himself upon me. Last night he asked me into his room, ostensibly to dictate a letter. However..." She shook her head. "Oh, it was horrible, horrible! His strength, his ghastly, overwhelming..."

"Please, there is no need to go on," Holmes said.

Wells interposed. In a trembling voice he took up the story. "I was nearby, Mr Holmes, when I heard Cicely's cries. I fetched the key and let myself into the bedchamber, and what I saw there..." He shook his head bitterly, his expression wretched. "I was beside myself with rage, sir, and blinded to the consequences took up the letter opener and... and plunged it into the horror's torso." He looked up, defiantly. "I am not proud of what I did, but I was spurred into action by my love for Cicely and by my revulsion at the ambassador's vile actions." He paused, then went on. "I opened the window and gouged a mark in the wall beneath, to make it appear that the murder was the work of an intruder. I then left the embassy and disposed of the weapon in the Thames."

He hesitated, then continued. "I do not regret what I did, for the creature had it coming to him, and like a man I will face the consequences. If you inform Scotland Yard of my actions, I will have my day in court."

Holmes smiled at this, and shook his head. "Well said, but it will take more than pretty rhetoric to persuade me that what you claim is the truth of the matter."

I stared at my friend. "What the deuce are you driving at, Holmes?"

Holmes turned to Miss Fairfield. "At our first meeting," he said, "I noticed the splashed ichor on your bodice which I took at first to be egg yolk." He paused. "Well?"

Miss Fairfield faced the detective foursquare, thought for a moment, then began, "I admit—"

Wells gripped her hand. "Cicely…"

"No, Bertie," said she, "the truth is better out. You are correct, Mr Holmes, Bertie did not kill the ambassador." She took a deep breath, then said, "When he pressed himself upon me, held me down with his tentacles and… and proceeded to… You must understand that I was beside myself with terror, and when I saw the letter opener on the bedside table, I…" She stopped, almost out of breath. "I did what I did, Mr Holmes, in self-defence, but I too will face the consequences if that is what you feel is right and proper."

My friend paced back and forth, his chin upon his chest, lost in thought. Then he stopped and faced the pair.

"As far as the human and Martian authorities are concerned," he said at last, "the affair is closed. The ambassador killed himself in a fit of remorse and guilt for his philandering with human women of ill-repute. The Martian judiciary will not arrive for another seven days, by which time what little evidence there is will be corrupted. While not condoning your actions, Miss Fairfield, I understand the terrible fear that drove you to commit the deed."

"You mean…?"

"In my opinion you have suffered enough. Nought will be gained by hauling you before the court, for while human law might have sympathy with your plight, I cannot say the same for the Martian judiciary."

She stared at him, open-mouthed, and tears glistened in her eyes.

"If I were you," Holmes went on, "I would attempt to put the terrible memories of last night behind you. Your secret is safe with Watson and me."

"I cannot thank you enough, Mr Holmes!" Wells said.

Miss Fairfield stepped forward and took the detective's hand. "Thank you," she murmured.

Presently we watched them step from beneath the boughs of the oak and, hand in hand, walk into the diminishing twilight of the heath.

In due course we started back to Baker Street. Holmes lit his pipe and pulled upon it ruminatively. I stared up at the stars scattered brightly across the heavens, lost in thought as I pondered the coming of the Martians and the many wondrous incidents that their arrival had entailed.

We strode on in silence as the darkness deepened around us, and at last, from all across London, near and far, there sounded the first of the tripods' strange and mournful cries.

"Ulla, ulla," they called dolorously into the warm night air, "ulla, ulla..."

# Part One

## The Martian Simulacra

*Chapter One*

*A Visitor to 221B Baker Street*

Two years after my friend's involvement in the affair of the Martian ambassador, Sherlock Holmes was called upon once again to render assistance to our extraterrestrial associates.

In the interim my friend had worked on a number of investigations, though none which I thought of sufficient interest to add to the already copious annals of his exploits. In between cases he had spent his time studying the intricacies of Martian electronics, poring over the *Encyclopaedia Martiannica*, and scanning the crime pages of the *London Gazette*. Often, late into the evening over a glass of brandy, he would regale me with what he had learned of Martian life from the encyclopaedia, as well as offering his own solutions to the crimes and scandals of the day.

I, for my part, divided my time between my club and a select group of private patients in west London. I was now sixty and slowing down. The old war injury was troubling me from time to time, and my concentration was not what it had been.

That very morning Holmes upbraided me on this score. "What

you should be doing, Watson, is not so much slowing down but speeding up."

"What on earth do you mean?"

He examined me over his toast. It was a brilliant summer's morning, not yet eight o'clock, and through the windows of 221B Baker Street I looked out upon yet another cloudless day. In the distance the cowl of a Martian tripod loomed, silent and brooding, high above Regent's Park.

"People of our age often make the mistake of thinking that they should reward themselves – grant themselves a gift for long service, as it were – by 'slowing down'." He pointed a thin finger at me. "But this is lazy thinking. Only by keeping active, physically and mentally, can we hope to keep senility and decrepitude at bay."

"That's all very well for you to say," I retorted, "the possessor of a relatively healthy body and a brilliant mind."

"I appreciate the effects of your war injury, Watson, but what I suggest is that you take up a hobby, embark on something new and mentally invigorating."

"But dash it all, Holmes," I said, "it's not as if I possess your mind, you know? What is it you advise me to do?"

He was saved from replying when Mrs Hudson entered the room, somewhat flustered.

"Oh, Mr Holmes! I know I shouldn't say this, knowing how you hobnob with them from time to time… But there's one of the slimy things downstairs – well, on its way up, right now. It gave its name, but for the life of me I couldn't make sense of its burblings."

"It will be Grulvax-Xenxa-Goran, I shouldn't wonder. Be so kind as to show him up, Mrs Hudson, and would you be so good as to prepare a pot of Earl Grey?"

She bustled out, and in due course the door opened and the Martian squeezed his bulk through the doorframe and shuffled into the room.

Holmes advanced and shook one of the creature's tentacles. He bowed, murmured a greeting in the Martian's own gargling tongue, then continued in English, "Grulvax-Xenxa-Goran, I am delighted to welcome you again to 221B. You know my good friend, Dr Watson."

I essayed a nod in the alien's direction, loath to match Holmes's greeting and grip a slimy tentacle. I hoped the creature would not be offended at this breach of etiquette. Grulvax-Xenxa-Goran had been promoted since our last meeting, and was now the ambassador to Great Britain, and a Very Important Alien.

The Martian sat down on the chaise longue, and presently Mrs Hudson entered bearing a silver tray with a teapot and three china cups and saucers. She retreated, averting her gaze from our guest, and Holmes poured the tea.

"Now," he said, sitting back with the saucer perched upon the bony prominence of his right knee, "how might I be of service?"

Before replying, the ambassador attended to his refreshment. Gripping the delicate china cup in one of his proboscis-like tentacles, he raised it to his beak and, rather than taking a small sip, tipped the entire contents of the cup into his maw. He made a gurgling sound, as if in appreciation, and Holmes refilled his cup.

"The matter is one of the utmost delicacy," said Grulvax-Xenxa-Goran. "We cannot allow the news to be disseminated abroad, for fear of causing panic."

Holmes nodded. "And the nature of the crime?"

"The gravest, sir, the very gravest. Murder."

"Murder," Holmes echoed, leaning forward. "And the victim?"

"None other than the esteemed philosopher, Delph-Aran-Arapna."

The name meant nothing to me, but then I took very little interest in the high and mighty among the ranks of the aliens. By the frown that creased my friend's aquiline features, I gathered that the name was taxing his powers of recall, too.

"Delph-Aran-Arapna was one of our finest thinkers," the Martian went on, "belonging to the Zyrna-Ximon school of thought. He was also a Venerable – that is, a citizen entering his one hundredth Martian year, which approximates to one hundred and ninety Earth years."

"Venerable indeed," Holmes assented. "And do the Martian authorities have any clues as to who might have wanted the Venerable dead?"

The ambassador poured the second cup of Earl Grey into his mouth, gurgled his appreciation, then said, "Delph-Aran-Arapna's views were seen, among certain sections of Martian society, as contentious. But as to why anyone might disagree with his ideas to the point of wishing his death…" He lifted a tentacle in an evident gesture of mystification.

"How was Delph-Aran-Arapna murdered?" Holmes asked.

"In the most despicable manner imaginable," came the reply. "A tentacle was severed and then…" The V-shaped beak ceased its movement, and for a few seconds Grulvax-Xenxa-Goran closed his huge, coal-black eyes. The alien was clearly moved by his recollection of the murder. "And then the philosopher was held down by his assailants while his severed limb was utilised to block his windpipe. He died in terrible agony."

Holmes murmured his condolences. "I have read somewhere – I cannot recall where – that such a killing–"

The ambassador interrupted. "Just so. The killing in the manner I have described is known amongst my kind as *lykerchia*. It means,

34

in English, 'to kill someone for the views they hold'. Such a heinous murder is, thankfully, rare amongst our kind, which is why this particular crime is considered so revolting – and why not one word of it must filter out to the citizenry of my planet. The authorities have covered up his murder with the story that Delph-Aran-Arapna passed away peacefully in his sleep."

"The views held by the murdered philosopher," Holmes said. "How might they have angered someone to the degree of provoking murder?"

The ambassador waved a tentacle. "I will gladly apprise you of the details once you have agreed to take on the case," he said.

Holmes inclined his head. "And might I enquire where the murder took place?"

"He was murdered in his home, in Kashera. That is, in the verdant foothills of Olympus Mons."

"I see," said my friend, leaning back in his chair. "Now, I take it that you have reason to believe that the perpetrator of this ghastly crime has fled to Earth – hence your request for my assistance in the matter?"

"We are confident that the killer is still on Mars," the alien replied. "It would be impossible for him to have left our planet, as voyages to Earth are strictly monitored. Only accredited politicians, the military and selected artists and musicians are accorded transit passes to your world."

Holmes tapped his chin and stared into space for a while, then asked, "And so you wish me to conduct an investigation into the murder of Delph-Aran-Arapna at a remove of some sixty-odd million miles?"

The Martian lofted a tentacle. "On the contrary, Mr Holmes. We are desirous of your presence *in situ*, so that you might better conduct your investigations. I am here to invite you, and your esteemed friend Dr Watson, to journey to Mars as our honoured guests."

The alien's words rendered me, for the time being, speechless; likewise Holmes, but not for long. "That is a most gracious honour indeed," he said. "And one which I must discuss with Dr Watson. I trust that you do not require an immediate decision? There are various details that require our attention – arrangements to be made and appointments postponed."

"I fully understand," the Martian said, "but I must stress that time is of the essence. A liner leaves the Battersea docking station at two o'clock tomorrow afternoon. Another ship does not leave, after that, for a fortnight. Needless to say, upon the successful outcome of the case, my government would generously remunerate you."

Holmes waved this aside. "Pray, let us not sully the offer at this juncture with talk of monetary reward. I will require a few hours to discuss the matter with Dr Watson, and then, in the morning, if I agree to take on the case, I should like to further question yourself and any of your colleagues you think might aid my investigations."

Grulvax-Xenxa-Goran stood and looked from me to Holmes. "I await your decision with anticipation," he said. "For now, farewell."

The alien lumbered from the room and I turned to my friend. "Well, Holmes," I said. "We're going, of course? We can't really look such a gift horse in the mouth, can we?"

An expression of abstraction passed across my friend's ascetic features. "On the face of it, you're right, Watson. How I have dreamed of setting foot upon the red planet. To think of it, Watson – to walk the red sands beneath the cerise skies of Mars. To look upon the plane of Utopia from the slopes of Phlegra Montes!"

"I sense a 'but' approaching, Holmes."

"But, Watson, Grulvax-Xenxa-Goran's request puzzles me somewhat. Very well, I assisted the Martians two years ago, but the crime occurred on our doorstep and to solicit my services then was the logical option. But to request that I investigate the murder of a Martian philosopher on his own planet, when the Martians' own detectives would be better suited to deal with the matter... It vexes me not a little."

"But what ulterior motive might they have?" I asked. "If, indeed, you suspect an ulterior motive?"

My friend shook his head. "That is just the problem. For the life of me, I don't know what I suspect, and this troubles me."

He crossed the room, opened the Martian encyclopaedia, and pored over it for a time. Perhaps five minutes later, he looked up. "I'm going to the British Library," he said. "There are one or two details I wish to check. It concerns me that, for all the comprehensiveness of the *Encyclopaedia Martiannica*, nowhere does it mention the philosopher Delph-Aran-Arapna. Now there is perhaps a valid reason for this, and if so then my doubts might very well be for nought. Inform Mrs Hudson that I will be back for dinner at six, would you?"

And, with this, Holmes flung his overcoat around his lank frame and hurried from the room.

# *Chapter Two*

*A Conversation in the Park*

I was in a state of febrile excitation and anticipation for the rest of the day. Unable to settle down and peruse *The Times*, after lunch I took myself from the house and wandered the streets until finding myself at Hyde Park.

A Martian tripod stood sentinel beside Marble Arch, something grave and monumental in its very silence and stillness. At sunset, this tripod and others ranged around London would begin their signature call: "Ulla, ulla, ulla, ulla..." The eerie double-note, plangent and melancholic, would eddy across the rooftops of the boroughs, as one tripod enigmatically called to another in an acoustic chain diminishing across London and, eventually, fading into the distance beyond Richmond.

I passed the tripod and continued on to Speakers' Corner.

A protest or demonstration of some sort was in progress there, and I slowed down to take in the swelling crowd and the speakers.

Five men and women stood upon a platform beneath a banner that declared: "*Terra for the Terrans! Free Earth Now!*" Among the crowd I espied homemade placards bearing such legends as: "*Martians Go Home!*" and "*The Occupation Must End!*"

A tall, ginger-bearded figure in his fifties, I judged, stepped up to a microphone and began his peroration, and as I moved closer to the platform I realised that the speaker was none other than the celebrated playwright George Bernard Shaw. Seated beside him as he waited his turn at the microphone, harrumphing through his moustache like some huge, disgruntled walrus, I recognised G.K. Chesterton. I smiled my amusement that it had taken the arrival of the Martians to bring these two literary giants, normally at polemical loggerheads, to some form of rapprochement.

"Domination of one race by another can never, ever, under any circumstances, be tolerated," Shaw was saying. "Look upon the sorry plight of those countries and peoples under the oppression of our very own empire. Ask the citizens of India and Africa if they welcome our rule, depriving them as it does of the opportunity to grow as nations, to express their sovereign individuality. I say that the same is true now, on Earth, as humankind grovels under the tyrannical heel of our otherworldly oppressors!"

Cheers greeted Shaw's words, and he went on to enumerate his grievances in more specific terms. I estimated the crowd now numbered a couple of hundred, made up of citizens from all walks of society: barrow-boys and costermongers rubbed shoulders with bowler-hatted bankers and businessmen in pinstripes. I made out dowagers and dustbin men, aristocrats and artisans; if nothing else, opposition to the Martians' occupation had had a democratising effect among the populace. Though it struck me that, perhaps, just as many people, and from just as broad a cross-section of society, saw the benefits that the Martians had brought to our world.

I was casting my glance about the crowd when I caught the eye of a rather striking young woman standing at my side.

She was attired in a jade-green ankle-length dress, with a lace cloche perched on her head at a jaunty angle. Her hair was golden, her face pale and breathtakingly beautiful, with a wide, smiling mouth whose full lips suggested to me a happy and generous nature.

She noticed my attention and smiled. "Mr Shaw performs his usual trick of revealing truths with uncommon insight, don't you think?"

"That all depends," I ventured, "on whether you consider the Martians' presence good or ill."

She looked at me. "Are you here to join the protest, Mr...?"

I offered my hand. "Doctor," I said. "Doctor John H. Watson, at your service. And you might be?"

She blessed me with a delightful smile and shook my hand. "Freya Hamilton-Bell," she said.

"And you are here because you side with Shaw, Chesterton and the rest?" I enquired.

She raised a finger. "But I asked you first, Doctor."

I laughed. "So you did! Very well, I am here through happenstance, as I was taking an afternoon constitutional. And as to whether I oppose the presence of the Martians... I must admit that I can see both the benefits and disadvantages." A thought occurred to me, and I indicated the cafe beside the Serpentine that served afternoon teas. "I wonder if you would care to join me in refreshment, Miss?"

"Do you know, I rather think I would, Doctor."

"Capital!" I said, and led the way to the cafe.

We took our seats and I ordered tea and cakes, Darjeeling for my companion and Earl Grey for myself.

"Now," she said as she raised the china cup to her lips and took a tiny sip, "those benefits you mentioned, Doctor?"

"It cannot be denied," I began, "that the coming of the Martians has revolutionised our understanding of the sciences, and the benefits accruing from this are indisputable."

She pointed an elegant forefinger at me. She was, for a woman of tender years, rather forthright, and I found this somewhat refreshing. "But who gains from this 'revolution', Doctor? Do you realise that the profits made from the increase in manufacturing go not into the coffers of our government, but straight back to our oppressors on Mars? Do you realise too that poverty on Earth has increased for the majority since the Martian invasion? Oh, the Martians might condescend to give us certain medicines and technologies and other gewgaws to keep the populace subdued, but without doubt the Martians are stripping our planet of resources for their own material gain."

I smiled to myself. "Now I understand your presence here, Miss Hamilton-Bell. You clearly oppose Martian rule."

"I shock you, Dr Watson?"

"Not at all. I am rather impressed by your argument, and the manner in which you express yourself. The term 'a breath of fresh air' comes to mind. From one so young and..." I faltered.

She frowned. "I detect a patronising note in your assessment, Dr Watson. My age and gender, I rather think, do not enter into the equation." She gestured towards the speakers. "Minds far greater than mine can see the iniquity of the Martian regime. But it does not take intelligence or insight to realise that the arrival of the Martians is founded on a great and terrible lie." At this she bit her lip, and it occurred to me that she had vouchsafed more than she thought safe to let slip.

"I am intrigued," I said. "Please, go on."

She hesitated, regarding her half-finished Darjeeling. At last she said, "The Martians would have us believe that the first wave of invaders were of a tyrannical political faction that had gained dominance on Mars through ruthless oppression of the populace, terrible wars and merciless pogroms. The invasion of Earth in '94, Martian leaders maintain, was but the logical consequence of that bellicose regime: they had subdued their own world and, seeking others to oppress, and more valuable territory to occupy, had set their sights on Earth. The story goes – or so our Martian overlords would like us to believe – that these initial aggressors were brought to their knees by a common terrestrial virus, and that the second wave of Martians were the more peaceable, liberal schism originally left behind on Mars. They further assure us that the two are distinct, and that our current Martian oppressors bear no relation to the former tyrants."

I sat back, hiding a smile of amusement at her fervour. It made her even more beautiful, I thought. "And you think differently, Miss Hamilton-Bell?"

She swept on. "They would have us believe that, with the invasion forces intent on the subjugation of Earth in '94, defences back on Mars were neglected and liberal forces then took advantage to wrest control of the scant armies left behind. They claim the liberals despatched a liner to Earth, and that a scientific team alighted in Africa in 1898 and manufactured an antidote to the virus that had put paid to the initial invasion."

"And according to you?"

She smiled, but without an iota of humour. She fixed me with a steely gaze. "The fact is, Dr Watson, that the Martians, the initial wave and the second front, are one and the same. It was merely a political expedient, promulgated by the second set of invaders, to claim that the original group were murderous tyrants. Oh, they worked it very cleverly. I would go so far as to say that they were politically brilliant – and we, sad dupes that we were, fell for their lies hook, line and sinker."

"You seem," I said, "certain of your rather... lurid accusations."

She smiled at me frostily. "I am as certain as I can be," she said.

"And how is that?"

She hesitated. "I would rather, at this juncture, keep my sources to myself."

"Very well," I said, and sipped my tea for a time. "But look here, if you were right, then surely we would have heard a rumour of it by now? The papers would be full of–"

"The papers," she said quickly, "are controlled by the Martians. The press barons are in cahoots with the ruling Martian elite. They print lurid accounts of life on Mars, shallow travelogues to amuse the masses, and trumpet the benefits the invasion has brought, and all the while the barons and the editors are mere patsies to our oppressors, raking in their millions with lies."

I sat forward. "You intrigue me. I hear what you say, but, without corroboration to back up your claims..."

"Without corroboration, Dr Watson, you think my stories the mere flights of fancy of an impressionable young woman?"

"Why, I think nothing of the kind!" I expostulated.

"But your entire manner, if I might make so bold, has been rather superior throughout our meeting. You have the air of someone allowing a child to chatter loquaciously, while you sit content in the assumption of your own superiority. Oh, I've seen your type before. What we need, once we've got rid of the egregious Martians, is another revolution to sweep away old, conservative values and traditional ideas!"

"I take it, Miss, that you are a suffragette?"

She glared at me and, I rather think, blasphemed under her breath, "*Good God!*"

She hurriedly gathered her bag and made to depart.

I reached out so as to delay her precipitate departure. "I wonder if we might meet again," I said.

She snatched her hand away, said, "That, Dr Watson, remains to be seen," and swept – rather regally, I thought – away.

I sat in silence for a while, digesting her words and feeling both chastised and, oddly, invigorated by the meeting with such a feisty young woman.

In due course I finished my tea and retraced my steps back to Baker Street.

# Chapter Three

*The Mystery Deepens*

I found my friend deep in a brown study when I returned. He was pacing back and forth, his chin sunk upon his chest and his fists thrust into the pockets of his smoking jacket. He hardly acknowledged my arrival, merely grunted at my greeting, and I knew better than to derail his train of thought.

Over dinner he emerged from his reverie, and I felt emboldened enough to enquire: "Well, Holmes, did you learn anything at the British Library?"

"The mystery deepens, Watson."

"How so?"

"I asked to see certain obscure Martian texts upon my arrival at the library," he said. "They were not the originals, of course, but rather translations pertaining to abstruse areas of Martian philosophy. I was certain that in these tomes I would find reference to the work, if not to the life, of the philosopher Delph-Aran-Arapna."

"Let me guess," I said, slicing into my pork chop. "There was no reference to be found, hm?"

"Your sagacity astounds me, Watson. You're right. There was no mention of the fellow in these texts, nor in more recent periodicals and journals. Although there was reference aplenty to other Martian thinkers, there was not a smidgen to be found on Delph-Aran-Arapna."

"Perhaps," I surmised, "he just wasn't of the first rank."

"Yet according to Grulvax-Xenxa-Goran," said Holmes, "he was feted as one of the finest Martian minds of the current era."

"So what the deuce do you think is going on?"

He pursed his thin lips thoughtfully. "That, my friend, we might very well find out when we set foot on the red planet."

"We're going?" I exclaimed.

"I telephoned Grulvax-Xenxa-Goran upon my return," he said. "Our berths are booked aboard the liner *Valorkian*, leaving at two o'clock tomorrow. One week later we will be on Mars."

"My word," I said. "You weren't deterred by finding no mention of what's-his-name?"

"On the contrary, Watson. My curiosity is aroused. It makes the puzzle all the more intriguing, does it not? Now the mystery is not only who might have ended the life of the Martian philosopher, but why all mention of the worthy has been omitted from every pertinent translation on Earth?"

"Of course, there might be a perfectly innocent explanation."

"You are right, there might be. I hope to learn more when I question Grulvax-Xenxa-Goran and his colleagues at the embassy in the morning. I have been granted an appointment at ten, for one hour. I will meet you at the Battersea docking station at one o'clock."

Mrs Hudson entered the room, cleared away the dishes, and asked if we wanted coffee. Holmes requested Turkish, and I joined him in a cup.

A while later, as we sat on either side of the hearth nursing our cups, Holmes said, "And how went your day, Watson? I see that you strolled around Hyde Park, listened to the speakers demonstrating against the Martian presence and, if I am not mistaken, took tea with a rather fetching member of the opposite sex."

I lowered my cup and stared at my friend in vexed admiration. "Confound it, Holmes! How can you possibly know?"

"Simplicity itself, my dear Watson. You returned with a copy of the *Weekly Sketch*, a periodical you purchase only when you take a turn around the Serpentine. That you paused to listen to the speakers at Hyde Park corner is a given, as I read the notice advertising the demonstration in yesterday's *Times*, and I have observed your enjoyment of public debate."

"But confound it… How do you know that I stopped for tea?"

"The Earl Grey tea leaves adorning your waistcoat, adhering there from a spillage, indicate that you paused for refreshment."

"Very well," I said, "but how can you possibly know that I met a rather charming young lady?"

Holmes cracked a smile. "Watson, old man, I can read you like a book: the light in your eyes, your somewhat dreamy abstraction, that witless smile that crosses your face from time to time when you consider the meeting. I have seen it again and again, over the years."

"Witless…?" I muttered.

"Am I wrong?"

I blustered for a time, then admitted, "Dash it all, Holmes. As a matter of fact I did meet a rather remarkable young woman."

He smiled to himself and murmured, "I do think you're smitten, Watson."

"Not in the least! Perish the thought," I said. "Admittedly she was a beauty, I'll give you that. But she was young enough to be my daughter – and her ideas were somewhat far-fetched, to say the least."

"Far-fetched?"

I outlined my conversation with Miss Freya Hamilton-Bell, and her opinion that our current Martian associates were one and the same as the original murderous mob.

"The notion is absurd," I said. "I can't begin to imagine how she got it into her head."

Holmes regarded the dregs of his coffee. "I have heard the theory mooted in learned circles on more than one occasion, Watson. Mark my words, there might be a grain of truth in the idea."

I goggled at him. "You really think so, Holmes?"

He set his cup aside. "Shaw and Chesterton are convinced that such is the case," he said. "Just the other week, G.K. bent my ear on the very subject at the Athenaeum. Perhaps, my friend, we might learn more on this matter, and others, when we set foot on Mars one week from the morrow, hm?"

"Indeed we might," I said.

His words set me to thinking, and that night, after we each retired to our rooms, I lay awake long into the early hours before sleep finally arrived.

*Chapter Four*

ᛦ

*All Aboard for the Red Planet!*

The Martian docking station at Battersea is one of the wonders of the modern world.

As one approaches from across the Thames, the station dominates the skyline of south London, a series of towers and bulbous domes – the latter a feature of Martian architecture – along with a dozen mobile launch gantries and as many docking rings where interplanetary ships make their landfall.

The station was a hive of industry, with a constant toing and froing of all manner of transportation. There was even a dedicated railway station to ferry passengers and goods from the newly arrived ships to the centre of London. A veritable hub of commerce had grown up around the port, with crowds of human stevedores bustling hither and thither. Glimpsed in amongst them, from time to time, one could observe the land vehicles used by the Martians when not riding in their iconic tripods: these were bulky, domed cars, which beetled busily back and forth on three wheels.

At noon precisely I stepped from my cab, found a porter, and had him transport my case through the busy concourse of the station to the vast, glass-covered embarkation lounge. This resonant chamber was occupied, for the most part, by Martians – no doubt diplomats, traders and the like, come to the end of their secondment on planet Earth. I wondered if they were longing for the red sands of their home planet after their sojourn on our strange world.

A dozen or so humans stood among the alien crowd, with chests and cases at their feet. These I took to be businessmen and civil servants. One fellow in particular struck me as familiar – a singular specimen of humanity, a little over five feet high but as broad as a bull across the shoulders. I was sure I had seen his barrel chest, great head and flowing black beard pictured in some periodical. He wore a tropical suit as if equipped for exploration, finished off with a sola topi.

I scanned the crowd, but of my friend there was no sign.

Through the glass roof I made out the gargantuan shape of a nearby Martian liner. Although it towered to a height of a hundred yards, it gave the impression of being squat, for it was perhaps thirty yards wide, its appearance made even broader by the addition of four scimitar-like tail fins which flared from its base. This was the *Valorkian*, the vessel that would transport Holmes and me to the red planet.

I had undertaken a little preliminary reading on the subject of interplanetary travel, and learned that we would pass the bulk of the week-long journey under sedation, with only an hour or so at take-off and landing being spent fully conscious. We would be able to look out upon our world as it diminished in our wake – and view our destination when we approached the orb of Mars.

I was daydreaming of our arrival there, and what adventures might await us, when I was hailed by a familiar voice and I turned to see Sherlock Holmes approaching, accompanied by a squat Martian.

"By a happy coincidence," said Holmes, "Grulvax-Xenxa-Goran begins a period of leave today, and will be making the journey, too. He has kindly offered to be our guide while on the red planet."

"It will be my honour to show you around our capital city," said the ambassador, "before your investigations commence."

"Most kind of you," I murmured.

"Now, if you will excuse me for a moment, I must ensure that all the relevant details are in order." And so saying, the alien scurried off towards a counter behind which stood a human customs official.

"Well, Holmes," I said when we were alone, "what did you learn?"

"Precious little," he said. "I informed Grulvax-Xenxa-Goran about the curious absence of all mention of the philosopher from the relevant literature, but he waved it away as of no concern. According to him, only a fraction of all information regarding Mars is translated. There is hardly time to render all information into English – or, he added, the need. For who, after all, would be interested in many of the more arcane aspects of Martian life?"

"And what did you make of his explanation?"

"Specious in the extreme, Watson. I know that the finest minds on Earth are eager to learn everything possible about Mars, its history, culture and philosophies, and the idea that all mention of one of its finest thinkers should be denied to mankind... No, Watson, I find the entire business decidedly rum."

Before I could ask why the Martians should have elided mention of the philosopher, he went on. "There was one other thing, Watson. Intrigued by your meeting with Miss Hamilton-Bell, and her strong opinions, I took the opportunity to look her up."

"And?" I asked eagerly.

He frowned. "Most odd, but like our enigmatic Martian philosopher, it seems that she does not exist."

"What?" I said. "Doesn't exist?"

"Or rather," Holmes went on, "the name with which she supplied you does not exist. I checked in all the telephone directories and gazetteers. It would appear that 'Freya Hamilton-Bell', Watson, is an alias."

I was about to question him further when, from nearby, a stentorian boom all but deafened me.

"Holmes, by Gad! As I live and breathe, what the deuce are you doing here?"

I turned to see the huge man I had noticed earlier bearing down upon us like a charging bull.

Holmes turned and, beholding our interlocutor, smiled his greeting. "Challenger, what a sight for sore eyes! You look set for an adventure into darkest Africa, sir."

The great man bellowed his mirth. "Africa? Perish the thought! I've charted that neck of the woods, old boy. Now I'm set for pastures new."

"Mars, I presume?"

"None other." He gestured through the glass roof at the *Valorkian*. "Leaving aboard that ugly tin can on the dot of two. And you?"

"Likewise," said Holmes.

"Capital! We should take tea – or whatever noxious beverage the Martians might serve – on our arrival."

Holmes made the introductions. "Watson, meet my old friend, Professor George Edward Challenger, zoologist, explorer and adventurer extraordinaire. Challenger, my friend and faithful companion, Dr John Watson."

"An honour indeed," Challenger said, gripping my hand.

I winced. "Delighted," I said, retrieving my hand and massaging life back into the crushed metacarpals.

"But what takes you to Mars?" Holmes asked.

"A spot of lecturing, followed by a bit of sightseeing. The Martians are more than eager to avail themselves of my expertise in the area of Terran fauna, don't y'know? I hope to climb Olympus Mons, if my hosts are willing, and I have a mind to sail the southern seas. I'd like to bag a monster said to haunt those waters, but getting the trophy home might prove somewhat problematical. And you? What takes you to Mars?"

I glanced at my friend, who said, "The Martians have roped me in to do a little investigating – but more on that later," he added as he beheld the return of Grulvax-Xenxa-Goran.

The professor tapped the side of his nose. "Understood, Holmes. Now, excuse me while I ensure my crates are properly stowed." And so saying he hurried across the concourse to where a porter was labouring with two vast wooden chests.

"Everything is in order, gentlemen," the ambassador said. "We should proceed to the check-in desk."

We passed through a perfunctory customs check, left the embarkation lounge, and crossed to the bulk of the waiting ship. Seen at close quarters, I was struck by the craft's size and latent power – and by its bizarre alien quality. Its carapace was dark and bulbous, and somehow appeared almost *biological*, like the epidermis of some great ocean-dwelling leviathan.

We stepped into its shadow, climbed onto a commodious elevator plate, and were whisked in seconds into the craft's arching atrium. Martians and humans alike scurried back and forth. I noticed, among the crowd, a dozen or so green-uniformed men and women who were employed by the shipping line as pursers and stewards.

Grulvax-Xenxa-Goran led the way to another elevator plate, and this one lofted us to a gallery that ran around the equatorial circumference of the ship. We proceeded along a narrow curving passageway until we came to a series of rectilinear portholes set into the outer skin. Straps hung on either side of these viewing portals, and our Martian guide advised us that we should take a firm grip on these when the ship took off.

In due course a thunderous rumble shook the vessel, and a motion like an earthquake almost knocked me from my feet. "Whoa!" I cried, and gripped the straps not a second too soon. The ferocious roar increased. I pressed my nose to the glass and beheld, in wonder, the grid-like streets of London growing ever more distant. Never before had I flown – not trusting the new-fangled air-cars with my life – but the sensation I experienced now was not what I might have expected flight to be. Rather, it was like being carried into the heavens by some vast, slow-moving elevator. As I stared out, all of London became visible beneath me, and I spotted familiar landmarks down below like an architect's scale models: there was Buckingham Palace, and here St Paul's; tiny cars whizzed back and forth, and citizens crowded the thoroughfares of the Strand and Pall Mall, overlooked here and there by Martian tripods.

Soon all detail was lost to sight, other than the pattern of the capital's streets, shot through by the great silver squiggle of the Thames. Fifteen minutes later we were at such an elevation that the coastline came into view, the bright blue of the Channel contrasting with the verdant hop fields and orchards of Kent.

A little later, as we sailed into the heavens high above Europe, Grulvax-Xenxa-Goran suggested that he show us to our berths. These were small cabins, barely larger than water-closets, and each contained a metal tank a little larger than a coffin. Our alien guide explained that we should undress, stow our clothing in the locker provided, and climb into the 'suspension pod', as he called it. He counselled us not to be alarmed when we were submerged, up to our necks, in an enveloping gel. This was necessary, he said, in order to reduce the risk of interstellar radiation. Presently a human steward would come along to administer a sedative.

The Martian departed, taking Holmes to his own cabin, and I closed the outer door and regarded the suspension pod with some scepticism. Taking a breath, I undressed, lifted the lid of the pod, and stepped gingerly into its confines. The pod was canted at a thirty-five-degree angle, at its upper end a wooden support for one's neck and head, and a feeding tube which hooked into one's mouth. No sooner had I settled myself into its length and pulled down the door, which covered my body but left my head free, than I felt a viscous fluid rise around my legs and torso. Cold at first, the fluid gel soon warmed, and the sensation, as it submerged me up to the neck, was not unpleasant.

An alarm pinged, no doubt alerting a steward to my readiness, and seconds later a uniformed young woman entered the cubicle bearing a small cup.

"Now drink this straight down, Dr Watson, and the next thing you know you'll be waking up high above Mars."

I took the cup and swallowed the milky sedative, and only then looked more closely at the stewardess.

"But..." I said as the sedative quickly took effect, a dozen questions on my lips.

For she was none other than Miss Freya Hamilton-Bell.

# Chapter Five

### A Most Curious Note

Her last words were prescient: it seemed that no sooner had my eyes fluttered shut than I was struggling feebly awake, the gel draining from the pod. As I sat up and pushed open the lid, I found it incredible to believe that a full seven days had elapsed. We were now more than sixty million miles from Earth, and in orbit around the red planet.

These thoughts were pushed aside by the vision that entered my head of Freya Hamilton-Bell, followed by a slew of questions. Had our 'meeting' in Hyde Park been as accidental as it had seemed at the time? What was Miss Hamilton-Bell, a self-confessed opponent of the Martian presence on Earth, doing here, working for the very Martians she considered her enemies? Had she purposefully manufactured our meeting aboard the *Valorkian*, and if so… why?

The alarm bell sounded, and I hurried to the locker and donned my clothing lest the young woman enter and find me half-dressed.

I need not have worried, however, for when a tapping sounded at the door, it was not Miss Hamilton-Bell but the ambassador.

59

"If you are quite ready, Doctor, would you care to join us on the observation gallery as we come in to land?"

"I'll be with you in a jiffy," I said as I finished dressing. In due course I adjusted my collar and joined the Martian in the corridor.

As we took an elevator plate down to the observation gallery, I said, "I was surprised to find that you employ human stewards aboard your ships."

"For the convenience of our human passengers," said Grulvax-Xenxa-Goran.

"And are these human employees resident on Mars?"

"For brief periods only," the ambassador replied. "They have what is known as a 'stopover', until they board the next returning ship for Earth."

The elevator plate reached its destination, and with an out-thrust tentacle my guide indicated that I should alight before him. I found Holmes a little further along the curving gallery, and beside him Professor Challenger. They were gripping leather straps on either side of a porthole, Challenger bellowing his appreciation of the view.

I grasped the strap next to Holmes, while Grulvax-Xenxa-Goran positioned himself before a porthole some way along the gallery.

"Developments!" I hissed as I peered out. We were passing high above a rust-coloured desert, with wind-sculpted dunes running off towards the horizon. Here and there I made out what I thought were vast silver lakes – though time and experience were to put me right on that score – and die-straight canals that carried precious water from the poles to the equatorial regions.

"This is astounding!" Challenger bellowed. "Why, look up to your right, Holmes! Now, is that great tumbling spud Phobos or Deimos?"

"The former, Professor. Deimos, which is smaller, you will observe in the heavens to our left."

To me he whispered, "What is it, Watson?"

I peered along the corridor to ensure that Grulvax-Xenxa-Goran was out of earshot: the Martian seemed absorbed in the view of his home world. "Freya Hamilton-Bell – or whoever she might be – is aboard this ship and working as a stewardess!"

"Not only beautiful, if your description is to be believed, but enterprising." He cogitated for a time. "It would appear, upon reflection, that your meeting in Hyde Park was not as accidental as you assumed at the time."

"That had occurred to me," I said.

"Did she have time to speak to you?"

I shook my head. "No, other than to tell me to drink the sedative, and that soon I would awake above Mars. But…"

"Go on."

"But it can't be just a coincidence, can it? I mean, if she did arrange our meeting in the park–"

"Then," Holmes interjected, "she must therefore have had intelligence that we had been invited to Mars, and ensured her presence aboard the *Valorkian* accordingly. My admiration for the woman increases by the second."

"But what can she want?"

"That remains to be seen, Watson. We must be vigilant."

I told him that the human stewards enjoyed stopovers before boarding the next scheduled ship to Earth, and Holmes digested this. "In that case we must ascertain when the next ship leaves for home, so that we know how long we have in which to expect word from her."

"You think she'll contact us?"

"Indubitably," said he.

My heart skipped at the thought, my excitation caused not merely by the idea of derring-do inherent in the situation.

"By Jove!" Professor Challenger ejaculated. "Just feast your eyes on that, my friends!"

I returned my attention to the scene far below, an endless expanse of sand that stretched to the far, curving horizon. Immediately ahead I made out a smudge or blemish that I took for a city, towards which we were hurtling. Directly beneath us was a huge grey circle in the sand, with a single silver filament connecting it to the city on the horizon.

Challenger called out to Grulvax-Xenxa-Goran and asked what the disc might be, and the Martian joined us and peered out.

"That, sir, is Hakoah-Malan," said he. "I suppose you would call it the planet's nerve centre."

"And the metal rail running from it?" Holmes enquired.

"A monorail connecting Hakoah-Malan to the capital of our world," the ambassador said, "the city of Glench-Arkana, directly ahead."

As the ship approached the city, I made out a veritable web of such monorails converging on the metropolis – and upon them, or rather *depending* from them, were carriages like bullets shooting back and forth. Enmeshed in this webwork was an agglomeration of black, carbuncle-like domes, soaring towers and other buildings, which extended for mile upon mile in every direction. In the centre of the city, like the bullseye on a dartboard, stood a great docking station occupied by a phalanx of mammoth interplanetary ships like our own.

"Behold the greatest metropolis in the solar system," Grulvax-Xenxa-Goran proudly informed us, "home to fifty million of my kind."

"Imagine," Challenger muttered. "Fifty million... That's more than the entire population of Great Britain – and all in one vast city!"

The ship decelerated, swung about, and came in low over the metropolis. I stared down at the boulevards thronged with Martian pedestrians and trilobite vehicles, and lined with buildings that emerged from the ground at odd angles, like daggers thrust into the earth. Several of these buildings were festooned with swatches of the red weed – *Hedera helix rubrum Martiannica*, as botanists labelled it – that had overrun London for a month after the first Martian invasion.

We approached the central docking station and came down slowly upon a vast metal flange, grapples like claws closing around the base of the vessel. The superstructure clanged and the roar of the engines gradually diminished into silence.

"Welcome to Mars!" Grulvax-Xenxa-Goran declared. "Now, if you would care to follow me."

We stepped aboard an elevator plate and descended to the vast arched atrium, where our fellow passengers, Martian and human, were gathered prior to disembarkation. I searched the crowd for the blonde-haired figure of Miss Hamilton-Bell, but in vain.

"You will find the gravity of my planet much lighter than that of Earth," Grulvax-Xenxa-Goran explained. "Also, the oxygen content of our atmosphere is not as great as that to which you are accustomed. I recommend you do not unduly exert yourselves, for fear of becoming light-headed."

Already the hatch of the ship was sliding open. I took a deep breath and was reminded of the rarefied air I had last breathed while serving my country in the Hindu Kush.

A flexible umbilical tunnel was manoeuvred up to the exit, and presently we followed our guide from the ship.

"It is mid-afternoon at this longitude," said Grulvax-Xenxa-Goran. "I will take you to a hotel, where you can rest and refresh yourselves. For the rest of the day you will be free to wander our great city. I will come for you at first light tomorrow and show you one or two of our great institutions. Then we will proceed north to the foothills of Olympus Mons, where our esteemed philosopher Delph-Aran-Arapna made his home before his untimely demise."

We emerged from the tunnel into a great terminus, busy with hordes of Martians. The chamber was undecorated, the walls a uniform shade of taupe, and I was reminded rather of the adobe interior of a shattered termite mound I had observed in Afghanistan.

We retrieved our baggage, whereupon Grulvax-Xenxa-Goran escorted us from the building onto a metal deck from which domed air-cars arrived and departed like bumblebees at a hive.

At this juncture we took our leave of Professor Challenger, arranging to meet him at our hotel – the Smerza-Jaran – in two hours for drinks.

An air-car carried us from the docking station, and I stared down at the teeming boulevards of Glench-Arkana. Crowds thronged the thoroughfares, and I beheld a teeming marketplace far below. A strange scent reached my nostrils, which I would forever associate with the red planet – an odour of indefinable spices mixed with an acrid tang that reminded me of hot, lathe-turned metal.

The air-car banked and approached a jet-black ziggurat, a stark silhouette against the mustard-coloured sky, which turned out to be our hotel. The vehicle came down gently and we alighted.

Grulvax-Xenxa-Goran remained in the passenger seat and lifted a tentacle in farewell. "I will collect you here at first light," said he.

I reached into my pocket, out of habit, in search of small change for the cab driver – but came instead upon a square of folded paper as the air-car powered up and flew off.

"Hello," I said. "What on earth…?"

I pulled out the paper, unfolded it, and stared in disbelief at what was written there.

"Well, Watson?" Holmes enquired, studying me.

Not a little startled, I read the note for a second time.

*My Dear Dr Watson,*

*You and Mr Holmes are in extreme danger. Please follow the instructions set down here, and then destroy this note. You must meet me at the Patava-Hutava eating-house, which is situated on a street called Gathra-Hakal to the north of your hotel, at eight o'clock this evening. You will undoubtedly be followed, but my comrades will ensure that this will be dealt with. You might not recognise me, therefore I will carry a green valise. When I have ensured that we are not observed, I will explain everything, and together we can decide what further action should be taken.*

*Yours sincerely,*
*Freya Hamilton-Bell.*

## Chapter Six

*Rendezvous on the Red Planet*

A t half-past seven we left the hotel and hurried through the bustling streets of Glench-Arkana. The day was drawing to a close, and beyond the horizon of domes and towers the sun was setting in a gorgeous laminate of lacquered orange and rose tints. We were the only humans abroad, and our passage down the alleys of the ancient city caused not a little commotion among the crowds. Martians turned and stared at us with their great inky eyes, and the air was filled with the twitter of their commentary. I glanced behind us once or twice – but if we were being followed, I saw no sign.

"But what on earth did she mean, Holmes, when she wrote that we might not recognise her? Of course we will – she's a rather striking specimen of womankind, mark my word. She'd stick out among the Martians like a veritable sore thumb."

"I rather think she was suggesting she would be in disguise," Holmes said.

"Disguise?" I laughed at this. "She would be hard pressed to disguise herself so that she wasn't obvious in a crowd of Martians!"

"We shall see," Holmes said, and indicated a narrow alley.

As planned, we were taking a circuitous route to the Patava-Hutava eating-house, the better to give Miss Hamilton-Bell's comrades an opportunity to delay anyone who might be following us. Holmes had studied a map of the area back at the hotel, and committed the tortuous route to memory. We passed down a thoroughfare given over to the sale of heaped spices and exotic fruit and vegetables. The street was packed with Martian pedestrians and domed bubble-vehicles: it reminded me, in its hustle and hubbub, of a Kabul marketplace.

At one point we heard a screech of brakes and turned to witness, a hundred yards in our wake, an altercation between the driver of a three-wheeled bubble-car and a pedestrian. Holmes gripped my arm. "Likely the work of Miss Hamilton-Bell's comrades," he said. "Hurry – this way."

We darted down a narrow passageway, emerged onto another busy thoroughfare, turned right and then crossed the street and dived down yet another alley. Holmes led the way at a brisk trot, and I followed, confident in my friend's sense of direction. By this time I was utterly lost.

Minutes later we came to a boulevard that I thought I recognised: in the distance was the stepped ziggurat of our hotel. Holmes ushered me down a side street and paused before an open-fronted restaurant above which was a legend in flowing Martian script.

"Here we are," said Holmes, consulting his pocket watch. "And just in time. I make it eight o'clock on the dot."

The eating area comprised a series of low metal tables surrounded not by chairs but by cushions. Perhaps half the tables were occupied by seated Martians taking liquids from silver fluted vessels and eating what looked like flaked fish from huge bowls. An aroma of spicy cooked meat filled the air. I scanned the restaurant, but of Miss Hamilton-Bell there was no sign.

Holmes led the way to a vacant table and we seated ourselves upon the cushions with our backs to the wall, the better to observe the entrance. He perused a drinks menu on the tabletop.

A Martian approached our table and spoke its gargling gobbledegook, to which Holmes replied in kind. The waiter scuttled away. "I ordered two hot spiced drinks which sound not too dissimilar to Kashmiri chai," he informed me.

Another alien approached, and I assumed that this one would take our food order. I was about to tell Holmes that I had little appetite when I noticed that the Martian was carrying a small green valise.

I gripped my friend's arm and hissed, "The game is up, Holmes. Miss Hamilton-Bell has been rumbled – the brute has taken her valise! Should we beat a hasty retreat?"

Holmes leaned forward and addressed the alien in his own language, to which the Martian replied and lowered himself to the cushions on the far side of the table.

"What did he say, Holmes?" I was frantic to know. "What has the accursed beast done to Miss Hamilton-Bell?"

"Lower your voice," Holmes ordered. "You are attracting unnecessary attention."

"But, dash it all, man!"

At this, the Martian reached a tentacle across the table and touched my hand.

"Don't be alarmed, Doctor," whispered the Martian in English. "It is I, Freya, and this is a rubber Martian suit."

"What the…?"

I stared at the hideous headpiece of the alien, and as I did so its ugly beak opened to such an extent that I could see into its maw – and what I observed there caused me first to choke, and then to splutter with laughter.

Miss Hamilton-Bell's uncommonly beautiful face grinned out at me, then gave a conspiratorial wink. The beak clacked shut, and she continued in lowered tones, "I am sorry if I alarmed you, but I was forced to don this disguise through direst necessity. It's dashed uncomfortable in here and hot into the bargain. I will be brief. My friends managed to waylay your tail, but the Martian authorities are so wily that they might have employed more than one agent to keep you under surveillance."

"You said that you would explain everything," I said.

"And so I will," came her somewhat muffled reply.

She fell silent as our drinks arrived, then informed the waiter she would not be requiring anything.

When the Martian had departed, Holmes said, "I take it, Miss Hamilton-Bell, that Watson and I were lured to Mars on false pretences?"

"Just so," she replied.

Holmes explained the spurious reason for our presence here. "My suspicion was aroused when I found no mention of the philosopher, one Delph-Aran-Arapna, in any Martian periodical, encyclopaedia or journal on Earth. It troubled me somewhat that my services should be sought by aliens who, undoubtedly, have their own excellent investigatory organs."

"Like many a human before you," she said, "you have been brought here as part of the Martians' masterplan."

Holmes frowned. "Which is?"

"No less than the total takeover of planet Earth and the eventual annihilation of the human race."

"Good God!" I exclaimed.

Holmes eyed the woman's disguise, deep in thought, then said, "If you don't mind my asking, Miss Hamilton-Bell, how did you become embroiled in opposition to the Martian government?"

I sipped my drink. Its unusual spices danced across my tongue, ending with quite an alcoholic kick. I drained half the flute, then gave my full attention to the woman's hushed words.

"I work," she said, "in the acquisitions department of the Natural History Museum in London, and travel here from time to time to liaise with Martian archaeologists. A year ago I was approached here in the city by a Martian unlike any I had come across before – both in his physical appearance and in his philosophy. This creature was shorter than the norm, his carapace a shade or two darker than the average Martian citizen of this latitude. My interlocutor hailed not from equatorial Mars but from the far north, adjacent to the polar regions. He was of a different race from the specimens you see here. His people are considered primitive by the majority, and even intellectually backward, not unlike the opinion that prevails today in Europe regarding Africans. He told me a terrible story of state repression, torture and genocide – and later I was to see evidence to support his claims: moving pictorial images showing the slaughter of innocents, the bombing of northern cities and towns. But this Martian had not waylaid me to complain of the injustice meted out to his fellows, but to warn me that this was but the start of the Martians' bellicosity."

"You mean…?" I began.

"The eventual wiping out of the human race," she said. "I witnessed enough, in time, to come over to the rebels' side and work for the cause of his people, along with thousands of like-minded humans."

"You mentioned in your note that Watson and I are in danger," Holmes said.

"I have intelligence that your lives will be endangered at some point over the course of the next few days, though I am lacking the precise details. But do not worry – my colleagues and I are working hard to ascertain the Martians' plans."

At that second a Martian advanced across the restaurant and paused beside our table. I sat back, fearing that the authorities were onto us, and had come to arrest our friend.

The alien leaned towards Miss Hamilton-Bell and spoke rapidly in lowered tones. At his words, she struggled upright, manoeuvring her tentacles with obvious difficulty. The newcomer held out a tentacle to steady her.

"Your presence has been reported to the authorities," she said. "My informant warns that security officials are on their way here as I speak. I must leave immediately. It is imperative that you inform Professor Challenger of what I have told you. He, too, is in danger. I will do everything I can to secure your rescue, gentlemen, but now I must make haste."

And, so saying, she scurried from the restaurant with the newcomer and was soon lost to sight amid the crowds in the street outside.

"Drink up, Watson," Holmes said, flinging a couple of notes upon the table.

I did as instructed, my head swirling with the rush of alcohol and from the import of Miss Hamilton-Bell's communiqué, and followed my friend from the restaurant. Holmes turned right along the alley, came to a boulevard, and hailed a passing cab. He gave the driver – this worthy much excited at the fact of his human fare – the name of our hotel, and soon we were beetling at speed along the busy street.

In due course we alighted outside our hotel and found the professor kicking his heels in the foyer. "Hell's teeth, Holmes! Where the blazes have you been?"

"We were delayed," said my friend. "We need to speak immediately, and in private. The hotel has a rooftop bar. This way."

"Confound it, man, you're babbling like the hero of a penny dreadful!"

But Holmes was already leading the way across the foyer and up a flight of stairs, and soon we were ensconced on couches on the elevated rooftop with a spectacular view across the city. A spangle of electric lights gave the aspect of a funfair, the spectacle matched by the fulminating constellations high above.

As I searched the heavens for the bright point that was Earth, Holmes gave the professor a résumé of what we had just learned from Freya Hamilton-Bell.

Challenger listened in silence, his huge face growing ever redder. As Holmes came to the end of his account, I thought that our friend was about to burst, or at least succumb to apoplexy.

"The fiends! The monstrous beasts! Do you know, I did wonder at my summons. I know I'm famous and all that, but why would a bunch of ugly Martians want to hear all about my travels in Arabia?" He stared from me to Holmes. "But what's all this about our lives being endangered – and what the blue blazes do the creatures want with us if we've been lured here under false pretences?"

"That, my friend, we shall no doubt learn in time." Holmes turned to me. "You are quiet, Watson."

"Mmm. Just thinking about Miss Hamilton-Bell – I hope she knows what she's doing, Holmes. I'd hate it if she were to succumb…"

"I wouldn't worry yourself on that score. From what I've seen of Miss Hamilton-Bell, she seems more than able to handle herself."

We sat in the clement evening and watched the last of the sunset, going over and over what we had learned and counselling ourselves to vigilance. As we talked, bolstering our confidence with our shared humanity amid so much that was eerily alien, I succeeded in locating the point of brightness that was planet Earth, and gained a measure of comfort from its presence.

It did not occur to me, not even for one second, that I might never again set foot on my home world.

# Chapter Seven

*Duplicity at the Museum of Martian Science*

I spent a fitful night in my narrow hotel bed, on a short mattress meant for the truncated bodies of our hosts. I tossed and turned, my dreams full of hideous Martian visages, these nightmare masks interspersed with visions of Miss Hamilton-Bell's singular loveliness. In my dreams she was a prisoner of the Martians, stripped of her uniform and chained in a dungeon, awaiting the depredations of her evil tormentors.

I awoke at dawn to find my friend's mattress vacated. Before I could bestir myself to worry for his safety, the hatch opened and Holmes ducked through, his arms laden with local fruit and a bottle of some refreshment.

"I purchased breakfast, as there is none to be had in the establishment and Grulvax-Xenxa-Goran did say that he would arrive for us at first light."

We sat on our bunks and ate the peculiar fruit – in shape resembling apples, but with a yeasty taste and the texture of soap. The liquid was pale green and milk-like; indeed, according to

Holmes it was the product of the Martian equivalent of the terrestrial cow – giant spiders, no less! – and had a spicy tang that made my eyes water.

"Do you think it wise to go along with Grulvax-Xenxa-Goran?" I said at one point.

Holmes ruminated. "Not to do so, Watson, would alert him to the fact that we know something is awry."

"I could always claim illness," I said, and indicated the soapy fruit. "You could say I've come down with food poisoning."

"I am curious to behold this Museum of Martian Science. What might the Martians be up to, Watson?"

"All this talk of the annihilation of the human race, Holmes… Do you think the girl was exaggerating?"

"Her claims are extreme indeed. But if she does rescue us, as she promised, then I have no doubt that she will be eager to substantiate her dire warnings with hard evidence."

We finished our singular breakfast, then descended to the forecourt to await the arrival of Grulvax-Xenxa-Goran.

No sooner had we stepped outside than a bulky air-car descended. A hatch like an insect's wing swung upwards and Grulvax-Xenxa-Goran gestured from the front seat.

In the capacious rear compartment of the vehicle, which was furnished with plush upholstered benches like a Pullman carriage, sat Professor Challenger.

"Our first port of call," the ambassador announced as we settled ourselves beside Challenger, "is the Museum of Martian Science. Professor Challenger's lecture is scheduled for this evening, and I thought he too might care to come along."

I exchanged a glance with Holmes, who said, "Capital idea. I am more than a little curious about the many wonders of your miraculous technologies."

The air-car powered up with a roar of engines, and in a second we were airborne.

As the city slipped away below us, my stomach turned at the thought of what might lie ahead. I recalled Miss Hamilton-Bell's words, and gazed with new hostility at our hideous host and his driver. The Martians were, at the best of times, ugly in the extreme, with their cockroach-coloured tegument, their greasy bristles sprouting from the crater-like follicles that pitted their hides, and their great inky, staring eyes. It had taken some time, after the second wave of Martians arrived on Earth with apologies for the behaviour of their more bellicose cousins, for humankind to look upon the extraterrestrials with anything like equanimity: it did not require much to cast them in the role, in my eyes at least, of the devils we originally thought them to be.

Grulvax-Xenxa-Goran turned in his seat and eyed us. "I understand that you elected to take a stroll before dinner last night?"

"That's right," Holmes said. "We passed a pleasant hour or so taking in the market streets in the vicinity of the hotel."

"And you were not... troubled by a disturbance in that district?"

I glanced at my friend. Was Grulvax-Xenxa-Goran referring to the distraction that had resulted in our minders losing sight of us?

"We did notice a commotion at one point," Holmes said, "an altercation between the driver of a car and a pedestrian."

"There have been instances of terrorist activity in the area," said Grulvax-Xenxa-Goran.

Holmes exchanged a glance with Professor Challenger and myself. "Terrorist activity?"

Our guide waved a tentacle. "Hotheads from the northern deserts," he said, "demanding greater access to water or some such." He changed the subject. "I trust you found a suitable dining establishment during your sojourn?"

"A pleasant little restaurant not far from our hotel," said Holmes.

"And you were not pestered by importuning individuals eager to speak to human beings?"

"Ah…" Holmes temporised, "we did speak to one or two individuals, but I hasten to add that their manners were impeccable. They were merely curious."

"In future," said Grulvax-Xenxa-Goran, "I would be wary of speaking to strangers."

Holmes gave me a significant glance as he settled back in his seat.

At length the air-car came down on the shelf of another ziggurat – the Museum of Martian Science itself – and we took an elevator plate down to the ground floor.

"I thought you might care to view the Hall of Technologies Past," said Grulvax-Xenxa-Goran, leading us through a high archway to a gloomy chamber the size of an airship hangar. As ever with the interior design of public buildings on Mars, the walls were daubed a uniform taupe and had the pitted appearance of something decorated by insects: we might have been inside a termite mound.

More interesting than the lack of decoration, however, were the examples of Martian machinery on display to either side of a central aisle.

First came bulky wheeled vehicles, evidently steam-powered, with high cabs and cauldron-like devices set at their front ends, not unlike the early steam-driven contraptions of the French inventor Nicolas-Joseph Cugnot. As we progressed along the aisle our host provided a running commentary. On Mars, as on Earth, warfare had proved to be the mother of invention. Again and again we passed ground vehicles and fliers whose purpose was to deliver projectiles, missiles and bombs. Soon we came upon early examples of the kind so familiar to every man, woman and child of Earth: the fearsome tripods. These early versions were smaller, on shorter legs, and with cabins large enough to admit just a single Martian driver.

As we moved from this chamber to the next, we came upon machines that, while they retained the basic shape of the tripods' domed cowls, were without the eponymous three limbs. "And these," Grulvax-Xenxa-Goran said, "are the latest Martian war machines, which dispense with the rather clumsy tripod locomotion. These are flying machines, which can circumnavigate the globe in a matter of hours."

We made noises to indicate that we were suitably impressed.

"And yet you chose to quell the nations of Earth with the antiquated, three-legged examples of the machine?" Professor Challenger asked.

Our guide was quick to correct him. "You refer, of course, to the accursed regime that initiated the unprovoked and unwarranted attack upon your world," he said. "The regime that we have since overthrown." Grulvax-Xenxa-Goran gestured with a tentacle back towards the tripods. "*That* regime judged that the tripods would be sufficient to subdue a race which had not yet developed aerial locomotion."

"And were proved correct," Challenger muttered into his beard.

We strolled on, examining what looked like artillery pieces and bulbous rockets. At one point Holmes asked, "How many races dwell upon your planet?"

"Just two, Mr Holmes. We of the equator, the Arkana; and the less populous race of the north, known as the Korshana people."

"And you live in harmony?" Holmes persisted.

"For the most part, though occasional militants from the Korshana people attempt to cause trouble."

"Ah," I said, "the 'terrorists' you mentioned earlier?"

"Just so," said Grulvax-Xenxa-Goran, hurrying us along.

We came to a torpedo-shaped vessel. Unlike every other vehicle we had seen so far, which had been fashioned from pitted materials the hue of graphite, this sleek device was silver.

Grulvax-Xenxa-Goran said, "And here we have the prototype of what we call a deep space probe, which we hope to launch on missions to the outer planets of the solar system before too long." He raised an inviting tentacle. "If you would care to step aboard."

Challenger squeezed his considerable girth through the tiny hatch, followed by Holmes. I brought up the rear, glancing back into the obsidian eyes of our host, who watched me inscrutably.

Within were three fold-down seats facing a console and a blank screen. No sooner had I taken the lead of my friends, and seated myself, than the hatch clanged shut behind me, effectively imprisoning us within the craft.

I leapt to my feet and searched for some kind of handle on the hatch, to no avail. I pummelled upon the metal surface, calling out, "What is this? Let us out at once, I say!"

Holmes was on his feet, his hawk eyes perusing the ceiling.

Challenger bellowed in rage and beat at the metal panels with fists the size of hams.

Seconds later I heard a peculiar hissing sound, and whirled around to see a mist-like vapour billowing down from the ceiling. My friends, being closer to the source of the gas, had fallen to their knees. I turned in panic and recommenced my frantic pounding on the hatch.

Then the gas reached me, and I, too, slipped into unconsciousness.

I was cognisant of very little during the next few hours, though I regained my senses for brief, hallucinatory periods.

At one point I was aware of being manhandled, gripped by numerous tentacles and carried along a lighted corridor. Then I was lying on my back, with a blinding light above me, and the gargoyle face of a peering Martian. A period of oblivion followed, and next I was aware of being moved at speed, not carried this time, but borne along on something wheeled. I felt tentacles gripping me, lifting me, and then I received the impression that I was being shackled hand and foot to some kind of metal frame.

I felt a constriction around my head, then passed rapidly into oblivion and did not resurface for many an hour.

# Chapter Eight

## ∽

*Imprisoned in the Desert*

"Watson! Watson, wake up."

"What the blazes…?"

"Watson," said Holmes. "It's good to have you back in the land of the living."

My friend knelt before me, a hand on my shoulder as I struggled into a sitting position. "Where the deuce are we, Holmes?"

"Where indeed!" came the bellow from Professor Challenger as he strode back and forth, having discarded his safari jacket. "It's infernally hot in here!"

Holmes assisted me to my feet and I took in our surroundings – or rather, I suspected, our prison.

We were in a great chamber, some fifty yards long by ten, constructed from the same adobe material as many of the other Martian buildings I had observed. There were no openings in the chamber, save one: at the far end was a semi-circular window as tall as a man at its apex, barred but otherwise open to the elements.

I made my way across to the opening, accompanied by my

friends, and we stared out upon an unprepossessing scene. A red desert stretched away for as far as the eye could see, devoid of other buildings and featureless save for the natural ripples created by the ceaseless winds. In the distance, on the horizon, rose a jagged range of mountains.

The iron bars were set perhaps nine inches apart, and though I turned myself sideways and attempted to squeeze through the gap, it was to no avail. Likewise Holmes, thinner than myself, attempted to force himself between the bars, with the same result. Challenger made no such futile effort: the gap could have been a yard wide, and would still not be big enough to admit his bulk.

I pulled off my topcoat and unbuttoned my jacket, then mopped my drenched brow with my kerchief.

"At least our gaolers didn't leave us without fluid," Holmes said, pointing to a nearby stack of cannisters. "Water."

The mere word made me realise how thirsty I was, and I crossed to the containers, opened one and drank. The water was warm, but served to slake my thirst.

Holmes was pacing the breadth of the chamber before the barred opening, watched closely by Professor Challenger.

"The very fact that the Martians have supplied us with water, but not food," Holmes said at length, "is interesting in itself, and tells me much: they do not wish us to die of thirst. They wish to keep us alive, but have placed us here for a specific reason. Also, we will remain here for a brief duration only."

"How do you ascertain that?" I said.

"If we were to be incarcerated here for any length of time," he said, "then we would have been supplied with food as well as water."

"Very well, but what do they want from us in the time we might be here – and, confound it, where exactly are we?"

Holmes turned to the opening and peered out, frowning. "We are situated on the Amazonis Planitia, perhaps two thousand miles north of the equator, as the mountain you see on the eastern horizon is none other than Olympus Mons."

"But why in Hell's name have they abandoned us here?" Challenger roared.

"I think we will find out," Holmes said, "in due course."

He resumed his pacing, and paused a minute later to ask, "Watson, what did you experience immediately after passing out in the silver craft back at the museum?"

I recounted my recollection of the bright light, and being examined by a Martian.

"And you, Professor?" Holmes asked.

Challenger shrugged his ox-like shoulders. "I was out for the count from the outset," he said. "I do recollect a bright light, but it's as if I dreamed it. I recall nothing else until I awoke in this confounded hole."

"What about you, Holmes?" I asked.

"I recall coming briefly to my senses to find myself lashed to a frame of chromium bars, while being examined by a Martian who then placed a tight band around my head... After that, nothing."

"But what were the ungodly beasts doing to us, Holmes?" Challenger roared. "By Gad, if I could get my hands on one of the slimy creatures!" And, miming his intent, his huge hands reached out and wrung the neck of an imaginary alien.

"You were asked here to give a lecture, Professor?" Holmes enquired.

"That's right. A couple of talks to the Martian Geographic Society on the subject of my more recent Arabian expeditions."

Holmes stroked his chin. "And did the invitation strike you as... odd?"

"It did cross my mind to wonder why Martians might be interested in Arabia, yes. I might pack the Royal Geographic Society with folk eager to hear my talks, but here on Mars…?" He shrugged.

"I was asked by Grulvax-Xenxa-Goran," Holmes said, "to investigate the murder of a philosopher who, it turns out, does not exist. Our incarceration, gentlemen, can only be linked to the larger picture."

"Which is?" Challenger asked.

"What else but the eventual annihilation of the human race?" said Holmes.

"But…" I said, "how can that be? The Martians are far in advance of us, technologically. Couldn't they merely wipe us out militarily, if that is their ultimate intent?"

Holmes's brow was buckled in an intense frown of concentration. At last he said, "They could, but perhaps they do not wish to annihilate us immediately. Invading armies often utilise the subjugated citizens of a defeated nation as labour – slaves, in other words. Perhaps that is the ultimate fate of our kind, and what is happening on Earth now, with the Martians displaying a benign, even altruistic face, is part of a 'softening up' process."

"And our kidnapping and imprisonment?" Challenger asked. "Where does that fit in?"

"On that sore question I am, for the moment, though I am loath to admit it, as clueless as yourself."

I moved to the opening and gripped the bars. With all my strength I pulled at them, hoping that the stone in which they were set might crumble – but it was a vain hope. The bars were immovable. And anyway, what purpose might be served by our escape from this chamber? We were in the middle of an inimical desert, two thousand miles from civilisation. Even if we were by some miracle to attain the city of Glench-Arkana, how might we find the means to leave Mars and return to Earth?

My spirit shrivelled at the hopelessness of our situation.

I sat with my back against the wall, sweat trickling down my exhausted face, and withdrew my fob-watch from my waistcoat. Therein I kept a photograph of my dear departed Mary, her sweet smile a boon to my senses in this time of need. I lost myself in a happy reverie of recollection, recalling our honeymoon in Brighton, and later holidays in the Scottish Highlands. Never had the memory of my country – even when serving in the sere plains of Afghanistan – provoked such a sense of sadness in my heart.

Holmes noticed my mood. "Chin up, Watson. I will refrain from offering such platitudes as 'Where there's life...', but the fact is that all is not yet hopeless. We must be vigilant, and grasp whatever opportunity comes our way."

I was of a mind to say that that was all very well, but the fact remained that we were imprisoned in the middle of a desert on a planet many millions of miles from home. But I held my tongue. "You're right, Holmes. There is always hope."

"That's the spirit, Watson," said my friend. He sat down next to me and stared at Challenger, who had slumped against the far wall and closed his eyes.

"That's odd," Holmes said.

"What is?" I asked.

"Watson, am I correct in stating that earlier, when we first met Professor Challenger in the air-car this morning, he was not wearing his sola topi?"

"Why... I can't rightly recall."

"He wasn't, of that I am certain," my friend pronounced, pointing. "And yet now he is."

I was about to ask Holmes what he might be driving at when

Professor Challenger opened his eyes suddenly, cocked his head, and said, "Am I going mad, or do I hear the approach of an infernal Martian air-car?"

Holmes bent an ear towards the opening. "I do believe you're right."

I jumped to my feet and peered through the bars.

Faint at first, and then growing louder, I made out the throb of an engine. I scanned the skies for any sign of the vessel, but saw nothing other than the slow tumble of Phobos far to the north.

Holmes joined me at the opening, and Challenger swore to himself as a vehicle passed directly overhead, the engine noise rising to a deafening volume.

"There!" cried Holmes, pointing.

A domed air-car came into view and settled on the sands a hundred yards before our gaol. At this distance I was unable to make out the pilot behind the tinted glass, and I waited with bated breath for the individual to show himself.

"This is it," Challenger said. "The blighters have come to proposition us – or threaten us. I fear that soon we shall learn our fate." He slammed a fist into his meaty palm. "But I for one refuse to go down without a fight!"

"It might not come to fisticuffs," Holmes said. "I advise caution until we learn what the Martians require from us."

"If they ever get round to it," I said, for whoever had piloted the air-car thus far was showing no inclination to climb out and approach our prison.

The air-car sat, a paralysed trilobite, under the ceaseless sun.

An hour elapsed, then two.

"This is intolerable!" Challenger raged. "Are they playing games with us, d'you think?"

"I am at a loss to second-guess their motives," Holmes admitted.

A further hour elapsed and the sun, moving overhead and slanting its light now from the west, shone directly into the air-car.

"Upon my word, Watson," Holmes said. "The vehicle is quite empty."

I peered through the bars. "You're right. There isn't a soul in the driver's seat, nor in the rear."

"But why should our enemies have sent an *empty* car?" Challenger mused.

"Perhaps not our enemies," Holmes said, "but our allies."

"You think someone sent it so that, were we able to escape this chamber…?"

"It seems an odd way to go about achieving our salvation, Watson," he admitted.

Again I fell to struggling with the bars, but I might as well have attempted to uproot an oak tree: they were immovable – and no matter how hard I tried, I could not force myself between the rods of iron. I gave up and slaked my thirst with water.

All was still and silent out there, and the only sound I heard was the occasional imprecation from the professor and my own thumping heartbeat.

And then, all of a sudden, the roar of an engine filled the air, and I rushed back to the opening, fully expecting to see the air-car powering up and taking off.

Instead, a second vehicle swooped down from the heavens, approached the opening and hovered before us.

Its pilot leaned forward, gesturing frantically behind the windscreen for us to move away from the opening.

"By Jove, Holmes!" I cried.

My heart surged with joy, for the pilot, our saviour, was none other than Miss Freya Hamilton-Bell.

## Chapter Nine

*A Simulacrum Revealed*

We hurried to the back of the chamber, and turned to watch as Miss Hamilton-Bell reversed the air-car away from the opening.

"How in damnation does she hope to get us out of here?" Challenger asked.

"By the only expedient open to her," said Holmes. "Watch."

She eased the air-car forward slowly; its bonnet came up against the bars. Through the windscreen I made out the young woman's face, her tongue-tip showing in concentration as she increased power and the air-car pressed forward.

As I watched, three bars bent, then popped from their moorings with an explosion of shattered stone and skittered across the floor. The air-car surged forward, sending more bars rattling across the chamber, then reversed from the opening and settled in the desert. In a trice Miss Hamilton-Bell leapt from the pilot's seat, climbed onto the dome of the air-car, and from there jumped through the opening and into the chamber.

She wore the green uniform of the Martian spaceship line, with the little pillbox hat perched on the side of her head, and I thought I had never seen a more beautiful sight in all my life.

"But how did you find us?" I blurted, rushing forward and taking her hand in gratitude.

"My comrades traced your progress from the museum and north to this prison," she said. "We then had to second-guess the motivation of your captors."

"That," said Holmes, "is what has been taxing my thoughts for some time. It occurred to me that we might very well be the bait in a cunning trap."

"In which case," I said in fear, "have the Martians succeeded?"

"You are correct, Mr Holmes," said Miss Hamilton-Bell. "The Martians did indeed sequester you here in an attempt to lure members of the opposition."

"But in that case..." I moaned.

"Fear not, Dr Watson." She smiled at me. "The Martians would not be satisfied with the capture of just a single rebel. They desire far more than that."

"I don't quite follow."

"When we learned where they had taken you," she said, "we decided to send in an air-car by remote control – to test the waters, as it were. If your Martian captors then pounced, we knew that this was a simple trap designed to capture one or two members of the opposition. If, however, they let it be, then we knew that a much more sophisticated operation was under way."

"And the latter has proved to be the case," Holmes said. "But what is that operation?"

Miss Hamilton-Bell paced back and forth. "For a long while the Martian authorities have attempted to locate the rebels' base.

They have followed my comrades, recruited spies, employed all manner of devious means to root out and destroy those Martians which oppose their draconian rule – but to no avail. We have always remained one step ahead of them. However... I suspect that we were observed, or overheard, by government spies in the restaurant in Glench-Arkana, and they devised a scheme to imprison you here as bait. No doubt they plan to follow us to the rebels' headquarters in the north."

Her lips formed a stern line as she looked at each of us. "We had a comrade working in the museum," she said, "who reported that you had all been scanned, and that you were unconscious for an hour or two afterwards. That was all the time they required to put their plan into action."

"Scanned?" I said.

She pulled something from the pocket of her jacket. It was a small, silver object about the size of a cigarette case. Set into its leading edge was what looked like a small glass bead. She directed the device at Professor Challenger and pressed a stud on its side. Instantly, the small bead glowed blue.

What happened next not only shocked but horrified me.

Professor Challenger, one moment at my side, at the next leapt forward with a deafening bellow and dashed the implement from the woman's grip. "No!"

The device flew through the air and rattled across the stone floor, and Challenger, like a man possessed, dived after it. I watched in shock, hardly able to believe my eyes, as Miss Hamilton-Bell – with lightning-fast reactions – leapt towards the professor and, with a display of startling acrobatics, swivelled in the air and lashed out with her right leg. Her shod foot caught Challenger in the midriff and with a mighty gust of expelled air he barrelled backwards and hit the wall. She lost no time in diving for the device, snatching it up, and backing away from Challenger as he staggered forward and gathered himself to attack.

"What's possessed you, man!" I cried. "She rescued us, for pity's sake! Can't you see that she's on our side?"

As Challenger surged towards Miss Hamilton-Bell, she drew a second device from her pocket and directed it at the professor. This was a handgun, and had the immediate effect of bringing Challenger up short.

His consternation was short-lived, however. In the act of raising his arms into the air, he dived sideways towards me, gripped me about the neck and then manhandled me so as to put my body between himself and Miss Hamilton-Bell. I was now, in effect, a shield.

Moreover, he fastened his meaty fingers around my neck and called out, "One move and Watson is dead!"

"Have you taken leave of your senses?" I choked. "Unhand me at once!"

His fingers increased their grip on my throat.

Holmes took one step towards me, consternation twisting his features.

"I never had you down as a traitor to the human race," said he. "You, of all men, I would have thought loyal to king and country. What are you thinking of, Challenger? What twisted motive has made you throw your lot in with the Martians?"

Miss Hamilton-Bell stepped forward. She, of all of us, seemed in charge of the situation: her demeanour possessed an enviable *sangfroid* as she smiled across at Challenger. "Would you care to answer Mr Holmes's question, or shall I tell them?"

"We shall prevail!" Challenger bellowed. "We invaded Earth for good reason, and we shall prove ultimately victorious! The perfidy of the opposition, in attempting to waylay our masterplan, is misguided and short-lived!"

"You say 'we'?" Holmes said. "How can you align yourself with our oppressors, Professor? Consider how the people of Great Britain might view you, a hero of the nation, a man decorated and feted for his unswerving devotion to the Empire, grovelling now at the feet of tyrants! What have they promised you, Challenger? Wealth, power – the means to explore the solar system at your leisure?"

Challenger growled, his fingers tightening on my oesophagus.

I fought for breath, but my lungs were bursting and my vision failing.

Miss Hamilton-Bell lifted the weapon in her right hand and aimed it in my direction.

"Dr Watson," she said calmly, "I apologise in advance."

And so saying, she lifted the handgun a fraction and fired.

I expected to hear the deafening report of a bullet, but heard instead the sharp crackle of an electrical current. And instead of a bullet, there issued from the handgun a dazzling blue light which missed me by a fraction and hit Professor Challenger square on the forehead. He cried out, electrocuted, and in that instant I too felt a jolt of electrical current conducted through his hands. Challenger released his grip on my throat and fell to the floor, choking. I staggered across the chamber. Holmes caught me and lowered me to a sitting position against the wall, and together we watched the next act of the drama play out.

Miss Hamilton-Bell strode across the chamber and stood over the prostrate form of Professor Challenger, staring down at him with neither pity nor revulsion on her face. Businesslike, she slipped the handgun under her belt and drew a knife.

She knelt before the professor and, as I watched in horror, thrust the blade into his throat. With a savage downward motion, she opened the man's torso from pharynx to abdomen.

I expected blood, of course, and was wholly unprepared for what did emerge from the gaping wound – which was precisely nothing.

Holmes left my side and joined Miss Hamilton-Bell, kneeling to closer examine her handiwork. I struggled to my feet and joined them, still reeling from the after-effects of the electrocution.

Miss Hamilton-Bell took a firm grip on the flesh to either side of the gaping wound and ripped open the chest cavity.

I stared, disbelieving, and attempted to work out quite what I was looking at.

Not blood and bone, or glistening musculature or adipose tissue, no – but masses of wires and circuitry and silver anodes.

"What the…?" I began.

She smiled up at me. "Not Professor Challenger," she said, "but an ingenious simulacrum."

"And thus the sola topi is explained," Holmes said under his breath. "I thought it odd that Challenger did not have it with him this morning, and yet did so now."

Miss Hamilton-Bell climbed to her feet, dusting her palms together and staring down at what I still thought of as Professor Challenger. "The Martians scanned you at the museum and created what they call 'cognitive copies' – in other words, copies of your minds, your personalities, which they then downloaded into mechanical simulacra, designed to resemble you in every detail."

Holmes nodded. "And then they switched the real professor for this copy in order to carry out their scheme to entrap you and your comrades?"

"Precisely," she replied, indicating the simulacrum. "My colleagues and I received intelligence that somewhere amid all that machinery is a beacon, relaying to the Martians its precise whereabouts."

"But what became of the real Challenger?" I asked.

"Our agents reported that the professor met his end shortly after he was scanned," she said. "Apparently he came round and attacked a Martian, and was summarily despatched."

I hung my head at the thought of the death of such a brave man. "May his death not have been in vain," I murmured.

"I second that sentiment," said Holmes, adding, "but if Challenger were an *exact* copy of the original, then how was it that he admitted to being on the side of the Martians?"

"The copies are exact," she said, "but overlaid on an autonomous mind, programmed to do the bidding of the Martians."

"Fiendish," I said.

Holmes regarded Miss Hamilton-Bell. "But something puzzles me," he went on. "Tell me, do the Martians know that you have these devices capable of detecting the simulacra?"

"We are confident, Mr Holmes, that they do not."

My friend frowned. "Then the mystery deepens. If the Martians assumed you could not detect a simulacrum, then why did they not simply kill Watson and me at the museum, as they did poor Challenger, and replace us here with our simulacra?"

Miss Hamilton-Bell shook her head. "Yes, that is odd. Perhaps it's something as simple as the possibility that your simulacra were not quite ready at the time, and they satisfied themselves by sending Challenger's copy, which was."

Holmes nodded to himself, but I could tell that he was far from convinced by the explanation.

"And now," said Miss Hamilton-Bell, "if you would be so good as to help me drag the simulacrum to the first vehicle..."

We bent and took hold of the unholy creature, and I must admit that the sensation of gripping its clammy ersatz flesh – fabricated from some kind of lifelike rubber compound – was altogether sickening.

Miss Hamilton-Bell and I took a foot each and, with Holmes gripping its arms, we hauled the body towards the arched opening and dropped it over the edge, then jumped down and dragged the thing across to the first air-car. Miss Hamilton-Bell opened the pilot's door and we heaved the bulk of the fake Challenger into the front seat.

Panting with exertion, she mopped sweat from her brow and stared about the cloudless sky. "Now," she said, "to send our enemy on a wild goose chase."

She ducked into the cockpit of the air-car, ran an expert hand across the control console, then stepped back smartly and slammed the door. We retreated as the engine powered up and the vehicle rose into the air, banked and accelerated in a westerly direction. Soon it was but a dwindling dot in the alien sky.

We crossed to the second air-car, and a minute later were speeding towards the northern fastness of the Martian rebels.

# Chapter Ten

*Miss Hamilton-Bell Explains*

I woke with a start sometime later, astounded that I had managed to fall asleep after so much excitement. Miss Hamilton-Bell called from the pilot's seat, "My apologies. We hit a little turbulence back there."

"That's quite all right," Holmes replied. "I was awake, though I think the good doctor's slumber was disturbed."

"I feel well rested," I said, stretching in my seat. "I say, how long have we been aloft?"

"A little over six hours," she said. "We should arrive at Zenda-Zakan in approximately fifteen minutes."

Holmes repeated the name. "The city of the rebels?"

"That's right – one of the few still inhabited."

I peered through the window to my left. Far below, the red sands stretched to the curved horizon, the only interruption being a low range of mountains to the west and, straight ahead, a lake similar to that I had witnessed from the *Valorkian* two days ago. However, as we flew over the 'lake' I saw that my vision had been tricked. The shimmering silver expanse was a vast plain of glass like the roof of a gigantic hothouse. Here and there across its scintillating surface I made out dark jagged gashes or rents where the glass had been smashed.

"What the blazes is that?" I asked, pointing.

"That is the abandoned city of Kalthera-Jarron," she said. "It was once the second largest city of the Korshana people, until the Arkana's attack. You see the damage where the atom-missiles struck? The chaos caused far below, in the city itself, and the loss of life occasioned, was truly horrific."

"But why were the Arkana and the Korshana at war?" Holmes asked.

She smiled sadly. "For the same reason that wars occur on Earth," she said. "The two peoples are ideologically opposed. This was not a war over territory, though that did come into it, so much as two implacably opposing views on how to manage the future of the Martian people."

"Intriguing," Holmes murmured. "And what were these mutually exclusive ideologies?"

"For you to fully understand that," she said, "first I must explain something about the cosmological situation of the red planet. You see, for as long as the Martian race has been technologically 'civilised' – that is, for the past five hundred years – scientists have been aware that Mars is moving slowly but inexorably away from the sun. This has the effect of making the surface of the planet ever cooler, while the atmosphere has become thinner. For a few hundred years, the ability of Martian scientists to do anything to effect a change in the situation was scant. However, with the advance of their science, methods have been devised whereby the future of the planet and its people was made secure – for a few millennia, at any rate. Engineers from the northern university at Zenda-Zakan came up with a means of making many of their cities hermetic by covering them with glass roofs, such as you saw back there. Also, scientists devised machines which could extract oxygen from the very rock itself, and in so doing employ the planet as 'lungs'. The northern cities underwent a transformation; it helped that many of them were already ensconced in rift valleys or fissures, so that they could be covered by the great glass 'lids'. The cities of the equator were built upon flat plains, however, and moving them and their populations to vast, prebuilt underground domiciles proved somewhat problematic, as well as costly. So the politicians of the Arkana came up with an alternative solution."

Holmes nodded sagely. "Allow me to hazard a guess – not something I am usually wont to do," said he. "The Arkana suggested that a wholesale removal of their people to the neighbouring world, namely Earth, might prove a more practical solution to their problems?"

"Exactly so," said Miss Hamilton-Bell. "They saw that Earth was an ideal refuge. It possessed just the right mix of oxygen and nitrogen in its atmospheric make-up, had bountiful supplies of raw materials, with vast uninhabited tracts of land, and a population that was technologically unsophisticated. So the peaceful solution of the northerners was abandoned, and preparations were made for the invasion of Earth.

"At the same time as the first armadas set sail in '94, bent on the bloody invasion of Earth, the Arkana resumed hostilities with the states of the north, in a bloodlust fuelled, no doubt, by the prospect of their imminent victory over we humans. But their triumph on Earth was premature. Little did they think that their invasion would be thwarted by humble Terran pathogens."

"And all on our planet duly rejoiced!" said I.

"In the years that followed," she went on, "the Arkana succeeded in creating antibodies to combat terrestrial diseases, and in due course they set off again for Earth. Since the first invasion, however, the Martians had taken the time to reconsider the modus operandi of their invasion. Rather than expend money and valuable resources on conquering Earth militarily, it was decided that they would occupy our planet by ostensibly peaceful means, and so they came masquerading as our altruistic benefactors – a ruse that pulled the wool over the eyes of the leaders of our planet."

She paused to point through the glass. "There, on the horizon, is what remains of the city of Zenda-Zakan. We will make landfall nearby and head for a system of tunnels where my rebel comrades have their base."

The air-car banked, and I held on as we swooped through the air towards the surface of the desert.

"And the ultimate aim of the equatorial Martians," Holmes said, "is to take control of our world until such time as all opposition has been wiped out and they can effect the mass transfer of their citizens to Earth?"

"That is the situation in a nutshell," said Miss Hamilton-Bell. "Already they are moving their efforts away from the war against the Korshana, and concentrating on Earth. Now we will land, take sustenance, and plan the next leg of our journey."

"The next leg," I echoed. "To where, exactly?"

"Back to Glench-Arkana," she said.

She frowned in concentration as she brought the air-car in low over the dunes, decelerated, and landed on a featureless swathe of sand. As we climbed from the vehicle, emerging into the warmth of the evening sun, I saw a dark patch in the side of a nearby dune, and no sooner had I set eyes upon this feature than a dozen or more small, dark-skinned Martians emerged from the mouth of the tunnel and scuttled across to the air-car. Amid much waving of tentacles and high-pitched Martian greetings we found ourselves surrounded by the Korshana people, and Miss Hamilton-Bell bent to embrace certain individuals and speak to them in their staccato tongue.

She laughed and turned to us. "They are overjoyed to see us," she explained, "as they feared that we'd been captured and killed. This way."

Buoyed along by the crowd, we followed her across the sand and into the shade of the tunnel. When my vision adjusted, assisted by globe-lighting that illuminated the tunnel at intervals of twenty feet, I saw that we were hurrying down what looked like a steeply sloping mineshaft shored up by metal girders. Soon the sandy surface underfoot gave way to ringing metal, and as if by some miracle – for surely we had descended a hundred yards beneath the surface of the planet already? – daylight shone ahead of us. We came out onto a great gallery running around the edge of a vast chasm, and I looked up to see an extensive honeycombed awning of glass, through which the setting sun cast its rufous rays. We were in the bomb-blasted city of Zenda-Zakan.

I glanced to my left, over the gallery rail, and wished that I had not given in to my curiosity. The chasm seemed bottomless, and my head swam with vertigo. Far below, I made out the ruins of gallery after fire-blackened gallery.

Miss Hamilton-Bell turned down a wide, burned-out corridor. She came to a double door and pushed it open, standing aside so that we could enter. The room was large and sunlit – its far wall comprised a single floor-to-ceiling window that overlooked the chasm and was illuminated by sunlight slanting in through the glass roof high above.

"You will find hot running water," she said, pointing to an arrangement of brass pipes and a large water tank. "I suggest that you refresh yourselves and meet me next door in thirty minutes. We have much to discuss."

With this, she took her leave.

I stripped to the waist, ran a tank full of hot water, and proceeded to wash myself with a great scouring sponge no doubt designed for tough Martian skin. Holmes, for his part, merely paced back and forth, lost in introspection.

I dried myself on a towel, donned my old and somewhat sweat-stained clothing, and joined Holmes at the window.

He was gazing down at the wreckage with a lugubrious expression.

"A race which can visit such death and destruction on its own kind," he said, "will have no qualms about wiping out the entirety of mankind when it suits them. The 'second wave' have treated us with kid gloves so far, Watson, but judging by what Miss Hamilton-Bell has told us, that will not continue. As soon as they have gathered sufficient materiel and turned their attention from subjugating their own…"

A communicating door opened, and a Martian appeared. He fluted something, to which Holmes replied in kind. "Miss Hamilton-Bell is ready," he said, "and a council of war has convened."

We followed the Martian into a large room dominated by a low, oval brass table. Around it, on cushions, were seated a dozen dark-skinned Martians, and as we crossed the room and took vacant cushions beside Miss Hamilton-Bell, twenty-four huge eyes charted our progress in silence.

As soon as we were seated, half a dozen voices spoke up, seemingly conversing across each other in high passion. It was a wonder that any sense could be made of the din, but Miss Hamilton-Bell pitched into the debate in the Martian language and held forth for long minutes, and a silence descended as all those around the table listened to what she had to say.

At last she gestured, and others spoke in turn, and she turned to us and murmured, "They are debating how we should proceed – they have two or three different proposals. I think it is only a matter of time before an agreement is reached."

"Which brings me back to my earlier question," Holmes said. "What are the Martians' motives in making copies of Watson and myself?"

"It is all part of their masterplan, Mr Holmes. To smooth the way for their ultimate invasion, they need the assistance of the human race itself – and how better to achieve that than to 'copy' certain individuals of influence?"

"You mean…?"

"Over the course of the past few years," she said, "many world leaders have travelled to Mars."

At her words, a great weight settled in my stomach, and an even greater weight upon my soul.

"I would venture to say," said Holmes grimly, "that almost every leader of note has at some point made the journey."

"And not returned," she said, glancing from Holmes to myself. "Oh, to all intents and purposes they come back to Earth with great tales of the scientific wonders they have beheld, and highfalutin notions of peace between our peoples, but…"

"But these are copies," Holmes said grimly, "simulacra of our leaders, planted to do the bidding of their masters."

My senses swam at the very idea, and at length I brought myself to ask the question, "But what became of the originals?

Why, just last year Asquith made the journey."

Miss Hamilton-Bell gazed down at her hands on the tabletop. "What do you think became of our prime minister, and all the others, Doctor?" she murmured. "Like Professor Challenger, they were copied and then despatched."

"But presumably," said Holmes, "the mechanical simulacra do not age? So how then might the Martians maintain the conceit?"

"By the simple expedient of periodically recalling the simulacra," she said, "and making adjustments to their appearance."

I closed my eyes briefly, sickened. Holmes, not usually given to profanity, swore quietly to himself, then leaned forward and said, "You mentioned earlier that we would return to Glench-Arkana."

Miss Hamilton-Bell held up a hand. "One moment, please."

She spoke in Martian, silencing the noise around the table. She fired off what sounded like questions to various individuals, and nodded at their replies.

Minutes later she turned to us and said, "As we speak, the Arkana are preparing to send the simulacra of yourselves back to Earth on the next ship, scheduled to leave Mars less than a day from now. Once arrived on Earth, your doubles will take up your old life in 221B Baker Street as if nothing untoward has occurred – conveying information to their masters and awaiting the call to assist the ultimate invasion." She looked from Holmes to myself, with steel in her bright blue eyes. "We must ensure that they do not succeed in transporting your simulacra to Earth. To this end, we will apprehend them and make the switch – insinuating yourselves in their place – without their guards suspecting a thing. We will then disable the simulacra, and you can proceed to Earth as double agents, so to speak."

"A tall order," Holmes opined.

"A tall order indeed, sir. The only alternative – and we might be forced into it, if all does not go well – would be to send you two back to Earth aboard a vessel we have readied here. But I will be honest and tell you that the vessel is old and not a little unsafe, and since the war killed many of the Korshana's finest scientists and technicians, our interplanetary vessels are not of the best."

"If we fail to make the switch with our doppelgängers in Glench-Arkana," Holmes said, "then to leave for Earth aboard the substandard ship is a risk that we must take. We *must* return to Earth, to continue the fight against our Martian oppressors."

"Hear, hear!" I called out.

Miss Hamilton-Bell gave a thin-lipped smile. "Excellent. We will spend the night here, and at first light proceed to Glench-Arkana and attempt to effect the switch. To that end…" She called out in Martian, and a pair of aliens who had been guarding the entrance hurried out and returned, a minute later, hauling what at first I assumed were three captive Martians.

They dropped the captives before the table – yet they were not Martians at all, but rubber suits.

"I am afraid," said Miss Hamilton-Bell, "that if we are to succeed in the next step of the operation, then tomorrow we must travel to Glench-Arkana in disguise."

I stared down at the macabre sight of the flopping rubber Martians prostrated at our feet, and I could not help but laugh.

## Chapter Eleven

*Disaster Strikes*

The following morning Miss Hamilton-Bell helped us into our rubber disguises, which opened via long lateral slits at the back of the head-torsos. While she held my suit steady, I stepped into the gap and worked my legs into the two thicker, central tentacles. I could not stand upright, of course, due to the short stature of the average Martian, but was forced to assume an uncomfortable crouching position, working my head into the space at the front of the suit and ensuring that I could see through the opening of the beak. A series of levers to my left and right worked the supernumerary forward and aft tentacles, as well as opening and closing the beak. Locomotion was achieved by moving one's lower legs in an excruciating series of shuffles.

Once we were installed in the suits, Miss Hamilton-Bell examined us closely and declared that we would pass muster, then donned her own suit.

"The situation is this," she said as she piloted us south. "The Martians are holding your simulacra in a safe house close to the spaceport. We have spies in place, monitoring the situation. The next ship will leave for Earth at four o'clock, eight hours from now. The simulacra will be transferred to the ship a few hours before it is due to depart."

I stared through the glass at the land passing far below. A canal arrowed towards the horizon, dotted with all manner of sailing craft.

"I have been contemplating the situation on Earth," Holmes observed sometime later, his voice muffled. "Our task of defeating the invaders is made all the more difficult due to the fact that among our own kind are the simulacra, scheming to further the ends of the Martians."

"The good news on that front," she replied, "is that, thanks to the network of spies in Glench-Arkana, we know who some of these mechanical imposters are. The difficulty will be to neutralise them and persuade the various governments on Earth of the Martians' intentions."

"On the face of it," I said, "that appears a hopeless task."

"All is not hopeless, Dr Watson," she said. "The forces of the north, though punished heavily in the war, are not defeated: they have armaments and citizens aplenty with which to oppose the Arkana. Also, among the ranks of the equatorial Martians there are those who oppose the barbarity of their fellows. Together we can overcome our oppressors and rid our planet of the Martian menace."

"Well said," Holmes applauded. "I for one relish the task ahead."

I stared through the glass and wished that I could be as sanguine as my friend, then settled back in my seat for the remainder of the journey south.

In due course the ugly spires and domes of Glench-Arkana hove into sight, sectioned by the spoke-like roads and monorails that converged on the central spaceport. Miss Hamilton-Bell brought the air-car down between a quiet canal and a terrace of low dwellings constructed of the ubiquitous dark grey material. The only splash of colour was provided by the red weed that climbed the frontage of the buildings.

To our right, beyond the canal, was the corrugated grey perimeter wall of the spaceport. Beyond loomed the towering nose-cones of Martian spaceships, standing tall beside ugly webwork gantries. Terminal buildings, bending like scimitars embedded blade-first into the ground, gave the skyline a wholly exotic appearance.

Miss Hamilton-Bell pointed a tentacle along the street. "The building with the green door is the safe house."

"What is the plan?" Holmes asked.

"Your simulacra are in the safe house," she said, "watched over by two security guards. However, in a little over fifteen minutes, two guards from the spaceport will collect your copies for the short journey to the ship that will take them to Earth. These guards are Korshana sympathisers. They will take custody of the simulacra in their air-car, and we will follow them to a quiet area of the city. There they will deactivate the simulacra and you will take their place. You will proceed with the guards to the ship, and in a week will once again be on Earth."

"But if we take the place of the simulacra, then presumably we will not be fed for the duration of the voyage? I for one don't fancy going a week without food or water!"

"Nor I!" I said.

"Do not worry," she said, "we will have agents aboard the ship who will ensure that you are supplied with food and drink."

"And you?" I asked.

"I will remain here, working for the rebel cause in whatever capacity I can."

As we waited, my thoughts strayed to Professor Challenger and all the other innocent humans who had been lured to their deaths on the red planet. I thought of Asquith, our prime minister, and William Howard Taft from the States, and the leaders from nations all across the globe. I recalled that just last year the press had made much of Field Marshall Kitchener's voyage to Mars – being the first military man granted the privilege – and before that writers such as Jules Verne and Joseph Conrad had accepted invitations to lecture there. I thought of Shaw and Chesterton, whom I had listened to in Hyde Park little more than a week ago: I wondered if they had been informed, by the rebels, of the imposition of the simulacra?

It struck me, as I sat in the back of the air-car, my pulse racing, that the situation was bleak: great forces were ranged against us, and our resistance seemed puny by comparison. At least – I cheered myself with the thought – we had feisty individuals like Freya Hamilton-Bell with whom to share the fight.

"Two minutes to go," she said.

In due course an air-car landed in the street outside the safe house, and two Martians climbed down from the vehicle and approached the building. One of them pressed a panel beside the door with its tentacle, then stood back and waited.

The door opened; a Martian appeared and ogled the pair with its huge black eyes. Conversation passed between the aliens, and I awaited the appearance of the simulacra. Truth to tell, I was more than a little curious at the notion of looking upon a copy of myself.

"What's taking so long?" Miss Hamilton-Bell said at one point. "The handover was arranged at the highest level – the authorities should have no cause for suspicion."

The two rebel guards passed what looked like official papers over to the house guard, who scrutinised the documents. A second house guard appeared, and the first passed the papers to him.

"Make haste!" Miss Hamilton-Bell urged.

At last, the house guards stepped aside, apparently satisfied, and gestured back into the building. At this, two familiar figures stepped through the doorway and joined the rebel guards.

The sight of Holmes and myself left me speechless. Holmes was as I had always seen him, an exact replica down to his long, measured gait and the alert way in which he held his head – but their version of myself? Was I really that short, and portly; and did I comport myself with such a rush, and on such short legs?

I did my best to banish vanity and watch as the bodyguards led the imposters across the street towards their air-car.

Just as I was thinking that the operation was going without a hitch, one of the house guards called out something that made the rebel pair stop in their tracks and turn. The house guards stepped into the street and faced the rebels. A lengthy altercation ensued.

"What's happening?" I asked.

"I don't like this one bit," was all Miss Hamilton-Bell would say.

As we watched, my heartbeat rapid, one of the house guards pulled a weapon from a bandolier slung around its torso and waved it at the rebels.

"I can only assume that they found some irregularity with the false documentation," she muttered. "I must do something. Remain here!" she added.

And so saying she extended a tentacle, opened the door, and before we could say a word to make her think again, slipped from the vehicle and hurried along the street.

I leaned forward, sweating all the more in the infernal Martian suit. "What the bally hell is she doing?" I cried.

Beside me, Holmes urged caution. "I am sure she has a plan of action."

Miss Hamilton-Bell approached the four aliens and two simulacra. As the house guards turned to address her, the rebel pair acted. One drew a weapon and shot the first house guard, then turned it upon the second.

"Look!" Holmes cried, pointing a tentacle.

I stared in horror as at least four further Martians tumbled from the safe house, drawing weapons and attacking the rebels – and attacking, also, Miss Hamilton-Bell. She threw herself to the floor and rolled towards the Martian, skittling it in short order and regaining her feet.

While this was going on, another air-car arrived upon the scene, a larger one this time, which disgorged half a dozen Martians – both Korshana and Arkana – who flung themselves into the melee.

The fighting was hand-to-hand now, with tentacles flailing and only occasionally a Martian able to use its weapon with any certitude.

Soon I found it impossible to tell friend from foe as squat aliens fought in the street. An incongruous sight amid the carnage, however, was the simulacra: either deactivated by the house guards, or finding themselves in a situation they had not been programmed to handle, they stood frozen like shop window mannequins while the battle raged about them.

At one point in the fight, Miss Hamilton-Bell fell to the ground and lay still. At first I thought that she had fallen victim to the assault, but Holmes cried out, "No! Look…"

The suit that contained the woman was moving, and I knew then what she was doing. Her freedom of movement hampered by the suit, she was attempting to squirm from it.

I was beside myself with apprehension, willing her to play dead.

Duly she succeeded in fighting free of the suit, and emerged – like a beautiful butterfly from an ugly chrysalis – into the fray.

Then she pulled a weapon and fired at an advancing alien.

She missed, and her attacker raised his weapon. Miss Hamilton-Bell, displaying her skill at ju-jitsu that she had first exhibited in the desert, pirouetted and lashed out a long leg, catching the alien in its face and sending it sprawling across the street. She ducked the blow of an advancing alien, raised her weapon, and fired. The Martian hit the ground, its tentacles thrashing.

We watched in mounting horror as yet another air-car descended. Six burly brutes jumped out and joined the fray, and for the next thirty seconds all was a whirl of confusion as shots rang out and perhaps two dozen aliens lashed at each other with flying tentacles. Miss Hamilton-Bell fought like a dervish, accounting for two or three Martians – and then turned to see three creatures advancing upon her.

"We must do something!" I cried.

"Agreed," said Holmes, opening the door and leading the way.

We tumbled from the air-car and approached the melee.

Miss Hamilton-Bell looked around her in desperation as the Martians advanced. I was willing her to take to her heels when the leading alien drew a weapon and, with a deliberation terrible to behold, fired at her from close range. She staggered backwards, clutching her chest – her eyes wide with shock – and tumbled to the ground. Her attacker pressed his advantage, advanced upon her recumbent form, and brought the butt of his weapon down on her skull with a crushing blow.

Sickened, I averted my gaze.

Seconds later I felt strong tentacles grab my arm. As I was

dragged away, I had one last brief glimpse of Miss Hamilton-Bell: she was lying immobile fifty yards away, her skull rent asunder.

I was frog-marched along the street and unceremoniously bundled into the back of an air-car the size of a pantechnicon. Holmes landed beside me with a grunt and the doors were slammed shut and locked. Seconds later the roar of engines and a certain buoyancy told us that we were airborne.

I thought of Professor Challenger, and all the other humans who had fallen foul of the merciless Martians, and though I knew that it was my fate to join them, I felt little personal fear, numbed as I was by what I had seen occur in the street.

Holmes was struggling from his Martian suit. His head and torso emerged, and he beheld my expression and said, "We could have done nothing to save her, Watson. Did you see how many of them there were?"

"At least we would have gone down with a fight!"

"The end result would have been the same, my friend."

I pulled off my suit and cast it aside in disgust, choking with emotion. "I'll tell you this much, Holmes. I will avenge her death. So help me God, I will! I will go down fighting, whenever the monsters show themselves."

A sound issued from the far end of the chamber, and Holmes said, "It would seem that you do not have long to wait."

I looked up as a tentacled beast shambled into the rear of the pantechnicon, then stopped a couple of yards away and regarded us with its glaucous eyes.

I rose to my feet, ready to leap at the first opportunity.

The monster's mouthpiece moved, and it addressed us in its meaningless, high-pitched jabber.

Meaningless to me, at least – but not to Holmes.

I was on the point of throwing myself at the creature when my friend gripped my arm.

I looked at Holmes in mystification. "What…?" I began.

He pointed at the Martian. "He says he is on the side of the Korshana, Watson. He apologises for the failure of the operation, and says that we should return to Zenda-Zakan forthwith, where his compatriots are readying a ship to take us back to Earth."

I passed the next few hours in a state of numbed disbelief, too grief-stricken to appreciate the miracle of my salvation, and then experienced a nascent guilt at having survived the ordeal while Miss Hamilton-Bell had not.

We reached the northern city of Zenda-Zakan and were ferried by land-car through the tunnels of the subterranean city until we emerged into an open-air bowl in the centre of which stood, proud yet battered, a small interplanetary ship.

We were escorted to our berths and submerged in the gel that would cosset us for the week-long duration of our flight to Earth, and the Martian rebel looked from me to Holmes and addressed my friend.

"What was that, Holmes?" I asked listlessly as I drank down the sedative offered by a second alien.

"He says that we will land somewhere in northern France, where the presence of the occupying Martians is scant. By that time, our simulacra will be ensconced in Baker Street. He will supply us with electrical guns so that we can despatch the simulacra when we reach London, and in due course an agent of the Martian rebels will be in touch to plan the way ahead."

I nodded apathetically. "Very well."

The Martian raised a tentacle in farewell and left the cabin.

I recalled Miss Hamilton-Bell's words about the safety of this vessel, and said, "Of course, Holmes, we might never make it home, you know?"

And a part of me, as I spoke these words, welcomed the thought of sliding into the balm of oblivion.

I was still gripped by grief when the engine thundered and the sedative finally took effect.

# Chapter Twelve

*Confrontation at 221B Baker Street*

I t was strange indeed to be back upon planet Earth, where the sky was blue and the gravity tugged greedily at my body. It took me a while, as we left the ship in a forest outside Dieppe and made our way towards the harbour, to take in the good fortune of our having survived the perilous voyage from Mars.

We travelled by a steam packet from Dieppe to Dover, and I considered the scale of the struggle against our oppressors that lay ahead. Perhaps my thoughts were still burdened by the fate of Miss Hamilton-Bell, for I had to admit that I had little appetite for the fight. It all seemed so hopeless, even futile, without the shining light of her indomitable spirit to guide the way.

At Dover we boarded a train for London, and a little over an hour later pulled into St Pancras, from where we made haste to the Diogenes Club and summoned Holmes's brother, Mycroft. My friend prevailed upon that worthy to put us up for the night, and Mycroft agreed, grudgingly, to lodge us at his Pall Mall townhouse.

Over a substantial dinner that evening, Holmes recounted

our adventures on Mars, then outlined our imminent assault on the accursed simulacra. On this latter point, however, Mycroft counselled us to caution, and suggested we go into hiding and think through our options.

Over a lavish breakfast the following morning, before proceeding to Baker Street, he again begged us to consider our actions. "You would be much safer assuming other identities and living incognito," he said. "Quite apart from the dangers inherent in broaching this pair, you will be forced into assuming your old roles – and how long might it be before the Martians learn that you are not indeed their simulacra? Then the fat will be in the fire."

Holmes considered his brother's words. "The alternative," he replied, "living incognito as you say, will mean that the world famous pairing of Holmes and Watson will be free to do the evil bidding of our overlords – and who knows what nefarious activities they might embark upon? At least, with the simulacra out of the way, we would prevent that. And if things take a turn for the worse, and the Martians become wise to our ruse, then we will do as you counsel, go to ground and assume other identities."

"So there is no way I might talk you out of this course of action, Sherlock?"

"No way at all," said my friend.

"In that case, allow me to assist you in bagging the pair," Mycroft said. "I will set up an immediate watch on 221B, to ensure that the Martians do not have your rooms under surveillance. Then, and only then, do we act."

At eleven o'clock, Holmes and I, disguised as chimney sweeps and with all the requisite paraphernalia in tow, and with blackened faces into the bargain, sat drinking strong tea in a workman's cafe around the corner from Baker Street. Mycroft was stationed in a cab a little way from 221B. From there he had watched the simulacra depart the house at ten that morning, and satisfied himself that there were no lurking Martians or their lackeys in the vicinity. A street urchin, with half a crown for his pains, was at the ready to convey Mycroft's word to us just as soon as the pair returned.

It was now noon, and we had received no word from the runner. I was in a state of nervous apprehension.

"All will be well, Watson. It will be, as the saying goes, a turkey shoot. The simulacra are expecting no assault, and likely will be unarmed. And," he patted his jacket pocket where he carried his electrical gun, "with these weapons we cannot fail."

I nodded, reassured by his words and the weight of the weapon in my own pocket.

Minutes later the cafe door opened and the urchin hurried across to our table. "Word from fatso," said the lad. "'The birds have returned' – whatever that means."

"Capital!" said Holmes and, tipping the lad a further shilling, we hurried from the cafe.

Never had my nerves been in such a state on approaching the familiar portals of 221B. My heart was pounding as we climbed the steps and Holmes rapped upon the door.

In due course Mrs Hudson answered the summons, and my heart leapt at the sight of her homely visage. She took in our disguises with evident distaste, until Holmes hurried forward, took her arm and whispered, "Not a word, Mrs H! It is I, and my companion is Dr Watson."

She looked flummoxed. "But, but…" she wavered, gesturing at the stairs. "Not twenty minutes ago, you–"

"All will be explained in due course," Holmes said. "Now, wait here until I give further word."

She nodded and backed against the wall. "Whatever you say, Mr Holmes."

I smiled at her as I passed, and followed Holmes up the staircase to our rooms.

He paused before the living room door, and his long fingers wrapped themselves around the handle. With his right hand he drew the electrical gun, nodding at me to do the same.

I pulled the weapon from my pocket and readied myself for action.

"After three," he whispered. "One... two... three. Now!"

He opened the door and burst into the room.

No sooner had we stepped into the room than the simulacra leapt from their chairs before the hearth and dived at us – so much for Holmes's suggestion that this would prove to be a turkey shoot!

In seconds the Holmes simulacrum had his fingers about my friend's throat, in the process dashing the electrical gun from his grip.

At the same time, the Watson simulacrum dived at me. I stepped nimbly to my left, avoiding its lunge, and fired my weapon. With fortune that, to this day, I find it frightening to dwell upon – for what might our fates have been had my shot gone astray? – the electrical charge hit the advancing simulacrum squarely in the chest and sent it reeling backwards. It hit the wall and slid to the floor, incapacitated.

Meanwhile, Holmes and his own mechanical copy were rolling around on the floor, the simulacrum's grip upon my friend's throat tightening all the while, Holmes's face a shade of puce as life was forced from him. For one second, as he lay on his back, his bulging eyes found mine and implored me to do something.

I raised my gun as the pair rolled. When the simulacrum was uppermost, its fingers in a deadly grip around Holmes's throat, I took the opportunity and fired at its head. The mechanical man arched with a strangled cry, then spasmed and released its grip on my friend.

Holmes struggled, coughing, from under the dead weight and I, half-delirious with relief, looked down upon the result of my handiwork.

"Sharp shooting, Watson. I owe you my life."

"Think nothing of it, Holmes. All in the line of duty, what?"

Holmes fell to examining the simulacra, declaring from time to time that he found the mechanical men fascinating.

"That's all very well, Holmes, but how the deuce are we going to go about getting rid of the pair?"

Holmes looked up at me. "Get rid of them? Why, they will occupy my working hours for weeks, if not months, to come. We will keep them in the storeroom, along with my stock of chemicals and other paraphernalia, and I will experiment upon them at my leisure. There is much to be learned, Watson, which will no doubt assist us in our fight against our Arkana foe."

He stood, moved to the window and stared out. High above Regent's Park, dominating the skyline, stood a Martian tripod – a sight that now confirmed in my mind all that was evil and duplicitous about our overlords.

"We face a stern challenge in the years ahead," said Holmes. "A terrible evil has swept the shores of our world, but I believe in time we can repel the invaders and once again reclaim what is rightfully ours."

"Here, here!" I said, quite stirred by my friend's eloquent call to arms.

# Chapter Thirteen

*At the Lyons' Tea Room*

L ater that afternoon, with the bodies of the simulacra safely stowed away and Mrs Hudson apprised of the situation and sworn to silence, we were taking a well-earned pot of tea when the telephone rang.

Holmes crossed the room and snatched up the receiver. "Yes?"

A tinny voice sounded, the words indistinct.

"That is correct," Holmes said, and then, "My word! Yes, yes, of course."

More words issued from the caller.

"We would be more than delighted. Yes, by all means. In thirty minutes, then." He replaced the receiver and paced a while in silent reflection.

"Who was that, Holmes?"

He turned and gave me a rare smile. "An agent of the rebel Martians," he said. "I was expecting a summons, of course, but not quite so soon. We have been called to the Lyons' tea room, Piccadilly, at four o'clock."

At three-thirty we took an electrical cab to the heart of London. Holmes was uncommonly silent for the duration of the journey, no doubt contemplating the many trials and tribulations that awaited us.

We alighted outside the tea room, and before we crossed the pavement Holmes restrained me with a hand upon my arm. I looked up at the louring cowl of the Martian tripod that defaced the Piccadilly skyline – but it was not this that had caused my friend to pause.

He said, "What happened on Mars hit you hard, my friend."

I smiled bleakly. "Quite knocked the stuffing out of me, old man. I know we must fight on, and I will do so, Holmes – as much for Miss Hamilton-Bell's sake as for ours, but it will be a melancholy–"

He stopped me. He was smiling. "Don't be so downhearted, Watson. All is not as it appears."

"What?"

"Prepare yourself for a shock, or rather a welcome surprise."

"What the blazes do you mean, Holmes?"

"I mean," said he, "that it is not only the equatorial Martians who manufacture the simulacra."

I blinked. "I don't quite follow…"

"The rebel Martians, our comrades in this battle, not only have the means to create simulacra, but have done so."

"Very well. That's good to know, but…?"

"Watson, you can be so slow at times!" Holmes laughed. "The rebels recruited humans to their cause. Not only that, but when an agent proved exceptional in the field, they created valuable simulacra so that these individuals might work as flight crew on the Martian ships to keep tabs on which humans were being lured to the red planet, while their originals remained to rouse the troops, as it were, on Earth."

"Good God, man!" I felt a little dizzy. His grip steadied me. "You mean to say…?"

He steered me across the pavement and into the tea room.

"The phone call was from the lady herself," he said – and he pointed across the room to where an uncommonly beautiful woman sat, recognisable to me despite her raven-haired disguise. "Miss Freya Hamilton-Bell," he went on, "the *original.*"

In a daze, hardly able to believe my eyes, I crossed the room.

Miss Hamilton-Bell rose, smiling at my speechlessness, and reached out to take my hand.

"Why…" I said, and, "Upon my word!" I gripped her hand and kissed her knuckles, tears springing to my eyes.

"I have heard reports of our travails on Mars, Dr Watson, Mr Holmes," she said as we took our seats.

"Forgive me," I said. "This is something of a shock. A most wonderful shock, I might add. I thought you dead – indeed, I saw you lying dead."

"My hapless simulacrum, Dr Watson," she murmured. "*I* live to fight another day, though from now on with somewhat greater circumspection. And I am gratified that you two stalwarts will be joining me in the fight."

The thought of the battle ahead now swelled my heart, and it was all I could do to restrain myself from embracing the woman in front of me.

"There is heartening news from my contacts on Mars," she said when we had settled ourselves at the table. "The Arkana have no notion that you fled to Earth, and are scouring the face of their world for you, which will buy us a little time."

"Good news indeed," said I.

"And now," she said, "I would like to hear, in your own words, all about your – *our* – derring-do on Mars. Spare me no detail."

And so, beginning on the morning of our summons to investigate the spurious murder of a non-existent philosopher on Mars, I regaled Miss Hamilton-Bell with a full record of our many and various adventures on the red planet.

# Part Two

*The Fight on Earth*

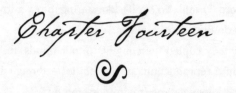

## Chapter Fourteen

### A Deerstalker and a Pair of Gloves

For the duration of the following day, Holmes undertook a minute examination of the Martian simulacra.

We fetched them from the storeroom and, pushing back the chaise longue and an armchair, laid out the bodies on the hearth rug. I must say that, on seeing them side by side, as unmoving as two corpses, I felt a shiver run up my spine.

"I must give it to the Martians," Holmes said before he began work. "One must admire the science that has gone into manufacturing the simulacra. Why, look at the verisimilitude with which they have reproduced your tegument, right down to the small mole on the left of your neck."

"Remarkable," I allowed. "I wonder..."

"Go on."

"I was about to say, I wonder how far the fidelity stretches. D'you think they reproduced the bullet wound on my shoulder?"

"Shall we investigate?" said Holmes, and began unbuttoning the simulacrum's waistcoat and shirt. He tugged back the material of the shirt to reveal the bare shoulder, and I stared down at the puckered, silver cicatrise just below the acromion where, more than thirty years ago, a Jezail bullet had brought me down.

"My word," I said. "Why, it's like staring into a mirror! But how the blazes do they do it, Holmes?"

"Just as they copied the contents of our minds, they somehow made faithful reproductions of our bodies – though I admit that their methodology escapes my understanding."

On his knees, he leaned close to the face of my simulacrum and inspected it minutely. "The workmanship is astounding, Watson. Why, look at the stratum corneum: the hair follicles and papillae!" He prodded its cheek with a bony forefinger. "And it feels just like human flesh," he went on. "Little wonder that we've been deceived by the hundreds, even thousands of imposters taking up the guises of the great and the good of Earth. If the mere logistical difficulties of vanquishing our Martian foe were not difficult enough, we must contend with these infernal doppelgängers."

"There are times, Holmes, when I almost despair and admit that the game is not worth the candle. Can we really overcome the might and the technical sophistication of the Martians?"

Holmes climbed to his feet. "One way we can start," he said, "is by understanding our foe. And to that end I will commence a thorough examination of these... these machines."

He moved to his cluttered workbench and returned with a razor-sharp knife. "Now, which should I cut up first?"

"How about your own simulacrum?" I said.

He gave me a penetrating look. "Why, Watson, you look a trifle squeamish. You must have attended an untold number of autopsies in your time."

"Yes," I said, "but none conducted upon my own double."

"Then I shall work on this one first," he said, and moved to his own simulacrum.

He unbuttoned the waistcoat, then the shirt and, as Miss Hamilton-Bell had done on Mars, he took the knife and slit the torso of the simulacrum from throat to abdomen. The integument parted like the flesh of a ripe fruit, revealing an intricate nexus of wires beneath. Ever the scientist, Holmes shook his head in silent wonder.

For the following three hours, he lost himself in examination of the machine. He dismantled the thing bit by bit, making meticulous notes in a ledger as he did so. From time to time he muttered something to himself, in amazement and grudging admiration.

As he worked, I perused that morning's *Times* from cover to cover, bringing myself up to date with the events of the world that had transpired while we had been on Mars. On the face of it, not much had changed: politicians spouted the same old party platitudes, natural disasters occurred with disheartening regularity, and England had drawn with Australia at the Oval. I found myself skimming the pages impatiently. In the past – before Miss Hamilton-Bell's revelations had opened our eyes – I would have devoured world events with undivided interest. Now I could not take the news reports seriously. The events on the world stage were but shadow play, and the reporting of those events so much trivial verbiage disguising the fact of the human predicament and the Martians' ultimate intent.

From time to time I looked up from the paper to see how my friend's investigations were progressing. He was totally consumed by the job at hand, intent on the intricacies of the problem before him. I had seen him thus on many occasions, though then the conundrum had been of a more chemical nature. Now he was faced with the micro-electrical wonders of another race entirely, and his questing mind rose to the challenge.

At one point he said, more to himself than to me, "Of course I'm interested in the machines' motive power, but what taxes my understanding at the moment is the question of autonomy. To what degree do these simulacra possess individual freedom to make conscious decisions of judgement according to their circumstances – or are they controlled, as it were, from afar?"

He lifted the electro-mechanical 'brain' from the split skull of his own lookalike and pored over the nest of filigree wires with the intense concentration of a jeweller assaying the quality of a fine diamond.

Lunchtime came and went. I had kippers, but food held no interest for Holmes. He agreed to take a cup of Earl Grey when pressed, but left it to cool at his side while his examinations proceeded.

Soon he had taken the entire mechanical substructure from the simulacrum so that only its sorry casing remained, a deflated parody of a human being that flopped grotesquely on the floor. He ferried the innards piece by piece to his workbench and examined the minute components under a microscope, from time to time muttering "Curiouser and curiouser" to himself.

At two o'clock, with the sun beckoning outside, I decided to take a breath of fresh air. When I informed Holmes of my plan to go for a stroll, he looked up absently. "Capital. I was about to ask you if you would be so good as to pop into Frobisher's on Savile Row and pick up one or two items."

"Frobisher's?" I said, surprised. Holmes had never been much interested in matters sartorial, and my curiosity was piqued. "Whatever for?"

He returned to his studies and murmured, "A deerstalker and a pair of leather gloves, the latter of the softest calfskin."

At this I could not restrain my laughter. "But Holmes, my dear fellow. What's all this about? A deerstalker? You derided Paget's illustrations in *The Strand* of you wearing the 'infernal headgear' – your exact words – and now you want me to purchase the very same!"

Squinting through the microscope, he said, "I still maintain that Paget's licence in adorning me with such was almost as heinous as some of the liberties you take in the reporting of my cases, Watson. However, on this occasion the idea of the deerstalker came to mind as the answer to a vexing problem."

"Which was?"

"All in good time, Watson. Now, to Frobisher's for a deerstalker."

"And a pair of gloves of the finest calfskin," I said. "And the headgear? Do you desire any particular material, Holmes?"

"A green tweed to match my topcoat," said he. "I take two sizes smaller than yourself, I seem to recall."

"But you won't tell me what all this is about?"

He fixed me with his piercing gaze. "All in good time, Watson. But I will say that it might very well be a matter of life or death. Now go."

And so dismissed, I took my leave of 221B.

It was a strange sensation indeed to be walking the sunlit streets of London a free man, after the trials and tribulations I had undergone on Mars. I passed down Baker Street and turned into Regent's Park, smiling at the governesses and their young charges who played with hoops and wheeled horses without a care in the world. Indeed, even the adult promenaders taking the air that afternoon did so in blithe ignorance of the true state of worldly affairs. I envied them, and a part of me wished that I had not been vouchsafed the intelligence that now assailed me as to the true malign motivations of our Martian overlords. Then again, would

I have gladly returned to a state of ignorant bliss? As I considered this, I thought of the indomitable Freya Hamilton-Bell – and I knew the answer. A terrible threat hovered over our world, such as had never visited us in all our history, and Miss Hamilton-Bell and other brave souls were risking their lives to fight the great injustice. How could I bury my head in the sand and wash my hands of all responsibility in light of this? I considered Professor Challenger, murdered by our tentacled foe, along with our prime minister, H.H. Asquith – as well as the hundreds of other innocent Earthmen and women likewise cast into oblivion to suit the Martians' evil masterplan – and my resolve was stiffened.

I would do whatever I could to thwart the ambitions of our overlords – even if that was the mere purchasing of a deerstalker and a pair of calfskin gloves.

Smiling to myself at my new resolve, I turned onto Savile Row and made my way to Frobisher's.

Thirty minutes later, on my return to Baker Street, I stopped before a newspaper vendor and perused the front page of *The Times*. A column at the foot of the page caught my attention. "Good grief…" I said. "Holmes will be interested."

I bought a copy and hurried home to find Holmes still bent over his workbench. I passed him the brown-paper parcel containing the gloves and deerstalker, and he took it absentmindedly and laid it to one side, much to my chagrin.

I sat down, opened the newspaper, and cleared my throat. "Interesting report here, Holmes," I said.

"Is that so?" he said with little enthusiasm.

"Indeed," said I. "It concerns none other than Professor Moriarty."

He looked up. "What did you say?" he demanded sharply.

"'Moriarty Lives?'" I read the headline, and went on, "'The evil mastermind Professor James Moriarty is alive and well and living in Shoreditch, according to several eyewitness accounts recently obtained by our crime reporter.'" I lowered the paper. "Surely this cannot be true?"

Holmes snatched the newspaper from me and scanned the report. "No more than sensationalist scandal-mongering," he muttered, tossing it aside and returning to his work.

"I certainly hope so," I said. "We've enough on our plates without having to contend with Moriarty."

Holmes did not deign to reply.

A short while later I pointed to the parcel on the end of the workbench. "Well, Holmes, aren't you going to tell me why the deuce you want the things? A matter of life and death, you said."

"And so it is," he said, tweezering a length of wire from the simulacrum's brain. "Bear with me for one second, old man, and all will be revealed. There! I have it." He sat back in his chair and expelled a great breath. "Now, be a good chap and have Mrs Hudson make me a fresh cup of tea, would you? And one for yourself, too."

"That's kind of you," I huffed.

When we were duly equipped with steaming cups of Earl Grey, Holmes remained at his workbench and I pulled up an armchair, the better to hear his exposition.

"As my investigations proceeded," he began, "I was primarily interested in the autonomy of these devices, as I mentioned earlier. Were they free agents, or under some form of control? The answer to this could have a drastic bearing on how we might proceed."

"And you found out?"

"It would appear that they are, to a degree, puppets, dancing to the whim of distant controllers. Oh, they have a fair degree of autonomy, or they would be unable to deceive their nearest and dearest, as well as their work colleagues. The content of their originals' minds have been reproduced so that they can function day-to-day, but I posit that the major decisions they would be called upon to take are decided by a remote operator in some kind of central 'telegraphic exchange', as it were."

"On Mars?" I enquired.

Holmes stroked his chin. "I think not. More likely here on Earth, in various centralised locations scattered around the globe where the simulacra are situated."

I gestured at the electrical debris littering the bench. "But how did you determine this?"

"By examining the simulacrum's brainbox, or cognitive nexus, as I call it. Housed within it is a small computational device, of the kind I have read about in Martian technical papers. In these devices, I surmise, reside the copies of their originals' minds, along with apparatus analogous to a telegraphic receiver. Quite simply, the Martian controller instructs the simulacrum what to do over and above its simple daily functions. For instance, Asquith might be going about his usual governmental duties in Whitehall when a command comes to deploy his naval fleet in the invasion of France – a facetious example, Watson, but you see what I mean."

"Devilish!" I said.

"Quite," Holmes agreed. "Now, I have discovered that the remote controller contacts his simulacra once a day – merely, I think, as a safety precaution. Checking up, as it were."

"You found out? But how?"

Holmes gave a humourless grin. "By the fortunate expedient of being in the process of dismantling the receiver when a communiqué came in from the controller at four o'clock. Evidently the simulacra are programmed with a full understanding of the Martian language – for the controller spoke thus. It is indeed fortunate that I have studied the lingo."

"Bless my soul, fortunate indeed! But what the deuce did it say?"

"The controller enquired as to the simulacrum's whereabouts, and then asked why your simulacrum, Watson, was not responding."

"Good Lord, Holmes. What the blazes did you tell him?"

"I thought on my feet, Watson, and said that your simulacrum had been discommoded in a fall and I was effecting repairs. I have no reason to believe that the operator did not believe me. At any rate," he said, "the operator went on to say – in the somewhat roundabout and long-winded way of the average educated Martian – that we should await instructions, and that in a day or two we would be called upon to act. He then said that he would be in touch tomorrow at the same time."

"'Called upon to act'?" I chewed my moustache. "Don't like the sound of that at all, Holmes."

"It remains to be seen just what 'act' in this case entails. We always have the option, I'm glad to say, of taking Mycroft's counsel and going to ground if needs be."

I gestured to the brown-paper parcel. "But why the deuce do you need the deerstalker and gloves? A matter of life and death?"

Holmes reached across the table and picked up two small metal devices, each the size of a woman's make-up compact. "Now undo the parcel, Watson, and pass me the deerstalker."

I did as he asked and watched, more than a little bemused, as he took a knife and slit the stitching of the cap's right ear-flap. "Excellent," he said, and inserted the silver device into the space between the silk lining and the tweed. Next, taking a glove, he slipped it onto his left hand and eased the second silver oval into the glove so that it sat atop his metacarpus.

"Will you tell me, Holmes, just what on earth…?"

He cast me a wry glance and took up the deerstalker. "Never have I dreamed of the day when I might voluntarily consent to donning such farcical headgear," he said, "but needs must when the Martian overlords drive."

So saying, he slipped the deerstalker over his thin skull and arranged the flaps so that they covered his ears and sideburns.

"Capital," he said. "Later I will take the receiver from the Watson simulacrum over there," he waved in the direction of my recumbent doppelgänger, "and insert it into the left ear-flap. In this way we won't be caught out by the controller's summons. This," he went on, raising his left hand, "is a simple microphone – which I located in my double's right metacarpus – by which I can reply to the controller."

I laughed. "Ingenious!" I said. "But you do realise, Holmes, what this means?"

He favoured me with a dour grimace. "No doubt you will take great delight in telling me, Watson."

"Indeed I will," said I. "You will perforce have to wear the 'infernal headgear' night and day."

"I rather hope that I can get away without wearing it while I sleep," he said.

A tap at the door interrupted us, and Mrs Hudson stepped into the room. Fortunately, the simulacra were hidden from her view by the chaise longue, though she did give Holmes – garbed as he was in the deerstalker and one glove – an odd look.

She held up a folded slip of paper. "One of your urchins, Mr Holmes. Just delivered this."

Holmes thanked her and took the note, reading it as she took her leave.

*Dear Mr Holmes and Dr Watson,*
*It is imperative that we meet as soon as possible. I am currently domiciled at a safe house in Barnes: 22 Willow Avenue. Take a roundabout route and I will hopefully see you at six.*

*Yours,*
*Freya Hamilton-Bell.*

My heart thumped – though whether at the gravity of the summons, or the fact that I would soon be in the company of the delightful Miss Hamilton-Bell, I was unable to say.

Holmes regarded his pocket watch. "Almost five, Watson. I have just enough time to take the receiver from your simulacrum, and then we will be off."

By and by we left 221B and took a cab on a devious route to Barnes.

# Chapter Fifteen

*At the Safe House*

No. 22 Willow Avenue proved to be situated in a terrace of cottages overlooking a bend in the Thames. Fragrant wisteria grew around the small doorway and a window box, replete with violets and pansies, stood upon the sill. It seemed an appropriately delightful address for Miss Hamilton-Bell to use as a hideaway.

Holmes rapped on the crimson paintwork, and a second later the door opened a bare two inches. I caught sight of a brilliant blue eye regarding us, and the door opened further.

Miss Hamilton-Bell smiled and stepped aside.

I removed my hat and bowed. "Wonderful to see you again," I said.

"The pleasure is entirely mine, gentlemen."

She led us into a fussy, overstuffed parlour done out very much in the Victorian fashion, with heavy, dark furniture, ormolu ornamentation, and maroon brocades. She saw me glance around the room, and explained, "The house does not belong to me, but to a well-wisher. My taste is altogether more modern and minimalist. Would you care for tea, or something a little stronger perhaps?"

We asked for tea, and she repaired to the kitchen and reappeared a little later bearing a tray with a silver teapot and three china cups. She poured, and I watched her as she did so. I decided that her dark hair – whether a wig or dyed – did not suit her: it cast her fair features into shadow and gave her an altogether melancholy appearance. That said, her beauty shone through as she smiled and passed my cup.

Holmes balanced the saucer on his prominent knee. "You wished to see us as a matter of urgency, Miss Hamilton-Bell."

"To begin with, I was wondering if you had given my words of yesterday serious consideration?" She looked from myself to Holmes.

I recalled what she had said in the Lyons' tea room – after I had recounted our travails on Mars – as she pleaded with us to forget our 'mad fool' idea of remaining *in situ* at Baker Street: her concern at the time had rather touched me.

"That we should," Holmes said, "desist in my scheme to take the place of the simulacra which were to replace us?"

"Precisely," she said.

Holmes sighed. "Miss Hamilton-Bell," he said, "I can only repeat my objections to the idea of our 'going to ground', as you would have it. Doing so would gain us nothing. However, by taking their places, we have an inside line to the very power base of the Martians. It might be possible, with cunning, to inveigle ourselves into situations which in future might redound to our advantage."

She heard him out, and then replied, "When you stood firm yesterday, Mr Holmes, and departed somewhat precipitately before I could object further, I contacted a sympathiser in the ranks of the Martians here in London. I visited him last night, and returned with... Well, I will show you. Please excuse me one moment."

She rose, gathered her skirts about her, and hurried from the room. I exchanged a glance with my friend. "Whatever could it be, Holmes?"

"I cannot see that it would be anything that might deflect us from our chosen course," said he.

Miss Hamilton-Bell returned holding a device that very much resembled the one her simulacrum had deployed in the desert prison on Mars. She pointed it at Holmes and pressed a stud on its side. A bright point of red light glowed at the forward end of the instrument.

"The red light," she explained, "means that Mr Holmes is human."

"I could have told you that," I laughed, "though there have been times when I've had cause to wonder."

"I think what Miss Hamilton-Bell means," Holmes interjected, "is that the device is able to detect whether the subject is either human or a simulacrum."

Tight-lipped, she nodded. "Just so. When our Arkana oppressors discovered that the Korshana had also developed the ability to manufacture simulacra in the fight against their tyranny, they came up with a simple device to detect the mechanical substitutes, and have been using them against us frequently of late."

Holmes smiled to himself, then said, "So you are trying to frighten me off the idea of maintaining this charade?"

Did I see anger flash in Miss Hamilton-Bell's eyes as she replied? "Not so much frighten you, sir, but warn you of the danger of continuing with your chosen course of action."

Holmes leaned forward. "Presumably these devices work by detecting something inherent in the simulacrum targeted?"

"That is correct," she said. "The light glows blue when the device detects the cylindrical battery which powers the simulacrum."

"And the red light is activated when it is unable to detect a battery?" said Holmes. "Therefore, all we have to do when we return to Baker Street is remove the batteries from the simulacra and ensure that we carry them about our persons at all times. Then, should any Martian use a detection device against us, they will be reassured that we are simulacra. I take it that no human has ever attempted to pass themselves off as a simulacrum?"

"To the best of my knowledge, that is the case," Miss Hamilton-Bell said. She went on with a wry smile, "In lieu of being unable to dissuade you to give up your foolhardy charade, I beseech you to take great care. The Arkana are ruthless, and would think nothing of killing you in an instant. But you need no telling. You know what became of your friend, Professor Challenger."

"I assure you that I, for one, will take no undue risk," I said.

"We are no good in the fight against the Martian tyrants if we are dead," Holmes said. "You can be assured that we will proceed with the utmost caution."

Accepting defeat when she was staring it in the face, she smiled to herself. "Then allow me to replenish your cups, and to move on to the other reason why I summoned you here."

"So you want more than to merely berate us?" Holmes expostulated with uncharacteristic mischief.

"Much more," she said.

She poured more tea, sat with her cup in her lap, and considered her next words. "Two years ago you had dealings at the Martian Embassy with a human scientific liaison officer, a Mr Herbert Wells." She paused. "We understand that Wells still works for Grulvax-Xenxa-Goran." She looked from me to Holmes. "We would approach Mr Wells ourselves, but we have certain understandable reservations about the wisdom of doing so. For one, we do not know if we can trust him – we have yet to ascertain the degree of his loyalty to his paymasters. But, as you can imagine, if we can apprise Mr Wells as to the true nature of the Arkana, and if we were able to recruit him to our cause, then he would, in his position at the embassy, prove an invaluable asset."

"And you would like Watson and myself," Holmes said, "to contact Mr Wells and ascertain the lie of the land, as it were?"

"As you have given yourselves so wholeheartedly to our cause, and insist on playing the parts of Martian simulacra, then I deem you to be in an advantageous position to re-contact Mr Wells and discover where his loyalties might lie."

Holmes nodded. "We will endeavour to contact him on the morrow," he said. "We have good reason – is this not so, Watson? – to believe that little love is lost between Mr Wells and the Martians."

Miss Hamilton-Bell cocked an eyebrow and enquired how this might be so, but Holmes told her that the less said, on this occasion, the better.

She sipped her tea, looking at Holmes a little oddly. "I wonder if I might ask a personal question, Mr Holmes?"

"And what might that be?"

"Could you tell me why, on this balmy summer's evening, and indoors to boot, you are still wearing your deerstalker and gloves?"

I laughed at this and slapped my thigh, and while my friend gave Miss Hamilton-Bell the full story concerning the dismantlement of the simulacra, and the concealment of the receivers and microphone in his hat and gloves, I looked around the over-furnished room.

I noticed, on the mantelshelf, the framed photograph of a dashing young man in military uniform: that of a captain in the Hussars, if my eyesight served me. When next a lull fell in the conversation, I indicated the picture. "A possession of whoever owns the house?" I asked, rather hoping that I might be right.

A shadow fell over Miss Hamilton-Bell's features. "No, Dr Watson," she said, "the photograph belongs to me."

"A paramour, perchance?"

She shook her head. "My brother," she murmured.

"Dashing fellow," I said. "Served in Afghanistan, judging by the background."

"Where he met his end," she said.

"Oh, I say – I'm sorry. I'm so dreadfully sorry. Those dashed Ghazis–"

She interrupted. "He died in Kabul fighting the first wave of Martians," she said, "eighteen years ago this July. I was twelve at the time, and he just twenty." She looked up, and then smiled with a radiance at odds with her previous words.

"And now," she said, "who's for more tea?"

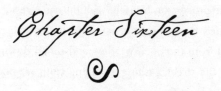

# Chapter Sixteen

*"A Much Greater Depredation…"*

The following morning, over breakfast, I found Holmes in a sombre mood. He chewed on his toast with an air of abstraction, and I ventured to ask if he had passed a sleepless night.

"On the contrary, my friend, I slept soundly. But I am sorely taxed by what occurred on Mars – namely, why the Arkana should have spared us when they saw fit to murder poor Challenger?"

I shrugged as I tucked into my scrambled eggs. "Perhaps it's what Miss Hamilton-Bell said, Holmes: our simulacra were not ready in time."

"Perhaps," he said, unconvinced, and resumed his moody silence.

After breakfast, Holmes moved to his workbench and spent some considerable time sifting through the innards of the Martian simulacra. At last he located two cylindrical units the size of fountain pens – the batteries that powered the doppelgängers – and passed one of them to me.

"Now keep it safe about your person at all times," he said,

slipping his own into his trouser pocket.

As a precaution, he pointed the simulacrum detector at me and pressed the stud. The light on the leading edge glowed blue. He repeated the process on himself, with the same result.

After lunch he scrawled a note and sealed it in an envelope, then leaned from the open window and called down to an urchin loitering in the street. Fishing a shilling from his pocket, Holmes descended to meet the runner.

"I have sent a note to Mr Wells," he said on his return, "asking him to meet us at five at the Piccadilly Lyons'."

"I was thinking, Holmes, about what the Martians might want from our simulacra. They told you, rather ominously, that they would be in touch."

He ruminated, his gaze distant. "I too have been vexed by this very question," he said. "I have been trying to work out how we might be of service to them, over and above rendering the obvious investigational assistance."

"Odd to think," I said, "that the Martians fabricated a duplicate of your mind every bit as perspicacious as the original."

"Odd, Watson? I find it disturbing. Do the scientific and technological capabilities of our oppressors know no limits? If we are up against a foe who can match and even trump every human achievement and ability…" He shook his head. "It would suggest that, in order to vanquish the Arkana, we will need, as well as fortitude and pluck, a hefty dose of luck – never a commodity on which I like to rely."

He spent the rest of the afternoon further disassembling the mechanical men, and a little before four o'clock I was startled, while browsing the newspaper, by his sudden exclamation: "Good God, what a fool I am!" So saying, he snatched up his deerstalker from the workbench and rammed it on his head, then found his glove and slipped it on.

A few seconds after four, he sat up suddenly and I heard the muted, guttural sound of a Martian voice issue from the receiver concealed in the deerstalker's right ear-flap.

Holmes raised his gloved left hand to his lips and replied, then fell silent as the controller spoke.

Minutes later the communiqué was over and Holmes sat back in relief.

"What the deuce did they say, Holmes?"

"A routine call to establish our whereabouts." He tapped the left ear-flap. "They also summoned you, or rather your simulacrum."

"They did?"

"And I replied in a somewhat different tone, repeating more or less what I'd stated initially, that we were at Baker Street, and that I was between cases at the moment and awaiting further instructions."

"Must admit I didn't notice the difference." I laughed. "All Greek to me, Holmes."

"Fortunately, we were not summoned to do their bidding–"

A knock at the door interrupted him.

"With luck, that will be Mrs Hudson bearing Wells's reply. Be a good fellow and see what he says, will you, Watson?"

I thanked Mrs Hudson, took the note, and read it aloud.

"*Dear Sir, I will be delighted to resume our acquaintance at said time and place. Your humble servant, Herbert Wells.*"

"Capital, Watson."

"Do you think you can convince Wells to come over to our side?" I asked.

"I am certain of it. After the affair two years ago, his latent animosity towards the Martians will be primed, needing only the lighting of the touch paper – in this case, the evidence of the simulacra and our personal testimonies – to ignite him to action. I perceive in Wells a person of boundless mental energy and enthusiasm, which need only to be channelled. He will, I hope, prove a worthy ally."

I sensed a slight note of circumspection in his tone. "However…?" I said.

"We must approach the meeting with caution, Watson. There is always the possibility that the Martians have done the same with Wells as they have with ourselves. Namely, that they have replaced him with a simulacrum. We will go armed with our electrical guns and Miss Hamilton-Bell's detection device."

Thus equipped, we made our way to Piccadilly.

Wells was already seated at a booth at the back of the tea room, spooning vegetable soup with a gusto suggesting near starvation. He climbed to his feet, wiping his straggling moustache, as we joined him.

"Mr Holmes, Dr Watson," he said in his high-pitched voice, shaking our hands, "a delight to meet you again."

"Likewise," said Holmes, taking a seat and ordering tea for two from the waitress.

I had quite forgotten how short of stature Mr Wells was, with a disproportionately bulky torso tapering down to spindly legs. His head was large, broad across the brow, and his deep-set eyes somewhat melancholy. Also, as he re-seated himself behind the table, I thought I detected a look of suspicion in his regard of Holmes and myself.

Which, I concluded, was entirely understandable. We had

discovered his part, two years ago, in the death of the Martian ambassador. He had every reason to be wary of our motives in arranging this meeting.

While I busied myself with the tea, Holmes slipped the detection device from his pocket beneath the lip of the table and was directing it at Wells. He pressed the stud, and I was relieved to see a red light illuminate the hem of the tablecloth.

"And how is Miss Fairfield – or rather," Holmes corrected himself, "should I be asking after the well-being of Mrs Wells? When last we met, you were on the verge of matrimony, as I recall."

Wells winced and stared into the puddle of his soup. "I'm afraid things went rather downhill on that front, Mr Holmes."

"Oh," I said, "I'm sorry to hear that, old chap."

Wells dabbed at his soup with a chunk of bread and chewed the sodden mass with little enthusiasm. "After her recent success–"

"Success?" I enquired.

"Under the name of Rebecca West," Holmes said, "Miss Fairfield has published a series of articles to much acclaim."

"That's correct, Mr Holmes. And I rather think that the praise went to her head. Added to which, my own failure in that department... I suppose there was resentment on both sides. I must admit that I felt a degree of envy of Cicely's success, and she was irked by this."

"You broke off the engagement?" Holmes asked.

"Not I," said Wells. "That was entirely Cicely's doing. You see, there was someone else."

"I say, I am sorry," I said.

Wells sighed. "There was this fellow employed at the embassy as a scientific advisor. I wouldn't have minded so much – well, that's a lie, I would have minded whoever had turned Cicely's head – but the fact was that this chap was in his fifties, apparently, and dashed ugly to boot."

Holmes murmured his commiserations, somewhat unconvincingly, I thought.

"Still," I said, "one must put it down to experience and soldier on, what?"

Wells's weak smile suggested that he'd heard this platitude more than once before, and had failed to be convinced.

"But I am sure that you gentlemen did not come here to listen to my tale of romantic woe," he said. "How might I be of assistance?"

"It is," Holmes began, "a somewhat delicate matter. We have of late come into some intelligence regarding our Martian... friends."

This had the effect of provoking Wells.

"Friends? They're no friends of mine, Mr Holmes. Oh, I might work for the ambassador, but there's no love lost in my regard for the Martians, considering what they're doing to our world."

Holmes leaned forward. "And what might that be?" he asked.

Wells licked his lips and looked around the tea room as if wary of eavesdroppers. In lowered tones he said, "I've been a member of the Fabians for some good time now, and it's public knowledge that Mr and Mrs Webb are openly antagonistic to the Martians and their regime on Earth."

"Yes," said Holmes, "I read a recent interview with Mrs Webb in the *London Illustrated News*, in which she expressed her concern about the financial management of our economy, and the Martians' influence upon it."

"She was being diplomatic in that interview," Wells said bitterly, "for fear of unduly antagonising the Martians. Did you know," he hurried on in hushed tones, "that the Martians are milking our economy dry? And not only ours, but the French and Americans, too."

He sat back and cast another weary glance around the room. "But I must be careful in my denunciation of our oppressors," he said, "given my position at the embassy…"

Holmes leaned forward. "The desperate economic straits you describe are not the half of it, my friend." He paused deliberately. "If you only knew the true state of affairs."

"The true state? What do you mean?"

"I mean," Holmes said, "that the financial plight of our country, indeed our planet, is but the precursor to a much greater depredation."

Mr Wells looked from Holmes to myself. His face had turned quite pale.

When he spoke, it was almost a whisper. "How do you know this?"

"We have ample evidence," Holmes said, "and our own experience. We recently set foot on the very soil of the red planet. There we were subject to a series of travails in which our very lives were threatened, and a friend of mine met his end at the hands of the Martians. We learned, from a young woman working to bring the Martian oppression to an end, exactly what the situation is."

"Can you tell me more?" Wells asked.

"Better still," he said, "I can show you physical evidence of the Martians' perfidy."

Holmes finished his tea and then, in the same furtive manner as Wells, cast a glance around the room. "We cannot be too careful. Watson and I will leave for Baker Street post-haste, and I suggest that in ten minutes you should set out for the same destination – taking a circuitous route and perhaps changing cabs more than once in the process."

Wells nodded. "Understood."

Holmes settled our bill, and as we left the tea rooms I said, "Do you really think we're in danger of being followed, Holmes?"

"I hope not, but I fear we might be. I am taking no chances. What we must remember, Watson, is that powerful oppressors sow division amid those they seek to cow – and one of the weapons they use to do so is the promise of power and money. I have absolutely no doubt that there are, living among us, benighted souls working against their kind for the reward of filthy lucre."

On that sombre note, we hailed a cab and made haste to Baker Street.

## Chapter Seventeen

*A Little Game at Wells's Expense*

Once again in our rooms, Holmes lifted my doppelgänger's skin by the scruff of the neck and carried it into the adjoining bedroom, and the sight of it hanging from his hand like an old dressing-gown turned my stomach. He returned and arranged the skin of the second simulacrum in the wing-back armchair. It presented a forlorn, withered sight as it sat with its back to the door, its sunken head reposing on the antimacassar, its empty eye sockets staring at the mantelshelf: a ghastly version of Sherlock Holmes robbed of all vitality.

"Whatever are you doing, Holmes?"

"A little game at Wells's expense," he said, "all the more to shock him into realising the terrible extent of the Martians' oppression."

"I would have thought the sight of the pair lying side by side on the hearth rug would have proved convincing enough, Holmes, but have it your way."

"I will repair to the bedroom and leave the door ajar, then observe his reaction as he beholds my double."

"I hope his heart is strong."

"If it isn't, then you'll be on hand to render medical assistance," he said. "How is your cardiovascular knowledge these days, Watson?"

I deigned not to reply. Sometimes, I reflected, my friend's sense of humour was mordant in the extreme.

In due course Mrs Hudson announced that we had a visitor, a gentleman by the name of Wells.

Holmes slipped into the adjoining room, and I crossed to the door and met Wells on the threshold, shaking his hand and asking if he'd care for a drink.

"A brandy, perhaps?" I suggested – to fortify him against the shock in store.

"Do you know what?" he said. "I think I will, but just a peg."

I poured three small measures – assuming Holmes would wish to join us – and, entering into the spirit of the venture, passed Wells the glass and gestured to the vacant armchair beside the hearth. "Take a seat, old man."

He moved around the wing-back chair containing the simulacrum, then stopped dead as he looked down at Holmes's double.

His reaction was not quite what I had expected.

He smiled, sat down and stared with interest – but not the expected shock – at the simulacrum. "I see they've immortalised Holmes, too – but how the blazes did you get your hands on this? A damaged specimen, perhaps?"

Holmes stepped from the bedroom, having observed Wells's anticlimactic reaction. "A damaged specimen?" Holmes echoed. "What on earth do you mean?"

Wells gestured at the deflated doppelgänger. "This," he said, peering more closely at it. "It doesn't seem of the best quality."

Holmes took the brandy I proffered and knocked back a

mouthful. "You've seen one of these before?"

"Oh, I know all about them," Wells said.

I exchanged a worried glance with Holmes. "You do?" he said.

"You see," Wells explained, "just the other day I happened to be crossing the courtyard of the embassy as a tripod was delivering a large packing crate. The ambassador hurried from the building to supervise the delivery, and I was about to leave them to it when I heard a tremendous crash. The crate had fallen from the elevator platform, hit the ground and split open, spilling its contents. Imagine my surprise when I saw what had tumbled out."

"And just what was it?" I asked.

"A lifelike dummy of Lloyd George," Wells said. "I asked Grulvax-Xenxa-Goran what it was all about, and he told me that the dummy was bound for the docking station at Battersea, whence it would be transported to Mars to feature in an exhibition of Great Britain's great and good. It had been delivered to the embassy for a last inspection before it was despatched." He took a mouthful of brandy, adding, "But I thought you summoned me here to show me evidence of Martian evil?"

I glanced at my friend. His expression was grim.

Without a word, Holmes entered the adjoining room and returned clutching my simulacrum. He dropped it on the rug at Wells's feet, and pointed to the piles of wire littering the workbench across the room.

"They are not 'dummies', as you called them, and they are not destined, along with Lloyd George, to grace some exhibition on Mars about Great Britain's eminent personages."

Wells blinked. "They're not?"

"I'm afraid that Grulvax-Xenxa-Goran pulled the wool over

your eyes," said Holmes. "What you accidentally beheld, when the crate split open, was the mechanical simulacrum destined to replace the real flesh-and-blood Lloyd George."

Wells swallowed, then gestured mutely at the simulacra. "And these?"

"Mechanical doppelgängers intended by the Martians to replace us on Earth following our murders on Mars," Holmes said, and went on to outline, in detail, our recent travails on the red planet.

Wells sat, stunned, when Holmes had finished speaking. At last he spoke up. "And you say that the Martians have been killing prominent humans and replacing them with, with..." Again he gestured at the simulacra.

"The better to assist the takeover of our planet when the Martian warlords deem that the time is right," Holmes supplied.

Wells uttered an oath, shaking his head in wonder. "I knew that the Martians were far from the altruistic benefactors they liked to make themselves out to be," he said, "but never in my wildest dreams did I think that... that..." He stammered to a halt.

He looked from me to Holmes. "And when might the takeover commence?" he asked.

Holmes shook his head. "That we don't know, but we were hoping..."

"Go on."

Holmes drained his brandy. "There is a resistance movement, Mr Wells. We are in contact with one of its members, the woman whose doppelgänger accompanied us to Mars. Also, there are Arkana Martians who sympathise with our plight and oppose what their fellows are doing. But in order to defeat the might of the Martians, we need to recruit new members in all walks of life—"

"And I," Wells interrupted, "working as I do for the ambassador, would be a prize recruit?"

"You state the case with admirable concision," Holmes said. "You doubtless have access, or can obtain access, to important papers, documents, communiqués and the like, which would be invaluable in shedding light on the Martians' intentions."

Wells was nodding slowly to himself, as if mulling over whether or not to throw in his lot with our cause.

I rose, crossed to the side table, and recharged our glasses.

"Well," Holmes said after a moment, "what about it? Are you with us?"

Wells remained silent, staring into his replenished glass. At last he said, in little more than a whisper, "I'm a fool... In fact, I'm seven kinds of fool, and a dullard to boot."

"Steady on, old chap," I said. "We've all been taken in by the tentacled monstrosities."

Wells set his glass on a side table and held his head in his hands. "Why didn't I realise what was going on?"

"As Watson said, we've all been taken in," Holmes said gently. "Don't berate yourself."

"But it's not just the Lloyd George dummy, or rather the simulacrum," he said. "Lord! Why didn't I see it before now?"

"See what?" Holmes asked, leaning forward.

Wells took a deep breath. "Earlier, in the tea room... I mentioned an advisor at the embassy – a human."

"What about him?"

"I should have realised that something was not quite right – I merely thought it odd at the time. You see, just last week I interrupted Grulvax-Xenxa-Goran and the stranger in the former's office. They were poring over papers, plans or blueprints, and

161

they appeared flustered on my entrance – and the ambassador scrambled with the papers as if to hide them from me, hurriedly introducing the fellow as a scientific expert." He shrugged. "I gained the impression that they were examining naval blueprints, but thought little of it at the time. But now…"

"Now?" I said.

"You see, this human was an advisor in some scientific capacity, obviously working closely with the Martians on something important. Dash it all, but I should have realised something was wrong about the fellow!"

"Do you know his name?" Holmes asked.

Wells smiled, but without humour. "Yes," he said. "He called himself Mr Smith."

Holmes grunted. "Very helpful," he said. "But can you describe him?"

"That's just it, Mr Holmes. I can't. You see, he was disguised."

"Disguised?" I echoed.

"On the three or four occasions I saw him, he always wore a black cape and a fedora – and his face was hidden by a mask. I was reminded of the Phantom of the Opera, and assumed that the mask concealed some hideous disfigurement."

"The chap obviously didn't want to be recognised," I said.

"Which makes his conduct all the more suspicious," Holmes said, then pointed at Wells. "In the tea room you mentioned that Miss Fairfield's head had been turned by a scientific advisor."

Wells sighed. "The very same fellow, Mr Holmes. I often saw them together at the embassy, and once in the street outside. I… I confronted Cicely about their liaison, and she admitted that she was attracted to him, even though he was older than her, and 'dashed ugly' – her own words – but claimed that the attraction was wholly intellectual. I didn't believe her, and perhaps because of this, inevitably, we grew apart."

Holmes rubbed his chin. "I need to interview Miss Fairfield and trace this mysterious Mr Smith. I take it you still see her daily at the embassy?"

"I don't," Wells said, "as she gave her notice two months ago. I have been seeing her from time to time since her departure. We sometimes dine at the Moulin Bleu on Wednesday evenings, though we haven't done so for a week or two."

Holmes rose to his feet and paced the room, lost in thought.

"I'll need her address, if you please," he said at last.

"By all means," Wells said, and recited an exclusive address on Cheyne Walk.

"Watson, we'll make a trip to Chelsea first thing in the morning and try to shed light on this Mr Smith, and his dealings with the Martian ambassador. I have the distinct feeling that he is up to no good."

"Seconded," Wells echoed in dolorous tones.

"Meanwhile, Mr Wells, keep your ear to the ground, and if you hear anything at all suspicious, or which you think might aid us in our cause, do not hesitate to get in touch – but don't go into detail over the telephone," he went on. "Merely state a time and a day, and we will convene at the Lyons' tea room in Piccadilly, understood?"

Wells nodded, and drained his brandy. "I wish I could say it's been a pleasure making your acquaintance again, Mr Holmes, Dr Watson, but in the circumstances…" He grimaced across at Holmes's simulacrum, still seated in the armchair, then looked away.

In due course Wells took his leave, and Holmes resumed his

pacing. I poured myself a third glass of brandy – a stiffer one, this time, as I was in need of its balm – and sat by the hearth lost in thought.

"This Mr Smith, Holmes. Don't like the sound of him at all."

Holmes paused in his pacing and stared across at me.

"And nor do I, Watson," he said. "Nor do I."

# Chapter Eighteen

*What we Discovered at Chelsea*

Eight o'clock the following morning saw us alighting from an electrical cab and staring up at the red-brick facade of a three-storey townhouse on the embankment. The house had been divided into three separate apartments, and a nameplate beneath the bell-pull indicated that Miss Fairfield occupied the upper floor.

Holmes hauled on the bell-pull and stood back.

The door was opened presently by an upright landlady with silver-grey hair and pince-nez perched on the bridge of her prominent nose.

Holmes informed this worthy that we were seeking Miss Cicely Fairfield, only to be met with a frown.

"Miss Fairfield left her rooms yesterday, and did not say when she might return." She touched a pearl brooch at her throat. "If I might ask, what is your business with the young lady?"

Holmes produced his card. "Sherlock Holmes, consulting detective. We have been hired by a certain Mr Wells to look into the whereabouts of Miss Fairfield."

At the sound of Wells's name, the landlady smiled. "Well, that's different... I like Mr Wells. He's a gentleman, unlike the other fellow."

At this, Holmes's ears pricked up. "The other fellow?"

"That's right, a Mr Smith he called himself. A big-headed chap in a cape."

"He was arrogant?" I asked.

The landlady smiled. "No, I mean that he possessed a rather large head on narrow shoulders."

"And was he wearing a fedora and a mask?" Holmes enquired.

"A hat, yes – but he wasn't wearing a mask."

"Did you by any chance get a close look at his face?"

The landlady shook her head. "I only saw him on two or three occasions, and he always had his collar turned up and his hat pulled low. Secretive, he was. The last time I saw him was yesterday, when he arrived in a cab for Miss Fairfield."

Holmes exchanged a glance with me. "She didn't happen to say where she was going?" he asked.

"She didn't say a word, but I remember thinking that she looked flustered, or worried. She was carrying an overnight bag, and Mr Smith was chivvying her along as if he had an important appointment to keep."

"What time was this?"

"No later than noon, I should say."

"Did you by any chance notice which company the cab belonged to?"

She frowned in concentration. "It might have been the Blue Star people, or was it the Kensington Company? Then again it might have been Robinson's. I'm sorry, but there are so many cab companies around these days."

Holmes nodded. "I wonder if you might show us up to her

apartment? It is a matter of utmost importance that we trace Miss Fairfield."

"Why, of course. If you'd care to follow me."

She led us into an immaculately decorated hallway and up three flights of stairs to the upper floor, then fumbled with a bunch of keys on a cord at her waist and opened the only door on the landing. Holmes thanked her, then closed the door gently on her enquiring glance.

"I don't like the sound of this," I said. "Miss Fairfield leaving in a hurry – perhaps against her will – with this Smith fellow…"

Holmes nodded, intent on examining the room.

It was a large open space with a bay window affording a wonderful view of west London. Unlike Miss Hamilton-Bell's hideaway, it was modern and sparsely furnished. What struck me straight away was the number of bookshelves placed against the walls, bearing hundreds of volumes on subjects ranging from sociology to ancient history, anthropology to geology. One bookcase was full of modern novels, another of poetry. A typewriter stood on a writing desk beside the window.

Holmes was on his hands and knees, minutely inspecting the hearth rug. Then he turned his attention to the fire grate.

"What are you looking for, Holmes?"

He muttered something along the lines of, "I'll know when I find it, Watson."

I moved to the first of three adjoining doors, which gave on to a small bathroom. I noticed that a cupboard above the sink was open, and that one or two bottles containing the kind of creams or embrocations that ladies find necessary had been knocked over: spaces testified to the fact that others had been removed.

I reported this to Holmes, then moved to the bedroom. A dresser still had one of its drawers gaping, and various items of clothing spilled from it. It did not take a detective of Holmes's perspicacity to work out that Miss Fairfield had departed in a hurry.

When I returned to the sitting room, Holmes was examining a piece of charred paper he had found in the fire grate. "What is it, Holmes?"

He turned a fragment this way and that with a pair of tweezers.

"Whatever it was, Watson, is now burned beyond all hope of recognition. It was a sheet of paper, eight-ounce vellum, of the finest quality. A fragment of typeface suggests an official document – in the Martian script, what's more."

He gestured to the deep pile rug before the fireplace. "I note the slightest impressions of three footprints in the shape of a man's shoes. I rather think that while Miss Fairfield was hurrying to collect a few necessary belongings, Mr Smith took the time to burn a document, ensuring that nothing, or at any rate nothing of import, survived the flames."

While he continued to sift through the ash in the grate, I approached the desk by the window. It appeared that Miss Fairfield had recently begun a piece of fiction, a short story or perhaps a novel. A sheet of paper was lodged in the platen, with the title *The Other Harold Gordon Webb*, followed by a paragraph describing the heroine's departure from a southern coastal town.

Holmes rose to his feet, dusting his hands together, and stared around the room. "What's that, Watson?" he said, indicating the typewriter.

"A story she'd just begun," I said, moving to the small kitchen. A single china cup stood on the table, half-full of black coffee. A smudge of lipstick on its gold-rimmed edge indicated that Miss Fairfield had been partaking of the beverage upon Smith's arrival, abandoning it upon her precipitate departure.

"Watson!" Holmes called from the other room.

I hurried into the sitting room to find him bending over the writing desk, his brow furrowed as he read what was typed upon the single sheet.

"Miss Fairfield is in danger," he said, indicating the paper.

"She is?"

"Read it, including the title!"

I did so, for the second time. "*The Other Harold Gordon Webb*," I read. "*Harriet Evans left Portsmouth, wondering if the heavy snow might impede the Hutchinsons. We only know it never gave…*"

I shook my head. "I don't quite see…"

Holmes tore the paper from the platen, read it again, then looked at me. "This is hardly the work of an accomplished writer, with several highly respected articles to her credit. Why, it's almost gibberish. The only explanation that occurred to me, Watson, was that it must be a code, a few innocent lines which could be left here and which would not arouse suspicion from Mr Smith were he to glance at them."

"A code?"

"Take the first letter of each word," he said, "starting with the title, and what do you have?"

I took the sheet and read the lines. "Good God!"

"Precisely," he said. "*To HGW. Help. With Smith. Woking.*"

"A plea to Wells to help her – Smith took her to Woking." I shook my head. "Woking?"

"It is of some significance to the Martians, Watson. It was, after all, where the first of their interplanetary vessels landed in '94. The Martians have a barracks there these days, as well as an engineering factory where they repair their tripods."

"My word... But why would Smith wish to take her there?"

Holmes ignored my question as he paced the room, lost in thought. He returned to the window and stared out in silence, his brow creased.

"Examine the evidence, Watson, piece by piece. Miss Fairfield met Mr Smith during the course of her work at the Martian Embassy. Wells states that she found herself attracted to his erudition. They met here on a number of occasions, as the landlady said that she saw Smith several times. On the last occasion, yesterday, Smith came for her at noon approximately. He was in something of a hurry, according to the landlady, and Miss Fairfield evidently packed in haste. And yet... and yet she had time to leave a cryptic plea for help on the typewriter, which must have taken some time to compose. Now, Watson, what does this suggest to you?"

I stared down at the typewritten sheet on the desk.

"That she knew she was leaving with him," I said, "perhaps the night before, giving her time in which to compose the note. Yet she did not know precisely what time, evidenced by her hasty packing, and by the half-finished cup of coffee."

"Exactly, Watson! She knew she was leaving with him, but was fearful of doing so – hence the note. Yet she made no effort, at any time before her departure, to flee the house and the attentions of Mr Smith. What does this suggest?"

I rubbed my chin, flummoxed. "Why, Holmes, I'm quite stumped."

"It suggests to me that poor Miss Fairfield was *compelled* for some reason to accompany Mr Smith, or she would surely have fled the apartment. It suggests that Mr Smith, therefore, had some hold over Miss Fairfield, making her compliant to his will."

"Good God!"

"Quite," said Holmes. "He had something on the poor woman. He was, I contest, blackmailing her. And the only blemish on her record, as far as we are aware, is her killing in self-defence of the former Martian ambassador."

"So Smith knew of this and used it against her?"

"That, Watson, seems to be the long and the short of the situation. Three questions emerge from this deduction. One, who is the mysterious Mr Smith? Two, how did Smith discover what happened in the ambassador's bedchamber two years ago? And three, what are his intentions regarding Miss Fairfield?"

I swore aloud. "In reverse order, Holmes," I began. "What are his intentions with the poor girl? Why, she is young and comely – I can only impute the basest motives for blackmailing and kidnapping her. As for how he found out about the ambassador's killing? Well, Mr Smith worked at the embassy – could he have had access to the former ambassador's personal papers, wherein he read of the Martian's feelings for Miss Fairfield? Perhaps he interrogated her, and she broke down and admitted her part in the killing? As for the identity of Mr Smith." I shook my head. "Why, he might be any Tom, Dick or…"

Holmes was staring at me with such an expression of foreboding that I fell silent.

"As for the last," said he, "I fear the worst."

"The worst?" I echoed.

"Examine the facts, my friend. Mr Smith is some kind of scientific expert who has willingly thrown in his lot with our oppressors. He is small of stature, yet large of head. He has been at pains to disguise his true features. He has – not for the first time in his long and nefarious career – broken the law in committing blackmail and kidnap."

I pulled the chair from under the desk and slumped down into it. "Please don't say what I fear, Holmes."

My friend stared out at a London that was bathed in sunshine, yet never had his features seemed so grim.

"I thought it impossible, Watson, despite the rumours that he – like me – had survived the plummet at Reichenbach." He shook his head. "I took comfort from the notion that he was dead, and thought the rumours that he was alive, and was up to his devilish games again, no more than that – cheap rumours dreamed up by press hacks eager for scandalous copy. But…"

"Go on," I said, despondent.

"But I fear," said Holmes, "that the mysterious Mr Smith is none other than Professor Moriarty."

# Chapter Nineteen

### News from Africa and the Middle East

It was just after ten o'clock by the time we arrived back at Baker Street. Holmes had been silent for the duration of the journey, lost no doubt in his own melancholic ruminations. I, for my part, dwelled on the calamitous turn of events: the double blow of Miss Fairfield's abduction, and our suspicion of who had perpetrated the diabolical act. Added to my impotent rage was the fact that Holmes's archenemy had thrown in his lot with the Martians. I had known the depths to which Moriarty was wont to stoop, but never in my wildest dreams had I ever thought that he might sink so low as to collude with the oppressors of humankind.

My introspective mood was lightened somewhat on our return to find a note awaiting us. Mrs Hudson said that a young woman had called but an hour ago, and had left it on finding that we were not at home.

"*Dear Mr Holmes and Dr Watson,*" Holmes read. "*Developments. Would you meet me at the cafe in Regent's Park at eleven? Failing that, the Euston Lyons' at five? Ever yours, Freya Hamilton-Bell.*"

"Developments?" I said. "I wonder if what Miss Hamilton-Bell has to report can match our news?"

"I hope it is of a more sanguine nature than our intelligence," Holmes said. "We could set off immediately and take tea in the park before her arrival."

"Capital! I'm famished."

Holmes cast me a wry glance as we left the house. "I never fail to be amazed at your unabated appetite, Watson, even in the direst of circumstances."

"One must keep body and soul together, old man. No good has ever come of stinting in the victuals department. I take it, therefore, that you will not be eating?"

"I might take a Chelsea bun with my tea," he allowed.

We strolled through the park, together with a host of citizens enjoying the clement weather. Ahead, looming over the oak trees, was a stationary tripod, a towering monument to the implacable might of the Martians. We gave it a wide berth and arrived at the kiosk some thirty minutes before our rendezvous with Miss Hamilton-Bell.

Holmes was as good as his word regarding his choice of refreshment, and while he absentmindedly bit into a Chelsea bun, I devoured a very passable Welsh rarebit. We sat outside in the sun and, but for the events of the morning, I might have considered the light meal a pleasant one.

"We must proceed to Woking once we have concluded our business with Miss Hamilton-Bell," Holmes said. "There is a train at twelve-fifteen, and we should go armed with the electrical guns and your service revolver."

"What do you think Moriarty might be doing in Woking, Holmes?" I asked between mouthfuls.

"No doubt he is on some errand at the behest of the Martians," Holmes replied. "That can be the only answer. As for what he might want with Miss Fairfield…"

"You don't think it might simply be a case of" – I hesitated – "of an older man desiring the fruits of youth, as it were?"

"It might very well be," Holmes said, "though I suspect that aside from this there is an ulterior motive. Also…"

"Go on."

His sweetmeat consumed, he filled his cherrywood pipe and puffed it into life. "Also, I am perplexed as to his need to disguise himself so thoroughly. Recall Wells's assertion that Mr Smith wore a facemask?"

I shrugged. "He's a notorious villain," I said. "A wanted criminal sought after from London to New York, Moscow to Melbourne. He obviously does not want to be recognised."

Holmes shook his head. "A cloak and fedora would suffice," he said. "A facemask is taking disguise to an extreme – indeed, it would attract attention, not deflect it. I suspect there is a reason for the mask that I have yet to fathom."

I looked along the curving path that approached the cafe as a familiar figure came into sight. Despite the travails of the day, my heart quickened at the sight of Miss Hamilton-Bell.

She was dressed in a jade-green crinoline dress, cinched becomingly at the waist, the get-up set off by a large sun hat of the same verdant shade. She turned not a few heads as she joined us at our table.

"Gentlemen, it is reassuring to see your friendly faces once again." She ordered Darjeeling with lemon from the waiter, then leaned towards us. "I have had a somewhat stressful morning."

"Then we have not been alone in facing adversity," Holmes said.

She looked curiously from Holmes to me. "I met a certain foreign contact at Marble Arch this morning. This gentleman hails from Paris, and liaises with agents in the Middle East and Africa. He bore disturbing news."

"No doubt concerning the Martian presence?" Holmes surmised.

"Just so. I will not beat about the bush. He informed me that he had received intelligence from agents on the ground in Kenya and Mesopotamia. They report that following the increased activity of Martian interplanetary ships arriving at Nairobi and Baghdad, a great army of tripods – of the military variety – have been clearing tribal peoples from vast swathes of land in central Kenya, and citizens from the plains east of the Euphrates. Also, tripods have been observed transporting building materials – sections of Martian geodesic domes and panels of their great curving towers – into these cleared areas. Their motives appear obvious."

"They are constructing cities for their own kind," Holmes said.

Miss Hamilton-Bell nodded. "If this were not bad enough, the Martians are using human slave labour to build these cities."

"Do you have any intelligence as to when the relocation might begin in earnest?" I asked.

"Sadly, no. But the day cannot be very far off. Among the Resistance, the feeling is that they will establish bridgeheads in these desert regions, and when these are occupied they will take over more densely populated areas."

"And the dispiriting fact," Holmes said, "is that the armies of Earth – the once mighty armies of Great Britain, Germany, France and China – have been greatly reduced in number by the simulacra stooges of their leaders, politicians and generals. We know that Asquith has been replaced, and Lord Kitchener."

"Among the military," she said, "more than a dozen senior

officers have been duplicated. And these are the ones we know about for certain. There are doubtless many others."

"You present a bleak scenario," I said.

"There are more dire tidings, my friends. A spy in the Martians' ranks has confirmed what we feared: the Arkana have brought their duplication machines to Earth. Formerly, these devices were made at great expense and used only on Mars. But recently, in the past few days, due to advances in their manufacture, they have been distributed beyond their place of origin – the easier to copy the great and good of Earth, rather than have them travel to the red planet."

"Good God," I said. "The battle has just become almost impossible!"

"But all is not lost," Miss Hamilton-Bell went on. "At least we know what the Martians are planning." She sipped her tea. "But what of your news? Did you manage to contact Mr Wells?"

"On that front," Holmes said, "the news is good. Not only did we contact him, but we succeeded in persuading him to work with us – not that he took much persuading. You see, there is little love lost between Mr Wells and the Martians."

He went on to detail his investigation into the death of the Martian ambassador two years ago, and Wells's and Miss Fairfield's involvement in the affair.

"I heard about the former ambassador's death, but accepted the reported version of events, that the Martian had taken his own life. Three cheers for Miss Fairfield, I say."

Holmes gave a mirthless smile. "I wish I could report happier tidings regarding that worthy," he said. "But my suspicions are that not only has the greatest criminal mastermind in human history sided with the Martians, but he has abducted the young woman into the bargain."

He proceeded to outline the events of the morning, and what we had discovered in Chelsea, in minute detail.

Miss Hamilton-Bell stared into her tea, unmoving, and only when Holmes ceased speaking did she look up and say, "But what can he want with Miss Fairfield?"

"I suggested his motives were no more than carnal," I said, "if you will excuse my saying so. But Holmes thinks otherwise."

"In my dealings with Professor Moriarty," Holmes said, "I have never heard, nor experienced at first hand, anything to suggest that he possesses what might be called a romantic nature. His affairs with his fellow humans are exclusively cerebral – or else sadistic. I fear that Watson might in part be right in imputing carnal motivations to Moriarty's abduction of the young woman – albeit desires tainted by the man's inveterate sadism, which thought is frightful – but I suspect that there is more to it than that."

"Might his interest," Miss Hamilton-Bell suggested, "be merely of the mind? Miss Fairfield is, after all, a highly regarded intellectual."

Holmes nodded. "And that," he said, "is what I fear."

In due course Holmes consulted his pocket watch and said that it was high time we were returning to Baker Street. We had to arm ourselves before taking the train to Woking.

"It is imperative that we do everything possible to find Miss Fairfield," said Holmes, "and, also, to prevent whatever Moriarty is planning."

Miss Hamilton-Bell looked from me to Holmes. "You realise, of course, the highly dangerous nature of your mission? If you were to be apprehended…"

"We will do all within our power to prevent that occurrence," said Holmes.

"I would advise against such rash action, at least for the time being," she said. "Allow me a little time to contact an agent who might assist you on the ground in Woking."

"I am afraid that time is of the essence," Holmes insisted. "I appreciate your concern, but I must stress that Miss Fairfield is in grave danger. And I assure you that we will go about our business with the utmost circumspection."

"In future it might become necessary," she said, "to avail yourself of the safe house in Barnes." And so saying, she passed a spare key to Holmes.

We bade a muted farewell with promises to contact her in due course with news of our exploits.

We hurried back to Baker Street, the young woman's scent stirring my senses, and the warmth of her hand – which I had gripped as she entreated us to take care – still lingering on mine.

Mrs Hudson apprehended us in the hallway before we ascended to our rooms. "Mr Wells – the gentleman who visited last night – he came knocking again just ten minutes ago and said he needed to see you urgently. I showed him upstairs and said you'd be back presently. I hope I did the right thing, Mr Holmes?"

"You certainly did," Holmes assured her, and hurried up the staircase.

We found Wells pacing the sitting room in a febrile state. "Holmes, Watson! I am delighted to see you."

I urged him to take a seat. "And you'll have a drink – you look as though you need one."

"Thank you. I don't know where to begin…"

I poured him a brandy. Wells slumped onto the chaise longue, and Holmes and I took our chairs to either side of the hearth.

"Allow me to hazard a guess," Holmes said. "You attempted to contact Miss Fairfield last night, and failed to do so. Moreover, you visited her apartment but an hour ago–"

"That's right, I did. But there was no sign of Cicely. How the blazes do you know?"

"Yesterday you mentioned that you and Miss Fairfield dined from time to time at the Moulin Bleu on Wednesday evenings. It is therefore reasonable to assume that you attempted to phone her last night, a Wednesday, and received no reply. Understandably concerned, you made a trip to Chelsea one hour ago." Holmes pointed to the man's breast pocket. "I spy the corner of an electrical cab ticket, zone one, with the printed time of your journey clearly discernible."

Wells knocked back his brandy. "And as I said, there was no sign of Cicely... What the deuce is going on, Holmes?"

I regarded my hands awkwardly, then looked up at Holmes who said, "We have discovered that yesterday Miss Fairfield went to Woking with Mr Smith."

"To Woking, with Smith? Why the blazes were they going to Woking, of all places?"

"That, sir, we have yet to discover."

"Did you learn anything else in Chelsea," Wells asked, "other than that Smith dragged Cicely off to Woking?"

Holmes hesitated. I could see that he was considering the wisdom of informing Wells – already in a distraught state – that his ex-fiancée had been abducted by none other than the archcriminal Professor Moriarty.

At last, deciding that the truth was paramount, he said, "We discovered the identity of the mysterious Mr Smith."

He rose to his feet and crossed to the crammed bookshelves on the far side of the room. He pulled out a fat volume – a history of criminality, I noted – and riffled through it until he found a small photograph lodged between the pages.

He returned to the hearth and passed the picture to Wells.

"The only extant photograph of Professor James Moriarty, a daguerreotype taken when he was arrested twenty-five years ago and held at Bow Street station – before he effected an ingenious escape."

Wells was staring down at the photograph with frank incredulity. "Moriarty?" he said, shaking his head as if in disbelief. "But…" He looked up and regarded Holmes. "But this isn't Moriarty… It's one of the Jones twins, either the elder or younger, I can't be sure."

Holmes turned pale. "The Jones twins? And who might they be? No, don't tell me, they worked for the Martians at the embassy, am I correct?"

Wells nodded. "That's right, they did. And a pretty secretive pair they were, too. Had an office to themselves on the third floor, and weren't to be disturbed. They left the employ of the embassy perhaps a month ago, so I understand."

Holmes all but groaned and turned to me. "Well, Watson, that explains why our 'Mr Smith' went to such pains to disguise himself while in the embassy."

"I don't quite follow, old chap…" I began.

"You see, Watson, 'Smith' couldn't be seen around the place as himself when the 'Jones twins' were also at the embassy – or Wells here and the other human staff might have started asking questions."

"You mean…?" I began.

Holmes nodded. "I do. I do indeed *mean*, Watson. I mean that Mr Smith and the Jones twins are three of the same – they are all Professor James Moriarty. The question is," he went on, "who is the real Moriarty, and which two are the simulacra? Not, I suppose, that it matters – the fact is that we now know that the Martians have, working on their side, the evil criminal mastermind Moriarty, plus two."

"I think this," I said, climbing rather unsteadily to my feet, "calls for a stiff brandy."

Later, Wells learned that we were making for Woking and insisted on accompanying us.

"You will do nothing of the kind, sir," Holmes said. "It would be foolhardy in the extreme to be seen with us in the very centre of Martian operations. Return home, and in the morning go to work at the embassy as if nothing untoward has occurred. We will be in contact at some point tomorrow."

We armed ourselves with the electrical guns, ensured that we were wearing the batteries, and bade Wells good-day outside 221B.

Minutes later we boarded a cab bound for Waterloo Station.

# Chapter Twenty

*The Attractions of Woking*

I must admit that, as our train pulled into Woking Station, I was feeling more than a little apprehensive at the thought of what lay ahead. We were entering enemy territory – an enemy that was not only merciless, but would not hesitate to bring about our end if our simulacra ruse was rumbled. Holmes had tried to reassure me that this was a reconnaissance mission only, but I was far from reassured as we stepped from the carriage and approached the ticket collector.

We passed through the barrier and entered the teeming concourse, and I stopped in my tracks and stared about me in wonder. All around were placards and notices advertising various attractions and exhibitions. One could visit Horsell Common, where the very first Martian cylinder had come to rest in '94, and go on a walking tour of the still deserted villages, which the first wave of ravaging tripods had destroyed; one could take a guided tour of the Martian Museum in the town centre, where such artefacts as the Martian Handling-Machines were on display, or visit the tripod manufactory on the outskirts of town.

While I was goggling at these gaudy advertisements, Holmes was studying a map of Woking. "See here, Watson," he said, pointing to a district to the south of the town centre. "This is the site of the tripod manufactory and the Martian Research Institute, situated in an old Victorian insane asylum. To the west is Horsell Common, and round about it the devastated villages."

"That's all very well," I said, "but how on earth are we going to go about locating Moriarty and Miss Fairfield? They might be anywhere."

Holmes turned and pointed. "We will begin our search with an enquiry – always, I find, an efficacious method of finding out what one wants."

The glass-roofed area was chock-a-block with a hundred hurrying citizens. "And whom might we ask?" I said.

Holmes nodded across the concourse. "How about that worthy, yonder?"

"A Salvation Army collector?" I said.

"In my experience I have found them eagle-eyed, Watson – always on the lookout for souls in need of salvation. And our friend Moriarty, with his suspicious eyes and shifty deportment, would easily qualify as such. If I couch my enquiry in a way that would trigger her piety and professional interest..."

So saying, he led me across to the diminutive, grey-haired, rosy-cheeked woman and slipped a shilling into her collection box.

"Why, thank you, sir. Most generous."

"Not at all," said Holmes. "Always glad to assist a worthy cause. I was wondering if I might solicit the Army's professional service?"

"We're ever eager to help those in need, sir."

"I happen to be searching for my daughter. Here is her

photograph," he said, passing the woman a portrait of Miss Fairfield.

As she screwed up her eyes and studied the photograph, I murmured to Holmes, "How the devil did you...?"

"I borrowed it from Miss Fairfield's apartment yesterday," he whispered in reply.

"Pretty little thing," said the woman.

"A runaway," Holmes said in woebegone tones, ever the thespian laying it on thick. "Worse, I fear she might have been in the company of an older man."

The old lady clucked in sympathy. Her face scrunched up in concentration so that it rather resembled a wizened apple. "I do believe..." she began.

"They would have passed through the station yesterday at around this time."

"Why, yes, I do recall them. I remember thinking what a pretty girl, but with such a look of concern on her face. And the fellow clutching her hand was fair dragging her along—"

"A somewhat ugly character, with a swollen forehead and sunken eyes?"

"The very fellow, sir. The very spit. I did wonder at the time what a lovely looking girl like her was doing with such a character. Under duress, it struck me."

"I don't suppose you know in which direction they went on leaving the station?"

"Well, I do know they took a taxi from the rank just there. The man bundled her into the back of the cab, and off they went."

Holmes looked through the station entrance to the taxi rank. "I don't suppose you noticed which cab they took?"

"Well, it was one of the Red Line cars, sir, 'cause I remember thinking how the girl's red coat matched the cab's paintwork."

"You've been extraordinarily helpful, madame. Thank you," Holmes said, and inserted another shilling into her collection box.

"Why, thank *you*, sir, and good luck," she added as we hurried from the station.

We crossed the pavement to the taxi rank, where a dozen cabs were lined up in the afternoon sunlight. I counted vehicles of at least three companies touting for trade, with among them four cars of the Red Line company.

Holmes spoke to the first Red Line driver, showing him Miss Fairfield's photograph, only to receive a taciturn shake of the head for his troubles. He moved on to the next Red Line employee and exchanged a few words. This fellow screwed up his eyes and examined the photograph for a duration, his lips pursed judiciously.

He passed it back to Holmes. "Was she with an ugly lookin' cove?"

"Indeed she was. I take it you saw them?"

The driver grunted. "Might have," was all he would vouchsafe.

With a show of legerdemain worthy of a stage conjurer, Holmes produced a crisp ten-shilling note and held it before the cabbie's staring eyes.

"And where did you take them, my good man?"

The driver made a grab for the note, but Holmes was too fast for him and withdrew the prize.

"Took 'em to the Martian place," the man said.

Holmes smiled. "The 'Martian place'? Very descriptive, sir. There are, at the very least, half a dozen sites in the vicinity that might be described as the 'Martian place'."

"Very well, then, it were the Martian Research Institute, okay?"

Holmes thanked the driver and handed over the ten-shilling note.

"You want me to take you there?"

"Not quite yet, but thank you."

Holmes drew me into the shade of the station, for the sun was fair beating down and he had dutifully donned his deerstalker at the start of the journey.

I stared at him. "'Not quite yet'?" I said. "But Holmes, you said that this trip was but a reconnaissance mission. You can't seriously be considering bearding the lion in his den?"

"Watson," he said, "do you recall the curious case of the Woking jewel thief, which a few years ago you wrote up for *The Strand* – rather melodramatically, I thought – as 'The Mystery of the Invisible Man'?"

"Of course I do, Holmes. One of my better efforts – but what the blazes–"

"You recall that I gave you the slip and vanished for a day or so, later reappearing to report that I'd come to this very town, assumed a disguise, and apprehended the 'invisible' thief as he was about to embark on his most daring heist?"

"Yes, but–"

"I availed myself of the services of a rather good costumier in town, Watson. This way."

Without waiting for me, he stepped out into the flow of traffic, halting a car with an imperious hand, and continued across the road. I waited until the vehicle had passed, the driver shaking his fist at Holmes, and joined my friend as he set off at speed along the High Street. After a hundred yards he turned down a side alley and paused before a narrow shopfront.

"Still in business, Watson, and open, what's more," and so saying he pushed open the door and stepped into the cramped premises.

Costumes of a dozen varieties and from as many countries were displayed on tailor's dummies, the scent of naphthalene hung in the air like cloying incense, and a hundred facemasks ogled us from the walls.

A shrivelled gnome of a man looked up from a ledger and exclaimed, "Why, as I live and breathe. Mr Holmes! It's been a while."

"Three years, two months and five days, if my memory serves, Mr Karbalkian. We have come to avail ourselves of your excellent services."

"It'd be an honour to assist," said the gnome.

Thirty minutes later we were attired, and made-up, in disguises that would have fooled our mothers. Holmes sported a tweed jacket and plus fours, a bald pate and his deerstalker. The addition of a gumshield and cotton wool stuffed into his cheeks, along with make-up that gave his face a puce complexion, completed the transformation. He looked like a somewhat dissolute country squire with a fatal predilection for fine port.

Holmes had supervised my own disguise, electing to further exacerbate my weight gain of recent years to the point where I resembled Tweedledee, outfitted in a ridiculously blaring checked suit and bowler hat. If Holmes passed as a disreputable minor aristocrat, I was an even more disreputable fairground crier.

As we completed our disguises in a cramped back room, Holmes said, "You have your electrical gun, your Webley and, most importantly, the simulacrum's battery?"

I patted my suit in turn. "Check, check, and check."

"Capital. We are all set, then."

"But set for what?" I asked somewhat fearfully as Holmes thanked Mr Karbalkian, settled the bill, and led me from the premises.

"What else but entry into the Martian Research Institute, Watson?" he said as we hurried back to the station and the taxi rank.

"I intend only what I suggested earlier – a reconnaissance mission."

"But how the blazes will we gain admittance into the institute?"

Holmes waved this aside. "We will unpick that knotty problem when faced with it," he said breezily as we reached the rank.

The cab driven by the rather grudging fellow who had earlier relieved Holmes of ten shillings was now at the front of the rank, and we slipped into its commodious back seat.

Holmes gave our destination as the Martian Institute and sat back as the car beetled silently from the rank and inserted itself into the stream of traffic flowing down the High Street.

I found it reassuring that the driver obviously did not recognise us in our disguises.

"The Martian Institute?" he grunted over his shoulder. "Don't normally get 'umans going to the institute, I don't. Plenty of smelly Martians, of course. Odd thing is, I had a couple o' 'umans in yesterday, bound for the Martian place. Ugly chap and his flighty piece. Bit of all right she was, mind."

"You don't say?" Holmes said, affecting a high-pitched tone.

"I do. And another odd thing is, I had this geezer asking after her just an hour ago. Waving his spondulicks around like he owned the world, he was." The driver chuckled. "Took his ten bob, I did, and told him I'd taken the couple to the institute – but I didn't tell 'em the whole tale."

"You didn't?"

"Didn't like the cut of his jib," said the cabbie. "Bit arrogant, he was."

I cast Holmes a swift glance, suppressing the urge to smile.

Holmes said, casually, "And what was the whole tale, good sir?"

"This ugly chap and his bit o' all right, they went to the institute like I said, but they didn't go in the main entrance, did they? No, slipped into a side door, furtive like."

"A side door?"

"That's right, just along from the main entrance it was." The cabbie grinned over his shoulder. "I reckoned they were sneaking in there for a bit of you-know-what!"

"Quite," said Holmes as we approached the high iron gate flanked by stone pillars. A gravelled drive processed up a slight incline to a foursquare grey building that had all the dour gravitas – even on this sunlit summer's afternoon – of the Victorian asylum it had once been.

We rolled up the drive and approached the building. A dozen Martian cars were drawn up in the turning circle, and beyond the bulk of the building I espied the cowls of several Martian tripods.

The door of the institute opened and three Martians shuffled out, their appearance against the quintessentially English backdrop of the country house striking me as somewhat incongruous, not to say grotesque.

I admit that, at this point, my heart was thumping and a hot sweat had broken out across my brow.

As the driver braked before the main entrance, Holmes leaned forward and pointed to a door ten yards to the right of the main entrance.

"Is that by any chance the portal by which the man and the girl entered yesterday?"

"The very one, sir," said the cabbie. "That'll be nine pence, thank you."

Holmes climbed from the cab, leaned towards the driver's window, and dropping the aristocratic tone said in his own voice, "The ten-shilling note I gave you earlier, my good man, will be more than sufficient remuneration."

Hiding a smile, I heard the driver curse Holmes roundly and set off at speed back down the drive.

"Frivolities aside," Holmes said, turning to stare at the grim facade of the Martian Institute, "the game is afoot, Watson. This way."

I followed my friend towards the black-painted door.

## Chapter Twenty-One

*A Multiplicity of Moriartys*

"The cabbie's letting slip Moriarty's use of the door was a stroke of luck, what?" I said as Holmes reached out and turned the door handle.

"Luck which has run dry, Watson. The door is locked."

Assuming as nonchalant a gait as was possible under the circumstances, there being a party of five Martians approaching the institute's entrance, we sauntered away from them towards the corner of the building. Holmes peered around the chiselled cornerstones, deemed the way safe, and gestured for me to follow.

I did so and, once out of sight of the Martians, leaned against the brickwork and mopped my brow.

"This is hardly the ideal pursuit for a man of my years," I said.

"*Pfaugh!* You should find such activity meat and drink, my friend."

"I prefer to indulge in a more sedentary banquet," I said, peering along the side of the building.

To our left was the east wall of the institute, stretching for perhaps thirty yards with windows set at regular intervals along its length. To our right, just yards away, was a high stone wall. Beyond the building, down the narrow perspective of the gravelled strip before us, I made out a lawn and ornamental garden and, beyond them, a cobbled courtyard. The one-storey buildings surrounding the courtyard must once have belonged to the asylum, but they had now been pressed into service as the Martians' Tripod Manufactory. A cacophonous metal clangour filled the air. Several tripods stood about the courtyard, eerily still, and sections thereof were piled beside the outbuildings. To my immense relief, no Martians were in sight.

Holmes took my elbow and indicated the nearest window, a few yards away. "We must proceed with the utmost caution, Watson. After me."

We approached the leaded window and Holmes squinted through the pane. He muttered an oath, and I too peered through the window.

I made out a classroom equipped with rows of desks. These were occupied by the unlikely figures of Martian students bent over their work, their tentacles busy with what appeared to be calculating machines. It was not the Martians, however, that had provoked my friend's exclamation – though the sight of the extraterrestrial pupils was somewhat bizarre – but the figure standing before a blackboard at the front of the class.

Their teacher was none other than Professor James Moriarty.

I ducked beneath the sill and stared at Holmes. "Good God!" I said. "Moriarty!"

"The man himself – or one of his simulacra."

He delved into the pocket of his jacket and withdrew the detection device that Miss Hamilton-Bell had given him yesterday. Crouching beneath the level of the sill, he lifted a hand, directed the device towards the front of the class, and depressed the stud.

The light glowed blue.

"As I guessed," Holmes said, "one of his mechanical copies. I somehow thought that the original Moriarty would not lower himself to act as a menial teacher."

"But is he the 'Moriarty' who came here yesterday with Miss Fairfield?" I wondered aloud. "There is a one in three chance of it being him, after all."

Holmes clucked at me. "I rather think not," he said, and before I could question him he was away, duck-walking across the gravel to the next window.

I joined him, my knee joints creaking woefully, and peered through. This room was evidently some kind of laboratory, with rows of benches bearing fulminating retorts, test tubes and Erlenmeyer flasks. A dozen Martians were at work before the benches, and passing among them was the familiar figure of the professor, pausing to instruct here, demonstrate there, and occasionally pausing to address the classroom at large.

Again Holmes activated the detection device and again the blue light indicated the professor was but a simulacrum.

We moved on to the next window.

Holmes peered through, while I nervously watched our backs. I feared that at any moment a Martian would appear around the corner and call on us to account for our skulking presence. And what then? Could we claim mere curiosity? I quailed at the thought.

"Take a look, Watson," Holmes said, "and see what you make of that."

I did as instructed, and beheld Professor Moriarty before a blackboard covered with abstruse mathematical diagrams and equations. The class this time comprised just three pupils, evidently partaking of an advanced lesson.

"The original?" I said.

"I'm afraid to say that I very much doubt it," Holmes said, and directed the detector at the teacher.

The light glowed blue. "Yet another mechanical copy," he said.

"But how many of the accursed things are there?" I exclaimed.

Holmes shook his head. "It is testament to the man's genius in various branches of the sciences and mathematics that the Martians, in many ways more sophisticated in these disciplines than ourselves, have seen the value of reproducing him. The very thought sickens me."

"What I'd like to know," I said, "is what in blue blazes the monster has done with Miss Fairfield?"

"Follow me," Holmes said, "and eventually we might find out."

Panting with the effort of emulating my friend's crouching shuffle, and casting fearful glances over my shoulder, I followed him to the next window, and then the next and the next. The scene in each was similar: in every classroom we beheld a simulacrum of Moriarty imparting the jewels of his wisdom upon his Martian disciples.

I looked ahead. There were but two further windows to investigate.

"I fear, Watson, that in order to locate Miss Fairfield we might at some point be forced to enter the building, if that is possible. Note that many of the windows are barred. If the postern doors are locked, like the one we tried, then only the front door remains as a point of entry."

"I must admit, I don't fancy breezing in through the front door," I said.

"Nor do I, Watson, but needs must."

We moved to the next window – the penultimate one along this side of the building – and Holmes peered through. "What-ho!"

he cried in a theatrical reprise of the aristocratic tone he had used earlier. "Success, of a sort. But I don't like the look of what's taking place in there, Watson."

I lifted my head and cautiously squinted into the lighted room.

"Good God!" I cried.

I found it difficult at first to fully comprehend what my eyes were relaying to my tired brain: the hunched figure of Professor Moriarty was bent over the sloping console of a silver machine the size of a grand piano, busy adjusting dials and verniers. On various screens on the console before him, moving graphs imparted who knows what arcane information, and from time to time lights flashed on and off. Moriarty's huge potato-like head moved back and forth in febrile excitation as his hands danced over the controls like those of some mad concert pianist.

It was not the professor, however, or what he might be doing, that captured my attention. For beyond the crazed professor was not just one Miss Fairfield, but two.

I sagged back beneath the level of the windowsill and said to my friend, "We've found her, Holmes, but a part of me wishes that we hadn't!"

I peered again, trying to comprehend what I saw.

The two Miss Fairfields were imprisoned side by side in a reticulation of chromium bars set against the far wall. They were spread-eagled, their arms and legs outstretched, shackled at ankle and wrist. The woman to the right wore a red summer dress, while the figure to the left was as naked as a newborn babe. On the heads of each woman was a device which resembled at first sight a crown or tiara, a silver strip connected to a medusa confusion of wires: these snaked from the head of the clothed Miss Fairfield, up over the frame and down to the second, naked woman.

"What the deuce is he doing to the poor girls?" I asked – though in my heart of hearts I could hazard a guess. I recalled the chromium frame from when we had been gassed in the Martian Museum of Science.

Holmes gave me a troubled look. "Recall what Miss Hamilton-Bell told us earlier," he said, "about the Martians having brought the duplication process to Earth? I fear – no, I know – that that is what is happening here. Moriarty is copying the mind of the original, clothed in the red dress, to the naked simulacrum. Now we know why he abducted her."

I cursed him. "At least now we've found the original Moriarty," I pointed out.

"But have we?" Holmes said. He raised the detector, pointed it into the room, and pressed the stud. The light glowed blue and I cursed again.

The Moriarty therein was yet another mechanical copy.

We ducked down below the level of the window and stared at each other.

Holmes appeared pensive. "But if the Moriarty in there is yet another simulacrum," he said, "where is the original, and what nefarious business might he be up to?"

"More importantly, Holmes, how the devil do we go about rescuing Miss Fairfield?"

"That is the question, for I'm sure that time is running out. I have no idea how long the duplication process might take, but he's had her here for a full day or more. There cannot be long left to run. And," he went on, his expression grim, "I am under no illusion as to the poor girl's fate once Moriarty has completed the duplication. He will kill her as all the other 'originals' were killed."

I fingered my revolver in the pocket of my jacket, and never had

I been more eager to press the weapon into service.

Holmes examined the window and its embrasure. "Like the others," he murmured, "it is barred."

"Our only option is to brazen it out and enter the building through the front entrance," said I.

"Are you game, Watson?"

"The stakes are high. I would never sleep again if we did nothing and Miss Fairfield perished at Moriarty's hands." I gripped my revolver, as if for reassurance. "I would rather die trying, Holmes, than do nothing."

"Well said, my friend. Very well, then—"

He stopped and looked past me. My heart sank and a dread horripilation crawled over my scalp.

"Holmes?" I whispered.

"It would appear, Watson, that we have been discovered."

Slowly, still crouching, I turned.

How the Martian had managed to creep up on us so silently over the gravel I could not fathom, but creep up he had. Now the terrible hideosity faced us at a distance of no more than three yards, staring with his great black eyes, his V-shaped mouth hanging open in what, if I were given to anthropomorphism, I would describe as gormless amazement. In his tentacles he gripped a weapon in the form of a golden tube, which he directed at us.

Holmes whispered, "Stand slowly, Watson, and raise your hands."

I climbed to my feet, my joints creaking in protest, and lifted my arms above my head in the time-honoured gesture of capitulation.

I harboured the hope that if our capture could be kept from the Moriartys, then we stood a chance of talking our way to freedom.

I did not, however, like the look of the golden weapon pointed directly at us.

Then the Martian lowered the weapon and, with another tentacle, directed a small, silver device in our direction.

I recognised the object as a simulacrum detector.

*Chapter Twenty-Two*

*A Fortunate Intervention*

"Now," I hissed at Holmes as the Martian pressed a stud on the side of the device, "we find out if our batteries work..."

I admitted that I was sweating as the Martian goggled at the device. He gripped it in the prehensile end of his slimy tentacle, and I was unable to make out whether the light thereon flashed blue or red.

"Fear not," Holmes replied. "All will be well."

"I wish I shared your confidence, Holmes," said I.

I expected the Martian to cry out at any second, alerting his cohorts to our presence. I glanced right and left, desperately seeking a way of escape.

Then the Martian spoke.

His arrowhead mouth clacked like castanets in the hands of a madman, and a stream of grunts and gurgles poured forth – but it seemed, despite my fear, that he was not summoning assistance.

Holmes replied in kind.

The Martian responded. I watched his singular mouthpiece as it opened and closed, its thick parrot-like tongue moving up and down like a clapper, a stream of drool spooling from its lower mandible.

I wondered if it were too early to assume that our batteries had worked and we had successfully passed ourselves off as simulacra.

Holmes replied. Under the make-up that he had made me apply, and the layers of extra clothing, I was sweating.

At this point Holmes lowered his arms, and the Martian let the detection device drop.

Later, Holmes was to report what had passed between himself and the Martian.

Upon apprehending us, the Martian had said, "By all that is sacred, what in the name of Phobos do you think you're doing?"

To which Holmes had replied, "We were merely passing, sir, and wished to witness the many wonders of your august institution."

"Do you realise the danger you would be in, my friends, if you were to be caught spying like this?"

"Spying? We were merely curious."

Then the alien had astounded Holmes by saying, "She said you would be venturing this way, one as thin as a rake, the other spherical."

"*Who* said we would be venturing this way?"

"Why," replied the Martian, "Miss Hamilton-Bell, who was fearful for your safety. She contacted me an hour ago. Since then I have been on the lookout, and it's fortunate indeed that I came across you before the guards caught you spying, though I must say I'm impressed that you can successfully pose as simulacra."

It was at this point that Holmes had lowered his hands to his side.

I, however, oblivious of the import of their little tête-à-tête, still thought that our safety was in the balance.

I glanced up and down the length of the building, expecting the Martian to be joined at any second by his compatriots – and then the game would surely be up.

Holmes's brief aside to me, however, dispelled my apprehension.

"All is well, Watson. Baro-Sinartha-Gree here is sympathetic to the Korshana cause, and is in contact with Miss Hamilton-Bell. Earlier she informed him of our journey to Woking."

I very nearly slipped to the ground in my relief.

He turned to Baro-Sinartha-Gree and said, "Do you speak English?"

"Badly," the Martian replied.

"We are in danger here, out in the open. Is there anywhere we can converse in private – our ultimate aim is to enter the building and free Miss Fairfield."

"Miss Fairfield?" Baro-Sinartha-Gree replied in confusion.

"You're not aware of Moriarty's kidnapping of the young woman?"

"I am a lowly mechanic working in tripod manufactory," he said.

I said to Holmes, "This is all very well, but why did Baro-Sinartha-Gree apprehend us with his fearful-looking weapon?"

Holmes relayed my query, and Baro-Sinartha-Gree clucked the equivalent of a Martian laugh and replied in broken English, hoisting the golden cylinder. "This is not weapon. This is pinion of tripod gyroscope."

"Perhaps," Holmes intervened, "we might continue this fascinating conversation in private?"

"This way," said Baro-Sinartha-Gree.

He leaned the pinion against the wall of the building and took off, dancing nimbly on his tentacles across the gravel and around the back of the institute. I expected to be seen at any second by

Martians less favourable to our cause. Baro-Sinartha-Gree led the way along the rear of the building and approached a door. We slipped inside after him and found ourselves in a stone-flagged corridor with not a Martian in sight. He opened a door to the right and ushered us into a storeroom equipped with shelves of stationery and office appurtenances.

Only when the door closed behind us did I allow myself to breathe a little easier.

At this juncture Baro-Sinartha-Gree explained to Holmes how he had come to throw in his lot with the Resistance movement. "I am an Arkanan, but in my veins throbs proud Korshana blood, thanks to my great-great-hive-father, who was Korshanan. When the Arkana invaded Earth, I vowed to do all within my powers to avenge the great wrong done by my people."

Holmes relayed this to me in precis, then proceeded to tell Baro-Sinartha-Gree about Moriarty's kidnapping of Miss Fairfield and how we hoped to win her freedom.

"He is alone with her in one of the rooms along the eastern side of the building where you found us," said Holmes. "If we can make our way there, without being observed, and overcome Moriarty…"

"Ah," said the Martian in his fractured English. "I have heard of this Moriarty."

"Do you know how many copies of him your people have made?" Holmes asked.

"Many simulacra," he said. "Maybe one hundred. Maybe more."

"That makes sense," Holmes said. "Why limit oneself to possessing one brilliant mind when you have the wherewithal to have dozens, hundreds even, at one's disposal? But think of the havoc he could wreak! Good God, one Moriarty was bad enough, but a hundred?"

He paused, then asked Baro-Sinartha-Gree, "And the original, the human Moriarty? Do you happen to know his whereabouts?"

The Martian lifted a tentacle. "I know only his simulacra are here, at institute."

Holmes nodded. "Very well. The time has come. We must confront the fiend's simulacrum and save Miss Fairfield. You have your electrical gun to hand, Watson?"

I patted my pocket. "And my Webley, too."

"I escort you along corridor," Baro-Sinartha-Gree said. "If anyone ask, I say you honoured guests, taking tour."

I slipped a hand into my pocket and gripped the butt of the electrical gun.

Baro-Sinartha-Gree opened the door, ensured that the way was clear, then led us from the storeroom.

We hurried down the stone-flagged corridor, my heart thumping, and came to another door. Through a square window-panel inset into the door I made out a corridor diminishing into the distance, with doors leading off on either side. The lecture rooms wherein we had seen the Moriartys were to the left. The second door along would give access to the room in which Miss Fairfield was incarcerated.

Baro-Sinartha-Gree pushed open the door and we followed, and to my great relief there were no Martians in the corridor.

We came to the second door on our left, and Holmes cautiously peered through the window-panel. He withdrew and nodded to me. "This is the room, Watson."

Baro-Sinartha-Gree murmured, "I wait here. Anyone come, I warn you."

"And when we have the girl?" I asked.

"You come with me, then. I take you from here."

"Take us? How?"

Holmes laid a hand on my arm. "This is not the time to quibble over details, Watson. Ready yourself. On the count of three, follow me."

I drew the electrical gun. Holmes said, "Now!" and pushed open the door.

# Chapter Twenty-Three

*Saving Miss Fairfield*

The expression on Professor Moriarty's ugly visage as we burst into the room brandishing our weapons was the epitome of surprise.

As he stared at us, his shock turned to disdain. "Why, if it isn't Mr Sherlock Holmes – with his faithful lapdog in tow. As disguises go, it's adequate enough to fool the unwitting. But as you know, Holmes, I am far from unwitting."

It was hard to credit that the criminal mastermind before us was not indeed the flesh-and-blood Moriarty. I had to remind myself that, in essence, this *was* Holmes's archenemy: just as his outer shell was a faithful reproduction of the original professor, so the mentation that resided in that ludicrously domed cranium was an exact copy of Moriarty's evil mind.

"Step away from the console, Moriarty," Holmes said, his electrical gun aiming directly at the professor's large head.

Moriarty's thin lips stretched in what could never be described as a smile; it resembled more a sneer. "If you take so much as one more step towards me, either of you, the girl dies. My hand is poised above the control that, at the merest touch, will terminate the duplication process and result in Miss Fairfield's immediate extinction. Likewise, if the process is interrupted before its completion, the result will be the same – the death of the girl."

"You foul specimen!" I spat, and looked to my left at the girl braced in the chromium frame.

She was unconscious, her head leaning to one side. At least she was spared the knowledge of the drama being enacted before her. To her right, the naked simulacrum was likewise inanimate.

Now that we were in the room, I was aware of the noise emitted by the process of duplication: a throbbing electrical hum issued from the cables that connected the original Miss Fairfield's head to her copy, a thrumming almost below the threshold of audibility that one felt as a pressure in one's diaphragm.

"I am prepared to do a deal," Holmes said. "I will allow you to finish the duplication, whereupon you will have your copy of Miss Fairfield. In return, we will take the original."

I knew that Holmes had no intention of letting Moriarty off so easily. I could tell by the calculating expression in his eyes that he was rapidly assessing the situation in order to buy himself a little time.

Moriarty gave a laugh that more closely resembled a cackle. "Oh, you poor fool! You cannot win, no matter what you do. The odds are stacked against you, Holmes."

"It would appear, Moriarty, that the odds are stacked against *you*. Once the process is finished, I will simply eliminate you and free Miss Fairfield."

Moriarty shook his misshapen head. "Oh, Holmes, I had more faith in your intellect than that. Apply the grey matter. The simple fact is that you can kill me – but so what? Do you think that I, a mere copy of the great man, am concerned about my own individual existence when I know that I will live on, not only in my original, but in the hundreds of copies that have been made?" He moved his left hand, indicating Holmes's electrical gun. "So you can brandish that silly weapon all you like, Holmes, and kill me with it if you so wish."

"And when I *have* killed you, Moriarty, and the scanning process is finished, then the girl is ours."

"And now I play my trump card," Moriarty said with a casual arrogance I found obnoxious in the extreme. "You see, in this instance I have adjusted the process so that Miss Fairfield will die at the very second the duplication is achieved. Why allow the original to live, when I have a copy identical in every detail to the original?"

Holmes flicked a glance at me and whispered, "He's bluffing, Watson. As soon as the process ceases, free the girl."

I gave a minimal nod, hoping that my friend was indeed right.

Playing for time, Holmes said to Moriarty, "But why do you want to copy the girl? What is she to you? Don't tell me," he sneered, "that your life-long cynicism has finally eroded and, in your old age, you have found... *love*?"

"Love?" Moriarty cried. "You should know me better than that, Holmes!"

"Then why do you want her?"

"Posterity," said the professor, surprising me. "Miss Fairfield is, you will agree, not only a first-rate intellect but a fine writer."

"So I have heard said," Holmes agreed. "But don't tell me, Moriarty, that you require an amanuensis?"

The professor laughed at this. "Not at all – I need someone with intellect and insight who might, at the end of my days, set down with truth and dispassion the momentous events and achievements of my life. I want the record set straight in order to counter the lies and vile calumny that you and others like you have peddled down the years."

"You're insane," I said. "As if a girl like Miss Fairfield would accede to record such a life of infamy."

"I want my true achievements, my genius, to be known by the word at large!"

Holmes interrupted the man's megalomaniacal oratory, gesturing towards the neighbouring room. "And the original Professor Moriarty himself? I see he has set his miserable copies to various tasks, while he skulks somewhere well away from danger."

"If you think you'll worm his whereabouts from me so easily, think again. As if I'd vouchsafe that priceless knowledge!"

I noticed Moriarty's glance flick quickly to his right. There, a wall clock indicated that the time was a few minutes to two o'clock.

I pondered the significance of his surreptitious sliding glance: did the duplication process cease upon the hour? Or was he expecting some interruption or other?

I wondered if Holmes had noticed Moriarty's interest in the clock.

The electrical gun was slick in my sweat-soaked palm. I had to resist the urge to lift the weapon and fire at the considerable target of Moriarty's head.

"I am curious," Holmes said. "When did the great man, as you call your original, offer his services to the Martians?"

Moriarty laughed. "Oh, you don't know the pleasure it gives me to deny the exalted Sherlock Holmes that knowledge! But I will say," he went on, "that it will be only a matter of time before you too are working for the Martians."

"As if my services could be bought!" Holmes laughed.

"Not bought," said the professor, "but taken. When you are captured, then the Martians will doubtless see you for the valuable commodity you are, and make multiple copies of you so that the famous Sherlock Holmes will be complicit in the ultimate victory of our alien overlords. Oh, the irony!"

"I'll have you know, Moriarty," Holmes said with not a little pride in his tone, "that we have already had our identities copied – and we not only effected our escape, but destroyed the copies into the bargain. Though," he went on ruminatively, "I presume that the vile Arkana, when they copied our identities, made backups so that they could easily manufacture a multiplicity of Watsons and myself."

"Would that were so," Moriarty said. "But simulacra can be made only from the original: copies made from copies were found to be prone to corruption–"

"Which is good to know," said Holmes, "but I assure you that the Martians will never capture us."

Moriarty glanced at the clock once again. It was two o'clock.

Seconds later, three things happened almost simultaneously.

The electrical thrumming suddenly ceased and a profound silence filled the room.

Holmes fired his gun and the electrical charge flashed across the room, hitting Moriarty in the head and knocking him from his feet. He fell to the floor and spasmed horribly, the flesh of his skull blackened and bubbling.

Then the door behind us swung open and a Martian shuffled into the room, squealing at the top of his lungs.

For a second I assumed the Martian to be Baro-Sinartha-Gree – until I saw that the creature was brandishing an electrical gun.

As the door swung shut, I caught a glimpse of Baro-Sinartha-Gree in the corridor, groggily picking himself from the floor and tottering around on rubbery tentacles in obvious disorientation. The last I saw of him, he had gained some coordination in his limbs and was staggering off along the corridor.

Holmes had turned at the sound of the intrusion, and he and the Martian faced each other in a static stand-off, each pointing his weapon at the other.

"Watson," Holmes said, "go to the girl and release her."

I had my gun trained on the Martian, too, as I backed towards Miss Fairfield. "If you shoot my friend, you're dead," I said.

He replied in excellent English, "If you fire that weapon, whoever you are, then I shall ensure that your friend dies. What are you doing here?"

"Come to retrieve what is ours," said Holmes as I backed, little by little, towards Miss Fairfield.

Her head had dropped forward, her chin resting on her chest. She hung in the frame from her wrists like a sacrificial victim. I noted with relief that her chest rose and fell, quashing Moriarty's claim that she would die upon completion of the duplication process.

I had reached the frame – but now I found myself in a dilemma: if I did as Holmes commanded and freed the girl, I would no longer have my gun trained on the Martian. The alien could take a chance and fire at Holmes, hoping to get his shot in before Holmes returned fire.

"You heard me, Watson," Holmes said. "I have the Martian covered. If he shoots, then so will I."

"Then," said the Martian, "we will both die."

"Holmes…?" I quailed.

"Do as I say," Holmes said in a steady voice. "I think I am more nimble on my feet than our friend here, more accustomed as he is to the lighter gravity of Mars. I could fire and be away before the fellow could move his ungainly bulk."

Fearful of what might happen next, I slipped the weapon into my coat pocket, knelt and quickly unfastened the leather straps binding the girl's left ankle, then her right.

I was conscious, as I did this, of a sound from beyond the barred window: a distant *clank-clanking* that, though familiar, I could not at that precise moment define.

Next, before I turned my attention to Miss Fairfield's shackled wrists, I glanced across at Holmes and the Martian: they were an eerily motionless tableau, staring intently at each other, weapons raised.

I unbuckled the strap fastening Miss Fairfield's right hand to the frame. She sagged, and I took her weight as she swung to one side, groaning. Holding her with my left arm, I reached out and managed to undo the remaining buckle one-handed.

The girl slumped in my embrace, her chin hooked over my shoulder. I was now rendered quite helpless in any battle that might ensue, but at least I had released the girl from the hideous contraption.

The steady *clank-clank* grew louder, and I knew then where I had heard the sound before.

"Well done, Watson. Now, move towards the door."

I saw Holmes's logic in issuing this instruction. Not only was it the only point of egress, but in moving myself and the girl towards the door I would be on the blind side of the alien: if I could hold Miss Fairfield with one arm and slip my right hand into my pocket for the electrical gun...

Outside the clanking grew ever louder, the deliberate iron tread of a Martian tripod.

I moved slowly towards the door, the girl sagging in my one-armed embrace.

A great shape appeared beyond the barred window, occluding the sunlight and pitching the room into sudden shadow. I saw the leading leg of the tripod, a mere yard from the window.

I slipped my right hand into my pocket and gripped the gun.

I was perhaps five feet from the Martian, and almost as far from the door.

"If you move any closer to the door," the Martian piped up, "your friend dies."

I stopped in my tracks, my heart thudding. The weight of the girl was becoming an increasing strain, and I was sweating profusely and feeling more than a little dizzy.

"Watson," Holmes said, "move towards the door."

I was about to obey the command when I was spared the effort.

Behind Holmes, the tripod lifted one of its great legs and slammed its plate-like foot through the barred window, sending glass, mortar and iron bars cascading into the room. To Holmes's eternal credit, he didn't so much as bat an eyelid: he later claimed that he surmised that Baro-Sinartha-Gree might attempt such a rescue – and, knowing my friend's powers of reasoning, who was I to gainsay his word?

No sooner had the tripod kicked an almighty hole in the wall, than the Martian fired at Holmes. My friend leapt, rolled, and returned fire, hitting the Martian square in its combined torso-headpiece. The alien squawked and hit the door with a thump.

Holmes strode across the room and helped me carry Miss Fairfield towards the gaping hole in the wall.

"One moment, Watson," Holmes said as we picked our way through the debris. "Give me your revolver."

I did so, wondering at his motives. He crossed to where Professor Moriarty's simulacrum lay smoking on the floor, took aim at its charred skull, and discharged six shots. The head exploded into a thousand fragments.

"Just to ensure that the simulacrum retains no memory of this encounter," he explained, returning and looping the girl's arm around his shoulder. "The last thing we need is the other Moriartys, or indeed the Martians, knowing that we were behind Miss Fairfield's rescue."

We staggered over a small hillock of tumbled masonry to the waiting tripod. Its elevator plate was lowered, and we stepped aboard and gripped the safety rail as it lifted us with a stomach-churning lurch from the ground.

The plate seemed to take an age to reach the tripod's cowl. I stared down, expecting at any second to see armed Martians come tumbling from the institute and open fire. One curious alien did appear around the corner at the front of the building, and glanced our way, but on seeing the tripod merely turned and shuffled away. I wondered if accidents with these vehicles were a regular occurrence at the institute.

We rose into the cowl and stepped from the plate, easing the still unconscious girl to the floor. Baro-Sinartha-Gree was ensconced in the pilot's couch, four of his tentacles hauling levers this way and that as the tripod started up and lurched away from the building.

I peered through an oval panel in the domed rear of the cowl, and looked down to see that a dozen or so Martians – accompanied by three Moriartys – had come to investigate the commotion: several were inspecting the gaping hole in the side of the building. I wondered how long it would be before one of their number worked out just what had taken place.

While I fell to examining Miss Fairfield, taking her pulse then arranging her in the recovery position, the tripod increased its speed. Having given the girl a thorough examination and assured myself that she was as well as could be expected in the circumstances, I peered again through the rear panel.

Several Martians were making haste towards the front of the building and boarding cars. I joined Baro-Sinartha-Gree and Holmes on the couch and reported this.

Excited, the Martian jabbered something in his own tongue.

Holmes translated: "He said, little good it will do them. The cars are restricted to using the roads. We are not."

I stared ahead through the forward viewscreen and saw what Baro-Sinartha-Gree meant.

The tripod was taking gargantuan strides across fields and meadows, startling grazing cows and sheep as it strode ever further from the institute.

Baro-Sinartha-Gree spoke again, and Holmes said, "He says he will take us across country and deposit us near a station on the London line. He will leave the tripod there and circle back to the manufactory on foot, where hopefully his absence will not have been noted."

"Will you please commend him on his admirable bravery," I said.

"I have done so already, and assured him that word of his valour will get back to Miss Hamilton-Bell."

Only then, with another glance through the rear viewscreen to ensure we were not being followed, did I allow myself to sit back and enjoy the journey. It was only the second time I had been aboard a tripod, and on the first occasion we had travelled at a more sedate pace through the streets of London. Now we were moving at speed, unhindered, through open countryside.

Much has been written about the singular means of the tripods' locomotion. In the early days of the Martians' appearance on Earth, engineers and scientists alike opined that the three-legged gait of the machine was impossible, much as the laws of physics decree that the flight of a bumblebee is likewise impossible, though manifestly bees do fly. So it was with the stilted perambulation of the tripods: how did they walk without stumbling and falling over? The answer was that they moved by means of what might be described as a hoick and a hop: with the left- and right-most legs planted firmly on terra firma, the middle leg swung forward, planted itself on the ground, and took the full weight of the vehicle while the left and right legs pushed off and swung forward in unison, the whole maintaining balance by dint of an onboard gyroscope. When the outer legs hit the ground, the middle one swung forward, and so on. This made for a somewhat lurching ride, but with each swinging step eating up perhaps thirty yards, progress was rapid.

We sat back as the tripod marched through idyllic pastureland and meadow, sharing the skies with starlings and startled rooks; we had the rare opportunity of staring down on the tops of oak trees, shortened in perspective. The countryside stretched away in serene silence, a rolling vista of fields crosshatched by hedgerows and veined by a silver stream.

At one point I heard a flustered exclamation from behind the couch, and jumped to my feet. Miss Fairfield was attempting to sit up, wiping her brow and appearing confused and exhausted.

"Where am I?" she asked, then stared at me. "Do I know you, sir?"

"John H. Watson, at your service, ma'am. We have met, but two years ago."

She shook her head. "That man... Smith–"

"You have undergone something of an ordeal, Miss Fairfield.

You need to rest a while, and all will be well, I assure you."

"But... but Smith. The frame! He... he fastened me into it, and... and that's the last I remember. Flashing lights... I tried to struggle, to free myself! I couldn't!"

I gripped her hand. "Please, don't fret. All that is over. You're free now. We are taking you back to London, where you will rest among those you can trust. We'll notify Wells, and arrange for your care until you're fully recovered."

Holmes appeared and knelt beside her.

She peered at him, her eyes narrowed. "I remember now. Two years ago, the affair at the embassy... Sherlock Holmes! You... you allowed me to go free."

"We did the right thing in the circumstances. The *only* thing," Holmes said. "Now, take the good doctor's advice and rest. Come, you will be more comfortable on the couch."

"The couch? Where are we? Oh!" she exclaimed as I helped her to her feet and she beheld the vertiginous view of the countryside far below.

We settled her beside Baro-Sinartha-Gree, and minutes later that worthy raised a tentacle to indicate a snaking train line in the distance.

"I stop here," he said. "Only short walk to station, through fields."

"And you?" Holmes enquired. "Are you sure you won't be implicated in the rescue?"

The Martian replied in his own tongue, the better to articulate his thoughts. Holmes paraphrased: "He said that we should not worry ourselves on his behalf. He's faced worse dangers than this while working as a spy for the Resistance."

Baro-Sinartha-Gree hauled on a lever and the tripod came to a grinding halt, once again poised steadfastly on all three legs.

We stood on the elevator plate, with Miss Fairfield held securely between us, and gripped the rail as we descended. I looked back the way we had come, but there was no sign of pursuing Martians.

Once in the high grass of the meadow, Baro-Sinartha-Gree pointed us in the right direction, then took our hands with the sucker of a tentacle. He uttered a short valedictory phrase, then turned and disappeared into the undergrowth.

"What did he say?" I enquired.

"To victory!" said Holmes as we set off for the station.

# Chapter Twenty-Four

❧

*Arrivals and Departures*

Holmes was pensive for the duration of the journey back to London. While Miss Fairfield dozed in the corner of the compartment, and I perused a copy of *The Telegraph* donated by a kindly old parson who had alighted at Weybridge, Holmes stared through the window, brooding.

Only as we were approaching Waterloo Station did I say, "Penny for them, old man?"

Holmes roused himself and gave a grim smile. "I was contemplating the bad old days and my encounters with Professor Moriarty," he said. "I considered my plate a full one then, Watson, with only one Moriarty at large. Little did I dream that one day we would be faced with a horde of the evil genius, in league with our alien oppressors."

We alighted at Waterloo and took a cab to Barnes, where we found Miss Hamilton-Bell still not returned from her day job at the Natural History Museum. Holmes let us in with the spare key, and I gave Miss Fairfield a cup of tea laced with a little brandy and saw her off to rest in a spare bedroom, saying I would look in on her in a couple of hours.

After we had changed from our disguises and scrubbed the greasepaint from our faces, Holmes declared himself famished and slipped from the house to fetch provisions. He returned a little later with a cob of bread, a jar of Patum Peperium, and a slab of Stilton. I made a pot of tea and we ate in the crowded front room, too tired to vacate our armchairs for the kitchen table.

On glancing at the mantelshelf, I noticed that the framed photograph of Miss Hamilton-Bell's brother was no longer in pride of place. I wondered at its absence, and mentioned it to Holmes.

He nodded. "I too noticed that it was no longer there. It can mean only one thing."

"It can? And what might that be?"

"That she is vacating the premises. Perhaps, as a matter of precaution, she must change location from time to time, moving from safe house to safe house around London so as to avoid detection."

I resolved to ask her about this when she returned, and settled back in my chair.

I was dozing, sometime later, when the opening of the front door awoke me. Miss Hamilton-Bell breezed into the room, pulling a sun hat from her dyed tresses and smiling at us as if she had not a care in the world.

She took in our exhausted forms and said, "While it is good to see you, gentlemen, you look dead beat. I take it that Woking was a signal failure."

Holmes managed to raise a smile. "On the contrary. It was, all things considered, a success. Thanks to you, we managed to wrest Miss Fairfield from Professor Moriarty's clutches. She sleeps upstairs as we speak."

Miss Hamilton-Bell sat down on the settee. "Thanks to me?"

"Had it not been for your alerting Baro-Sinartha-Gree to our imminent presence in Woking, who knows what disaster might have ensued."

"So he did find you!"

"Not only did he locate us, but his assistance proved invaluable."

She helped herself to tea, and Holmes recounted the entirety of our adventures, from our arrival in Woking to our precipitate departure from the institute aboard the Martian tripod.

"While we achieved the aim of rescuing Miss Fairfield," he finished, "we also discovered the grim fact of Moriarty's multiple duplication. It makes the task of defeating the Martians, my dear, all the more difficult."

She was smiling somewhat primly to herself, as if in receipt of a secret she would take pleasure in duly imparting.

"What?" I said. "You look rather pleased with yourself."

"Might it," ventured Holmes, "have anything to do with your imminent departure from these premises?"

She regarded him wide-eyed. "However can you know of that, Mr Holmes?"

"Simplicity itself," he said, indicating the mantelshelf and elucidating his line of reasoning. "I also observed that you have cleared away the various perfumes, soaps and the like from the bathroom cupboard."

She finished her tea and replaced the cup on its saucer. "Gentlemen, we are approaching the end game, and I am hopeful of success."

"Success?" I said. "The planet is overrun by merciless extraterrestrials, hundreds if not thousands of our eminent politicians, soldiers and others have been killed and replaced by copies obedient to the Martians, and the dastardly Professor

Moriarty is abroad in number... and you speak of success?"

Her superior smile remained.

"The young lady claims that the end game approaches," Holmes said, "and I for one am eager to hear more."

"First, gentlemen, let me tell you about the gains we have made in recruiting members of the armed forces, as well as politicians, to our cause. Several of my colleagues have been working to this end for a number of months – their task made that much easier when we received the detection devices from our contacts on Mars. Formerly, for obvious reasons, we were loath to approach eminent members of the army and navy. Now we are able to identify every simulacrum in an eminent position, and have about them men and women ready to take their place when the time arises – and it will be soon. Also, several of my comrades have infiltrated the government broadcasting department, ready when given the order to disseminate radio bulletins to the nation detailing the Martian perfidy and exhorting citizens to join the uprising."

"While this is heartening to hear," Holmes said, "it hardly betokens the success of which you speak. The threat of Moriarty alone is inestimable. I have had dealings with him in the past, and can report that he is a foe not only evil but intellectually brilliant – and now, moreover, he is not a single individual, but perhaps a hundred or more."

Miss Hamilton-Bell hesitated, her hands folded on her lap. She looked up, from myself to Holmes, then said, "Tomorrow, gentlemen, I leave Earth bound for Mars."

I nearly choked on my tea. I sat up, mopping my waistcoat with a handkerchief, at the same time spluttering my objections. "Leave? For Mars? Have you taken leave of your senses? The Martians killed your simulacrum on Mars – and they will gladly do the same to you if you so much as set foot on their home world!"

She stopped me with a raised hand. "Dr Watson, if I may interject."

"Why, of course. My apologies. I... I am concerned for your safety, needless to say–"

"And I appreciate that concern, though I think that I should make one thing clear before I go on."

Holmes leaned forward, his eyes gleaming. I wondered if he were ahead of me once again, and had an inkling of what she was about to say. "And that is?"

"The Martians are aware of me as Miss Hamilton-Bell, but they do not know me in any of my other guises."

"I was aware that 'Hamilton-Bell' was a *nom de guerre*," Holmes said. "But you have others?"

"Several, though the less said about these, perhaps, the better. My colleagues at the Natural History Museum know me as Dr Amelia Davis. For the past two years," she went on, "I have been liaising with my opposite number at the Martian equivalent of the Natural History Museum in Glench-Arkana."

"Liaising?" I said. "To what end?"

"To arrange the loan of an ancient Arkanan artefact known as the Keld-Chenki stone, a menhir inscribed with a sacred religious text and treasured by the Arkana race. It will form the centrepiece of an exhibit of ancient Martian carvings at Kensington later this year."

"And you are going to Mars to supervise its transport?" I said.

Before she could reply, Holmes said, "But there is obviously more to your trip than merely assuring the safe conduct of a Martian menhir to Earth?"

She inclined her head. "As we collect the stone, sympathetic Martians in Glench-Arkana will deliver a device which we plan to secrete within the packing crate."

"A device?" Holmes asked.

"Namely, an electromagnetic pulse generator."

Holmes leaned back, smiling. "I begin to see..." he said in admiration.

I looked from him to Miss Hamilton-Bell. "Would you mind explaining to a simple doctor of medicine...?"

"The first electromagnetic pulse generators were developed by Korshanan scientists soon after the conflict with the Arkana almost a century ago," said Miss Hamilton-Bell. "Since then, they have been adapted and refined, and can emit high energy waves which disrupt – indeed, render wholly inoperative – all electrical devices within range: telephones, wireless devices, tripods–"

"And simulacra!" I cried.

"Precisely," she said. "Once we have the generator in London, it will be taken by one of our operatives in an air balloon high above the capital, and activated. Within seconds, the capital will be in chaos. All simulacra will be revealed for what they are, and the army will stage a coup the like of which has never before been seen on British soil. This will be repeated in cities all around the world, with electromagnetic pulse generators that have been ferried from the red planet over the course of the past few months. Also, when my ship leaves Mars for Earth, the massed armies of the Korshana will begin a military assault on Glench-Arkana and other Arkanan cities."

"Now," I said, "I see what you meant when you said that the end game is approaching."

"Very soon, my friends, we will begin the long fight to rid Earth of our Martian oppressors."

"Which is all very well," I said, "but are you sure you'll be safe journeying to Mars? I mean to say–"

She reached out and laid a delicate hand on my liver-spotted metacarpus. "Dr Watson, I appreciate your concern, but I assure you that all will be well. The Martians suspect nothing. As Dr Amelia Davis, I have travelled to Mars on numerous occasions, and I am well known in Martian academic circles as a friend of the Arkana."

Over the course of the next hour, Miss Hamilton-Bell went into more detail concerning the imminent uprising, quizzed on various points by Holmes, who wanted to know every facet of the proposed rebellion.

At one point I said, "If two of your guises are Miss Hamilton-Bell and Dr Amelia Davis… pray tell, what is your true identity?"

She smiled. "Perhaps for reasons of security it would be wise if you were to continue to think of me as Miss Hamilton-Bell," she said.

A little later I recalled my ward, and slipped upstairs to check on Miss Fairfield. She was sleeping soundly, and I retreated without rousing her.

"Is she well?" asked Miss Hamilton-Bell on my return.

"Sleeping like a top," I reported.

"It would be best if Miss Fairfield made this her home for the time being," she said. "I will have someone stay here and look after her while I'm away."

"To that end," Holmes said, "we should perhaps inform Mr Wells of what happened to Miss Fairfield. He might, perhaps, be of a mind to effect a rapprochement. I should contact him forthwith. I wonder if I might use your telephone?"

While Holmes was in the hallway, Miss Hamilton-Bell poured more tea and asked further questions concerning our exploits in Woking that afternoon, information that I was only too happy to relay.

On his return, Holmes reported, "Mr Wells is meeting us at

seven this evening. He sounded preoccupied, and said that he had some important information to impart."

"He didn't say what?" I asked.

"Not over the telephone." He glanced at the clock, and said that it was almost time for the communiqué from our Martian controllers.

As the hour approached, Holmes excused himself and moved to the kitchen, and presently we heard the sound of him conversing in the Martian tongue.

Miss Hamilton-Bell raised an eyebrow. "He speaks the language like a native born," she said.

"Holmes never does things by halves," I replied. "If he sets his mind to doing something – and his skills are numerous – he endeavours to do it to the best of his ability."

"He is something of a polymath, then?"

I smiled. "He would be gratified to hear you say that."

Holmes returned, and I could tell from the lugubrious cast of his features that all was not well.

"Holmes?" I said, my heart racing.

He took his place in the armchair beside the hearth before replying. "We have been summoned to the embassy at eleven tomorrow morning."

I swallowed, fearful of his answer to my question. "Do you think they've rumbled us, Holmes?"

He stroked his chin with a long forefinger, his grey eyes distant. "I could not discern this from the tone of his voice – it was Grulvax-Xenxa-Goran himself who contacted me – nor from the content of the command."

"What did he say, precisely?"

"He was brusque, sparing no niceties in conversation with what he considered, quite understandably, to be no more than an automaton. He simply said that we were to present ourselves at his office at eleven tomorrow, and there ended the conversation."

"But is there any way that our guises might have been seen through?" I asked.

"I am asking myself the self-same question," Holmes replied absently.

"Surely Moriarty's simulacrum could not have communicated the fact," I said, "as you blew its cranium to fragments."

"I am of the same opinion."

"And the Martian who barged into the room upon the hour?" I said.

Holmes shook his head. "I assume that I only wounded the creature, but even so there was no way he might have seen through our disguises – even if he were aware of the Holmes and Watson simulacra in the first place."

He fell silent, and an awful possibility presented itself to me. I wondered if the same had occurred to Holmes.

"There is always the possibility," I said, "that Baro-Sinartha-Gree's part in the affair has been discovered and that the truth was… extracted from him."

My friend nodded. "That had crossed my mind." To Miss Hamilton-Bell, he said, "Is there any way you might contact Baro-Sinartha-Gree in order to ascertain his well-being?"

"I will try to reach him by telephone," she said. "He works an early shift at the manufactory, from dawn until two. He should be at his lodgings in the grounds of the institute by now, if all is well."

She repaired to the hallway where, in due course, we heard her speaking Martian. She spoke, was silent, then spoke again.

I gripped the arms of the chair, considering Baro-Sinartha-Gree's valour and hoping against hope that he had not suffered because of us.

Miss Hamilton-Bell returned to the room, somewhat downcast.

"Well?" I enquired.

"Baro-Sinartha-Gree is not at his lodgings. I spoke with a flatmate, who said he has not been seen since this morning."

My stomach turned. "If he has been tortured, and the story extracted from him…"

"But would that necessarily account for your summons to the embassy?" she asked.

"Perhaps the Martians would have checked our rooms in Baker Street first," Holmes said, "and on finding us absent then contacted us with the summons."

"In that case," said Miss Hamilton-Bell, "you should think twice, both about returning to Baker Street this evening, and of course about meeting Grulvax-Xenxa-Goran at the embassy tomorrow."

"She's right, Holmes. It's not worth the risk, if poor Baro-Sinartha-Gree has been tortured and was unable to hold his tongue."

"You should go into hiding for the time being," she said. "Discretion is the better part of valour, after all – and you have already more than distinguished yourselves today. You are welcome to make this your base for as long as you wish."

Holmes thanked her, then consulted his timepiece. "If we are to meet Wells at Euston, Watson, we should be making a move."

After I had looked in once more on Miss Fairfield, and instructed Miss Hamilton-Bell that upon awakening our patient would be in need of a square meal, we said our goodbyes and took a cab into central London.

Holmes had slipped once more into one of his ruminative moods. He did not speak until we alighted at Euston, and as we hurried through the crowded streets, he took my elbow and said, "There are never sanguine tidings without corresponding misfortunes. I relished word from Miss Hamilton-Bell of the imminent uprising, and relished more our part in it. If our dissimulation has been rumbled, however, we will be unable to play a full part in proceedings."

"Oh, I don't know, old man. I'm sure she'll find us something to do." How could I admit to my friend that, for my part, I was not a little relieved at the thought that our rendezvous with the Martian ambassador in the morning might be postponed? The only cloud on that particular horizon was the thought of what might have happened to poor Baro-Sinartha-Gree.

We arrived at the tea room a little before the hour, and I was in the process of ordering tea for three when I saw Wells bustling through the door and making a beeline to our table. His brow was furrowed and his mouth matched the lugubrious droop of his moustache.

He joined us and asked, "What of Woking, Holmes? I would have asked you over the telephone, but did not know whether my employers might be listening in." He reached across the table and gripped the material of my friend's sleeve. "Did you locate Cicely?"

Holmes assured him on that score. "Not only did we locate Miss Fairfield, and effect her rescue, but we also installed her in a safe house where she will be well looked after."

Wells sat back and blew out his cheeks with relief, and for the second time that day Holmes gave a full account of our doings in Woking.

When my friend had finished, Wells declared, "You are miracle workers, and no mistake. You cannot begin to imagine my worry. I was beside myself."

"You might look in on Miss Fairfield at some point," Holmes said. "I think she will be eager to see you. I did not tell you at the time – not wishing to increase your concern – but Miss Fairfield left a cry for help at her apartment before she was taken by Moriarty." He went on to tell Wells about the enigmatic code she had left in the typewriter. "Were you in the habit of visiting her there?" he asked.

"Before our little contretemps, yes. In fact, Cicely gave me a key to the apartment, which I've yet to return."

I smiled. "She obviously still harbours feelings for you," I assured him, "if she addressed her *cri de coeur* to you. She must have thought you'd come seeking her, sooner or later."

"This is all very well," Holmes said somewhat impatiently, "but you said you had information you wished to impart?"

Wells lowered his teacup and dried his moustache on a napkin, nodding. "That's right, Mr Holmes. In the course of my duties this morning I intercepted a communiqué from Grulvax-Xenxa-Goran to one of his Martian operatives, concerning yourselves."

Holmes lifted an imperious hand, for all the world like a tired traffic policeman. "I fear to ask... Has our cover been blown?"

Wells looked more than a little confused. "No, nothing like that. What the devil made you think...?"

I sat back, chuckling with relief. "For a while, Mr Wells, we feared that the truth of our identities had been tortured from Baro-Sinartha-Gree – the Martian who saved our bacon with the tripod."

"If not that," Holmes said, "then what was the purport of the communiqué?"

Wells nibbled his moustache. "I caught only the briefest glimpse of the telegram, you understand, and my Martian isn't of the best. But I got the gist of it–"

"If you would please come to the point," Holmes interrupted.

"Yes, of course. Well, what it said was that you were to be summoned to the embassy at eleven in the morning–"

"We know that," Holmes said testily.

"–and then called upon to effect a kidnapping."

I leaned forward, staring at him. "What!"

Wells repeated himself. "That's all I read, 'a kidnapping'. There was more, but Grulvax-Xenxa-Goran entered the office a few seconds later."

"Good grief!" I said. "My word… Miss Hamilton-Bell suggested we go into hiding not an hour ago, and I think a wiser piece of advice has never been proffered. Let's return to Barnes. What do you say, Holmes?"

My friend was sitting back in his seat with a certain look on his face that I had had the misfortune to witness in the past: his expression comprised six parts smugness and four parts condescension. He would soon expound upon the reason why my statement was wrong, and what his alternative assessment of the situation might be.

Wells finished his tea, bade us farewell and good luck, and hurried out to catch a cab.

When he had gone, I said, "A penny for them, Holmes."

"Watson," he began, "we will soon be commanded in our roles as Martian simulacra to perform a kidnapping of an eminent British worthy, no doubt. I suggest that this is a mere prelude to their being copied and then summarily murdered. Also, the very fact that we have been summoned precludes the notion that our cover has been blown. Do you agree so far?"

"Well, that would certainly seem to be the case."

"So if we decided that, as Miss Hamilton-Bell said earlier, discretion is the better part of valour, and make ourselves scarce… What would be the net result of this?"

"We'd save our ruddy skins!" I declared.

"And the kidnapping of the said eminent worthy will be assigned to someone else – whether Martian or simulacra hardly matters. The result will be the same: an innocent human will suffer, perhaps to be replaced by his mechanical double. I, for one, have no intention of letting that happen."

"Yes, very well. You have a point, I s'pose," I said. "But what do you suggest we do?"

"What else? We keep the rendezvous with Grulvax-Xenxa-Goran in the morning, listen to his instructions, and then – once we have informed the victim of his fate, and suggested that he make himself scarce – we do the same and go to ground. Do you agree, my friend?"

"Well, all things taken into consideration, and given the danger to this person… Yes, Holmes, I suppose that's the only honourable course of action, in the circumstances."

"Excellent," said he.

"But I must say that I'm not at all looking forward to meeting the ambassador one little bit," I admitted.

# Chapter Twenty-Five

## At the Martian Embassy

I spent a troubled night beset by dreams of being chased by giant Martians, and in consequence woke late the following morning. Holmes was already at breakfast when I joined him, bleary eyed and not a little out of sorts.

"The day is brilliantly sunny, my friend," he greeted me. "How about a spot of breakfast? Mrs Hudson has surpassed herself. Why, these devilled kidneys are exceptionally delicious."

"I think I'll just have coffee and toast," I said, too feeble even to glance at *The Times* folded beside my place at the table.

"Suit yourself," he said, "but it goes without saying that we need to fortify ourselves for the day's events with a decent breakfast."

"You're rather looking forward to this, aren't you?"

"And you're not. That much is evident from your dyspeptic appearance."

I sighed and poured myself a cup of coffee. "While I agree on an intellectual level with the gist of your argument – I see the sense of saving this innocent soul, of course – I fear what might await us in the embassy."

"That we might be uncovered as not being simulacra at all?"

"In a nutshell, yes."

Holmes waved this away. "You have no need to concern yourself on that score, Watson. Grulvax-Xenxa-Goran has no reason to suspect us. As far as he's concerned, we're a pair of obedient mechanical men there to do his bidding. The audience will be swift and to the point: he will issue his orders, give us our target, and dismiss us. What do you fear?"

Where to begin? "That the embassy will have some detection device that will see through the batteries we carry. That something about us, detectable only to the Martian eye, will give us away. That the ambassador will address me in Martian, expecting a reply, and I shall collapse on the floor in a gibbering heap."

"In that case leave the speaking to me, Watson."

"Thank you, I certainly will."

Holmes reached across the table and tapped my arm. "My friend, have faith. Would I ever drag you into a situation where I was without a strategy of escape?"

"Hm… I suppose not," I allowed.

"Good," he said. "All will be well, believe me. Oh, I sent a runner with a note to Miss Hamilton-Bell at first light, saying that to the best of our knowledge Baro-Sinartha-Gree had not been apprehended, and that our guise as simulacra was still intact – and wishing her good luck on her voyage to Mars."

"She's a girl in a million," I opined. "She ought to be made a dame when all this is over."

"And I for one will be having a quiet word in the king's ear when the Martians have fled with their tails between their legs – if, of course, he hasn't been replaced by a simulacrum! Now drink up, Watson, and let's be off."

Ten minutes later, with the batteries stowed discreetly within our jackets, we hailed a cab for Grosvenor Square.

The day was gloriously sunlit, as Holmes had mentioned at breakfast, but I took little delight in the fact as the cab ferried us to the embassy. The crowds thronging the thoroughfares of the capital, going about their daily business, served only to remind me of the singular and perilous aspect of our mission.

We reached the square and were about to make our way up the gravelled drive to the embassy when a car of impressive dimensions, with jet-black coachwork and a union flag fluttering on its bonnet, swept past us and entered the grounds.

It drew to a halt outside the building and two security personnel in bowler hats leapt out, one scanning the environs for danger while the other smartly opened a rear door. A stooped, grey-haired figure clambered out and stood blinking in the sunlight.

"None other than Asquith, our exalted prime minister," Holmes said. "Or rather his mechanical double, no doubt fulfilling an appointment with his Martian controllers."

We watched as, escorted by his minders, he made his sedate way up the steps and into the embassy.

"To think, Holmes, that a puppet of the Martians has been in power since his triumphal return from the red planet."

"And to think," he said, "that what happened to Asquith is but one example in thousands." He consulted his watch. "One minute to eleven. We should be making our way inside."

During the cab ride, Holmes had issued murmured instructions as to how we should comport ourselves. We were to be silent until addressed, and maintain fixed stares ahead; at no point should we exhibit idiosyncratic mannerisms that might denote us as human.

He reminded me of the simulacra of ourselves we had seen on Mars: they had been like soulless automata and would remain so, he said, until called upon to play the part of themselves in human company. We should comport ourselves likewise as we entered the lion's den.

We paused before climbing the steps, and Holmes murmured, "You recall the phrases I had you commit to memory, Watson?"

He had thought it prudent, after breakfast, to teach me a few basic Martian phrases, such as "Yes, certainly," "No," "I understand," and "That will be done," in case the ambassador addressed me in his own tongue. So that I would know what to reply to the Martian, Holmes would discreetly display an outstretched finger: one finger for "Yes, certainly," two for "No," et cetera... I fervently hoped that I would not be called upon to make a reply.

We entered the building and Holmes led the way across the marble floor to a human seated behind a desk, stating that we had an appointment with Grulvax-Xenxa-Goran at eleven.

The flunky replied that we might have to wait a while as the ambassador was in an important meeting, then summoned a bellboy – another human – who escorted us up a curving flight of stairs and left us in an anteroom. A pair of gold-painted doors led to the ambassador's office at one end of the chamber, and at the other a window gave a view of trees to the rear of the building. We settled ourselves on a padded bench to await our summons.

At one point I began to speak, but Holmes silenced me with a raised finger. I subsided into a sweating silence, conscious of my heartbeat and my mounting apprehension.

Perhaps fifteen minutes elapsed, though it seemed more like an hour.

At last, some thirty minutes after the time of our appointment, the double doors opened and the figure of H.H. Asquith appeared, clutching a folder of documents under his arm. He shuffled past us without a glance and descended the staircase.

If anything, my heartbeat increased and my mouth was infernally dry: I hoped that my distressed manner would not give me away.

Then Grulvax-Xenxa-Goran appeared at the door, uttered a brief command in his own tongue, and trotted back into his office.

We followed him inside.

The Martian seated himself behind his desk and gestured with a tentacle to a pair of seats.

We sat down. The ambassador spoke in Martian, and my friend replied in kind. I stared nervously through the window behind the alien, wishing that I could understand the exchange taking place. Ignorance, in this instance, was not bliss but served only to heighten my apprehension. Any one of the Martian's guttural utterances might have intimated, for all I knew, his suspicion of our duplicity.

Holmes later detailed the dialogue verbatim, and I have set it down as follows.

"We approach a critical juncture in the taming of this world..." the ambassador had said.

Holmes had deemed it prudent to remain silent. He reported that the tone of the ambassador's words suggested that he was musing to himself rather than addressing minions.

"We have stepped up the duplication programme, and will soon move on to the next phase. Not all humans are amenable to our presence here. Indeed, there is a growing resistance movement."

"So I understand," said Holmes.

The Martian raised a tentacle and tapped a sheaf of papers on the desk. "I have here a list of targets, some fifty-odd. All are engaged in stirring up anti-Martian sentiment, disseminating propaganda and propounding pro-independence rhetoric. These people will be replaced over the course of the next few weeks, and I assign you to the task of overseeing their abduction and replacement. Here is the list."

The ambassador picked up the sheaf and passed it across to me. I took it with a trembling hand and scanned the first page, then turned it and perused the remainder of the list. It was in Martian, of course, and meant nothing to me. After a suitable interval, I passed the document to Holmes.

He read the list, then looked up at the ambassador. "Are we to pursue the abductions in the order listed here?"

"Exactly as set down therein," said the Martian. "Come."

He rose, shuffled around the desk, and led us from the room. I exchanged a look of mystification with Holmes, who rolled up the document and slipped it into his pocket.

I was still sweating profusely, but had shed some of my initial fear. There was nothing in the ambassador's attitude so far to suggest that he thought us anything other than the simulacra employed to impersonate Holmes and Watson.

We followed him from the office and into a lift.

Holmes stood to attention at my side, staring ahead, and I maintained a similar posture as we descended. At such close quarters with the alien – he was standing at my side, his puckered integument almost brushing my sleeve – I was aware of his musky body odour, a little horsey with spicy undertones, and the fact that he was constantly muttering to himself.

The lift bobbed to a halt and the doors parted.

The ambassador led the way into a whitewashed basement stacked with timber crates. He ushered us over to two such, placed side by side. Each was perhaps six feet long, and they resembled coffins. He reached out a tentacle and lifted the lid of the first, and I found myself holding my breath as I waited to see what might be revealed.

A body lay within a nest of straw – or rather not a body, but what I took to be an immobile simulacrum.

The personage was of considerable girth, with triple chins and a straggling walrus moustache. I had seen the original in Hyde Park a few weeks ago, on the day of my first meeting with Freya Hamilton-Bell: none other than the writer G.K. Chesterton.

The ambassador shuffled to the next crate and lifted the lid, and I was not in the least surprised to behold, nestled in the straw, the simulacrum of George Bernard Shaw, as thin and wiry as Chesterton was corpulent, his ginger beard trimmed to a neat point.

I felt my anger rising. Of course, I knew that the Martians were casually eradicating and replacing the great and the good of our world, but to have the evidence of their crime displayed so flagrantly before us brought a rush of blood to my face.

Grulvax-Xenxa-Goran reached into the pocket of a belt he wore around his midsection, just below his arrowhead mouth, and produced a vial in the sucker at the end of his tentacle.

He held it out to me and gargled a few meaningless words.

I opened my mouth, feeling dizzy. Behind the alien, Holmes was holding up four fingers…

Four fingers? Now what the deuce did that signify?

I thought, for a second, that I was about to pass out – and then I had it. Four fingers: *That will be done…*

I recalled the throat-achingly complex series of sounds required to speak these words, and uttered them while taking the vial from the Martian. To my ears, I sounded like a man gargling with hot oil while being beaten with a cricket bat. How could a simple phrase like 'That will be done' translate as a speech that lasted at least fifteen never-ending seconds?

My hand was shaking and I was aware that I was stuttering like an imbecile. I expected the Martian to speak again, to ask what the blazes was wrong with me, and I think I closed my eyes in dread at his reaction.

Imagine my relief, not to say incredulity, when I opened my eyes to see the Martian turning to address Holmes, who later translated the following exchange.

"A harmless sedative," said the Martian, "two drops to be added to a glass of water for each man. Chesterton and Shaw will be speaking in Hackney this evening, as usual spouting their anti-Martian rhetoric – it seems the only thing that they can bring themselves to agree upon! I understand that both writers are acquainted with the original Sherlock Holmes."

"That is so."

"In which case the process should be simple. Invite the pair back to Baker Street after the meeting, and then sedate them. We will have transport standing by at ten o'clock to take the unconscious bodies to the institute at Woking, where the duplication will take place. We will arrange the disposal of the bodies in due course, you need not concern yourselves with that side of the operation."

"I understand."

"And then the double-act of Chesterton and Shaw will go about their lives as before our arrival here, penning their banal fictions and abstaining from criticism of our regime. Whereupon the final phase of the subjugation of planet Earth, and the mass migration of our people, can begin."

At this point Holmes later told me that he was tempted to ask Grulvax-Xenxa-Goran about the 'mass migration', but resisted the urge for fear of arousing the alien's suspicion.

We followed the ambassador back into the lift.

"Tomorrow you will proceed to sedate and arrange for the collection of the next subjects on the list," said Grulvax-Xenxa-Goran as we ascended.

The lift doors parted and we stood outside the ambassador's office.

"That will be all," he said in dismissal.

I offered up a silent prayer of thanks as we descended the staircase and hurried from the embassy.

Never had I felt a greater relief upon leaving a building, nor greeted the sunlight with such exultation. I felt like a man reprieved from a death sentence, and I admit that I was a little light-headed as we hurried along the street.

"There is a coffeehouse just around the corner," said Holmes. "There we can relax and discuss the situation." He stopped in his tracks and stared into the sky.

"Observe," he said, taking my arm.

I looked up. Rising high above the capital – a dark, dart-like speck in the clear blue heavens – was a Martian interplanetary ship.

"The midday flight from Battersea," he said, "aboard which will be Miss Hamilton-Bell."

I stared at the hurtling craft, the dazzling sunlight bringing tears to my eyes.

"Godspeed," I murmured to myself.

## Chapter Twenty-Six

*Conversation at Willow Avenue*

Such was my relief at having extracted ourselves from the embassy – from the very jaws of the enemy – that I was little short of jubilant as we settled ourselves at a corner table in the coffeehouse. The imminent danger, I thought, was over: we would discharge our duties to Chesterton and Shaw this evening, then lie low until Miss Hamilton-Bell's plans of rebellion came to fruition. Our duty done, we could relax in the knowledge that our lives were safe.

These were my naive assumptions on that sunlit summer's morning. Little did I foresee the trials and tribulations that lay in wait.

Holmes lost no time in providing me with a word-for-word translation of the dialogue that had occurred in the embassy, and its sobering ramifications.

"So the top and the bottom of it," I said when he had finished, "is that we must inform Chesterton and Shaw of the mortal danger they face."

"Succinctly stated, Watson. On the face of it, a simple task, given the pair's animosity towards the Martians. However, I know that Shaw is a stubborn character and might need some persuading of our story. Although I have met him on one or two occasions, he does not know me well, and will be suspicious."

"And Chesterton?"

"I am better acquainted with that worthy, having joined him in many a drink at the Cheshire Cheese, and he might be more easily convinced by our fantastical story. I noted in yesterday's *Times* that the public meeting at which they are due to speak commences at eight this evening. We will go along to Hackney and buttonhole them before the event."

"And then," I said, "we can attend to the business of finding a suitable bolthole for the interim."

Holmes fixed me with his piercing grey eyes. "You forget one thing, Watson," he said, whipping the Martian document from his inside pocket and spreading it on the tabletop before us. "The list of innocent people whom the Martians wish to duplicate and then eradicate."

I stared down at the strange Martian script – the individual letters resembling the stick-like characters of ancient runes – as Holmes produced his propelling pencil and fell to work translating the names into English.

After Chesterton and Shaw, next on the list were the suffragettes Emmeline Pankhurst and Emily Davison. They had set aside their quest for women's equality of late and thrown in their lot with Chesterton, Shaw and the other more vocal opponents of the Martian presence on Earth. Next came the politicians Winston Churchill and Stanley Baldwin, followed by Virginia Woolf and Rudyard Kipling – unlikely bedfellows, those two, I reflected – the painters Ursula Wood and Walter Sickert, and a number of prominent army generals.

The list went on, the famous and feted of British public life – and many names I did not recognise – all of whom had been vocal, to a greater or lesser degree, in their denunciation of the Martian presence. Some had merely questioned Martian policy in newspaper interviews, while others had written trenchant articles denouncing the alien presence: and for these supposed sins the Martians had seen fit to sentence them all to death. I could think of no greater symbol of the evil of the Martians' regime than the document that now lay before us.

Holmes finished writing out the names, some fifty-five all told, and stared down at the result.

"At least now we know those they wish to target," said he. "It's also useful to know that none of these have been duplicated already, and so they can be trusted implicitly."

"But how do we go about warning them all?"

"It is a pity that Miss Hamilton-Bell has already departed." He shook his head in self-censure. "What am I thinking, Watson? I am growing mentally lax in my old age. Didn't she say that she would have someone stay with Miss Fairfield in Barnes? This 'someone' will obviously be a sympathiser. This afternoon we will take the list to Barnes and apprise them of what transpired at the embassy."

"And then?"

"Then and only then, Watson, once we have warned Chesterton and Shaw this evening, will we go to earth, change our appearances, and then assist the sympathiser in Barnes in alerting those worthies on the list. This will occupy us until Miss Hamilton-Bell returns from Mars in a fortnight."

"Never has two weeks seemed so far away," I said.

"I think, once we are busy with the list, time will fly. *Tempus fugit*, Watson. Also," he went on, draining his coffee and gesturing for me to do the same, "*Melius festinatione faciet.*"

"Meaning," I said, "we'd better make haste and head to Barnes."

"But not before calling in at Baker Street and packing what we might need. I will inform Mrs Hudson that we'll be away for a while, or else she might worry unduly."

We took a cab thither, and while Holmes went below stairs to inform Mrs Hudson of our indefinite absence, I packed a bag and armed myself with my Webley and the electrical gun. I had taken to wearing the battery about my person at all times, though after tonight its use would be redundant: it would be a great relief to no longer play the part of a Martian simulacrum.

Later that day we climbed from a cab at Willow Avenue and hurried up the garden path to the terraced cottage.

A young woman of pixie-like proportions and a suspicious mien opened the door a cautious six inches and peered out at us.

At Holmes's hurried introductions, she smiled, gave her name as Lily Lenton and ushered us within. "Mr Holmes, Dr Watson. Freya told me all about your exploits, and mentioned that you might be back."

"And Miss Fairfield?" I enquired. "She is well, I trust?"

"She is, all things considered. She is resting at the moment."

"I take it that Miss Hamilton-Bell left without mishap?" Holmes said.

"She departed for Battersea at ten this morning," Miss Lenton said. "She gave me a note to pass on to you."

She crossed to the crowded mantelshelf and slipped a white envelope from behind a carriage clock, handing it to Holmes. He read the note quickly and passed it to me.

In a beautiful copperplate hand, she wrote:

*Dear Mr Holmes and Dr Watson,*

*These are a few lines in appreciation of everything you have done for the cause, not least of which is the saving of Miss Fairfield's life. I hope to see you again in a fortnight, when we might together celebrate the liberation of our world. In the event of my not surviving this mission, however, I would like you to carry on the fight regardless, and be assured that I met my end doing the only thing possible in the circumstances; to wit, attempting to ensure that our world is one day free of the accursed Arkana.*

*Your ever humble servant,*
*Freya Hamilton-Bell.*

I refolded the letter and replaced it in the envelope, quite moved, and turned my attention to what my friend was telling Miss Lenton about our meeting with the Martian ambassador. He withdrew the Martian document from his coat pocket and passed it to her.

She scanned the list of names and shook her head, her eyes wide with shock. "But... but I know both Emmeline and Emily – we met in the Movement" – by this I took her to mean the Suffragette Movement – "when I was just sixteen." She touched her throat with tiny, childlike fingers. "I am shocked, sirs. I knew that the Martian presence on Earth was more than iniquitous, but little did I realise..."

"I will leave the list with you," Holmes said. "Perhaps it would be wise if we were to return here tomorrow? If you could gather members of the Resistance so that we might coordinate the task of informing the intended victims, that would be more than helpful."

"I will do that, Mr Holmes," she said. "Perhaps if we arrange to meet here at three tomorrow afternoon?"

This duly agreed upon, I excused myself and went upstairs. I knocked on the bedroom door and upon hearing a summons entered to find Miss Fairfield sitting up in bed, a portable writing table propped on a cushion before her. She looked radiant as she smiled at me, with her mass of gypsy-dark hair and intense charcoal eyes. Her ordeal of the day before might have been a month behind her.

"Why, Dr Watson, this is an unexpected pleasure."

"Must look in on one's ward," I said. "You're looking well, my dear."

"I am very well, thanks to you and Mr Holmes. To think…" She shook her head, her handsome brow buckling in consternation at the thought of what had occurred yesterday.

I sat beside the bed. "Best not to dwell on what might have been," I counselled. "All that's in the past. Fact is, you're safe now."

"I would never have gone willingly with Smith," she said. "But…"

"He was blackmailing you, I take it? Holmes and I suspected as much."

"He intercepted a letter I wrote to Herbert, in which I mentioned the night of the… the incident with the former ambassador. Mr Smith suggested that it would be wise for me to accompany him to Woking, and once we arrived at the institute… he drugged me and… and oh, it was terrible!"

"There, there…" I soothed. I took her pulse, finding it normal, and changed the subject. "I take it that Mr Wells has visited?"

She coloured prettily. "He called yesterday evening." She pointed to a bunch of daffodils on the bedside table. "I told him that I would have preferred a good book, but thanked him anyway. He said that you had convinced him of the perfidy of the Martians, and his conversation with Freya last night only served to stiffen his resolve to join her cause. He is due here again at eight."

"Holmes and I have much to do before the day is out," I said, hearing footsteps on the stairs. "I'll let you get back to your writing."

Holmes appeared in the doorway, enquired after Miss Fairfield's well-being, then said to me, "It's time we were making tracks, Watson."

"Quite," I said, taking Miss Fairfield's hand and telling her that we would drop in again tomorrow.

"Oh – there is one thing, Doctor, Mr Holmes," she said, waylaying us as we were about to leave. "About... about what happened yesterday. According to what Freya told me, I am given to understand that Mr Moriarty was endeavouring to make a... a simulacrum copy of me? Can that be true?"

"I am afraid so," said Holmes.

She looked nonplussed. "A copy? But why on earth...?"

Holmes explained that the vainglorious Professor Moriarty wanted someone to act as his biographer, someone to put a positive gloss on his lifetime's misdeeds.

"And," she asked, "do you know if he succeeded in duplicating me?"

I looked at Holmes, who said, "As the duplication process finished just prior to our escape from the institution, it would appear that he did indeed succeed."

Her eyes clouded. "Oh, to think," she murmured, "that somewhere out there..."

"Try not to dwell on that," I said, and indicated her writing table. "Continue with your work, then take my advice and get some rest, hm? That's the spirit!"

We withdrew, made our farewells to Miss Lenton, then hurried to the High Street where we caught a cab to Hackney.

# Chapter Twenty-Seven

*A Public Meeting Interrupted*

We arrived at the assembly rooms half an hour before the speakers were due to take the stage. A goodly crowd was already gathered in the hall and citizens were still flocking in from the street. Those assembled, I noted, comprised a wide cross-section of society, from flat-capped workers to bowler-hatted city gents, alongside a number of bonneted women in the audience. Above the stage, a great banner proclaimed, *Citizens Against Martian Rule!*

"My word, Holmes, there must be at least two hundred in the audience!"

"Approximately three hundred and twenty," said my friend. "All the seats are taken, and there are ten rows of thirty seats. Some twenty men and women are standing at the back of the hall."

He made his way to the stage, where an official in a bowler hat and a high, starched collar was arranging chairs behind a table.

Holmes caught the man's attention and showed his card. "Sherlock Holmes, Consulting Detective. It is urgent that we speak with Mr Shaw and Mr Chesterton immediately."

The official looked at his pocket watch. "I'm afraid you'll have to wait, sir. They always cut it fine. Mr Shaw will be at his club, fortifying himself with carrot juice as we speak. You might find G.K. across the road in the Marquis of Granby, quenching his thirst."

"To the Granby, Watson," Holmes said, taking my arm and almost pulling me from the stage.

We pushed our way through a press of eager citizens still piling into the hall, emerged into the evening sunlight, and crossed the road to the public house.

We found Chesterton ensconced in a mahogany nook to the rear of the snug, a foaming pint before him and three empty glasses nearby testifying to his thirst. He was tucking into a huge, sizzling sausage as we joined him, feeding it into his mouth from a greasy newspaper poke. He was a large-boned man in his late thirties, with a heavy face running to fat, decorated with an unkempt moustache flecked with sausage grease and beer foam.

"Holmes!" Chesterton called out. "A surprise and a delight, sir!"

My friend introduced me. "An honour, Dr Watson!" Chesterton said. "You will join me in a drink? I can heartily recommend the porter."

"We must speak on a matter of urgency, G.K.," Holmes said. "I'm afraid that time is pressing–"

Chesterton waved this away. "They'll wait, old man. What's five minutes between friends? And it isn't as if they've never heard what we've got to say. D'you know, Holmes, I sometimes wonder if the game is worth the candle – if we're merely spouting hot air to keep the idle entertained. I sometimes think the Martians are here to stay, y'know?"

"It is that which I wish to speak to you about," Holmes began, but

Chesterton paid him little heed and, chewing on his sausage, said, "Dr Watson, I've read your tales in *The Strand*, and fine they are too–"

"G.K.!" Holmes said, becoming irate. "Please, listen to me. You're in danger–"

"Danger?" Chesterton blinked. "But we are all in danger of damnation, sir. Our souls are perilously and precariously balanced between salvation and temptation, between the ills of this world and the promise of the next." He quaffed half a pint in three gargantuan gulps and held aloft his glass to the publican for a refill.

"The danger," Holmes said, "is the Martians."

The publican duly ferried over another brimming pint. "And it is a danger I have been warning the world about for nigh on a decade," Chesterton said. "The perfidy of that Godless horde!"

He was interrupted by a rapping on the window at the far end of the room, and we looked up to see the sharp features of a ginger-bearded George Bernard Shaw peering querulously through the pane. He raised his wristwatch to the window and tapped the timepiece meaningfully with a long forefinger.

In playful salutation, Chesterton raised his pint to the playwright and accounted for half its measure.

Shaw vanished, only for his lanky frame to push through the door and make for our table, his motion given impetus by the way he leaned forward from the waist.

"Sirs," he nodded to Holmes and myself. "G.K., loath though I am to frequent such premises, I really must impress upon you the need to drink up. It's five to the hour and we speak at eight."

Holmes rose to his feet and gripped Shaw's tweed-clad arm. "Sir, as I've been trying to inform G.K., I'm here on an errand of utmost urgency. Your lives are in imminent danger."

Shaw's piercing blue eyes regarded Holmes with incredulity.

"Danger? What's all this…?" he began.

Chesterton said, "You'll have no luck attempting to save Shaw's soul, my friend. The Fenian is a heathen."

"It's not your souls I'm trying to save, both of you – but your skins. Now please listen to me," Holmes went on. "The Martians wish you dead. The fact of the matter is that they have tired of your opposition, and have arranged for your assassination and that of other like-minded opponents to their rule."

Shaw took a seat and stared at Holmes. Even Chesterton was silent now, chewing somewhat lugubriously on his sausage.

"And when might the attempt on our lives take place?" Shaw asked.

"The Martians will abduct you at ten this evening and take you to Woking, where you will be duly despatched."

"At ten, you say?" Chesterton asked, peering myopically at his pocket watch. "But that's two hours away, and we have an audience to entertain."

The worse for the consumption of five pints, Chesterton rose to his full height, swayed from side to side until he gained his land legs, then surged from the table and made for the door.

I gripped Shaw's arm. "For pity's sake, sir, try to talk sense into him, I implore you!"

Shaw unfolded his thin frame from the table and hurried after Chesterton, waving his cane as he went. They left the public house and we gave chase, Holmes muttering imprecations beneath his breath. Chesterton was already halfway across the road, breasting the traffic with the wind in his cape like a full-masted galleon on the high seas, with Shaw trailing in his wake. We dodged between cars and horse-drawn cabs and followed the scribes as they trotted down an alleyway next to the assembly rooms and entered the building through a side door.

I followed Holmes along a drab corridor, then through a swing door, which gave onto the wings of the stage. We stopped there, hidden from the audience, and watched with impatience as Chesterton barrelled onto the stage to a vigorous round of applause, followed by a flustered Shaw.

The bowler-hatted official glanced at his watch with relief, rose to his feet, and as Chesterton and Shaw took their seats at the table, said, "Ladies and gentlemen, it is my great pleasure this evening to introduce two of the country's finest men of letters..."

The crowd broke into another deafening round of applause as Chesterton rose to his feet, clutched his lapels with beefy fists, and peered into the auditorium through his pince-nez.

"What now?" I hissed.

"Our hands are tied." Holmes looked at his watch. "It is a little after eight. The meeting is scheduled to finish at nine." He stroked his chin, fretting. "Reluctant though I am to take them back to Baker Street, that would be one way of proving to the dunderheads that they're in mortal danger."

"By showing them our simulacra shells?"

"Precisely. But we'll be cutting it fine, what with the ambassador sending a car at ten."

He fell silent and turned his attention to the stage.

Chesterton was in full oratorical flow. "And yes, we have had our differences in the past: I find my esteemed friend's socialism entirely suspect, for it cannot give the people what they need–"

At this point Shaw interrupted, with a mischievous glint in his Irish eyes, "While capitalism, my learned friend, gives people what they do not need!"

"As you know," Chesterton continued, as if reading from a

script they had played out many times before, "I am no proponent of capitalism – but let me not get started on the manifold virtues of distributism. We are here tonight, Shaw and I, united despite our differences – yes, speaking as one mind – against the greatest danger this country, nay, the world at large, has ever faced. And that danger is the odious oppression of the beings from the fourth planet, the red planet – and I sometimes wonder, my friends, at the etymology of that sobriquet: is it solely to do with the hue of the soil, or does it have other, more sinister, connotations?"

As he went on, setting out his philosophical and economical opposition to the occupation of the Martians, I became aware of a stirring towards the back of the hall. Two silent figures had entered the chamber, and more and more of the audience were turning to stare at the latecomers. A murmur of comment swept through the gathering, the murmur turning to a babble, which soon threatened to drown out the speaker.

I took my friend's arm. "Good God, Holmes!"

A great hush settled over the audience, and even Chesterton had spluttered into silence.

All eyes were on the new arrivals.

Two squat, tentacled Martians stood at the rear of the hall, staring with their inscrutable, jet-black eyes. Their presence had a strange effect on the atmosphere in the auditorium: it was as if the temperature had plummeted by ten degrees. The silence stretched, and with it the tension.

Shaw glanced at us in the wings, concern showing in his bright blue eyes. Holmes raised a cautious forefinger, as if counselling against precipitate action at this juncture, and Shaw gave a minimal nod.

The practised raconteur that he was, Chesterton adapted his

oration to the circumstances. "Am I given to understand that what was billed to be a public address has become, with the arrival of our august occupiers, a debate? If so, sirs, then pray join us on the stage. I am eager to hear what you might have to say, and to hear you out with interest... Sirs, please accept my invitation."

The audience stared at the Martians in spellbound silence. The aliens turned to each other and I saw their mouthpieces open and shut. Then one Martian remained at the back of the hall, looking on, while the other shuffled on its writhing tentacles down the central aisle and climbed the six wooden steps to the stage. He rounded the table and stood between Chesterton and Shaw. The bowler-hatted official, with trembling fingers, adjusted the microphone to the Martian's height and rapidly retreated.

I glanced at Holmes. "What the devil can the creature want?" I whispered.

Chesterton, seated now, leaned forward. "You have us at a disadvantage, sir. Your name, if I might make so bold?"

The Martian leaned towards the microphone. "I am Tavor-Borima-Venn, military attaché to your esteemed kingdom."

"We welcome you to the stage," Chesterton said. "I don't know whether you arrived in time to hear my argument–"

Tavor-Borima-Venn interrupted. "I am well aware of the gist of your polemic. Do you think we are in ignorance of the thoughts of those that oppose our presence here?"

"Sir, I am unable to fathom the depths of your ignorance," Chesterton said, to nervous laughter from the audience, "though if you are cognisant of our argument, then you must surely have a counter-argument, which I am eager to hear."

I glanced at my watch. It was eight-fifteen. I wondered how long this pantomime might last, and wondered too why the military attaché had seen fit to attend the meeting. Had the ambassador become suspicious of Holmes and myself, and sent the attaché along to ensure that we carry out his instructions?

The Martian spoke. His English was impeccable in its eloquence, though with a gravelly note which added a certain menace to his words.

"We, my race, the people you know as Martians, came to your world twelve years ago in the spirit of conciliation, after a schism of our kind – a criminal minority – had invaded Earth. But I have no need to detail what you already know. What I do need to stress, and will do so, is the spirit of peace and cooperation which my kind, the Arkana, extend to the people of Earth. It is an undeniable fact that in the twelve years of our presence here, we have showered untold technological and scientific gifts upon mankind, making the material lot of the average citizen far better–"

Shaw leaned forward. "While the betterment of the material lot of humankind is a moot and debatable point," he said, "I am sure that my friend, G.K., will agree with me when I state that the invasion of our world by unwanted extraterrestrials has had untold psychological, not to mention physical, consequences. Ever an opponent of imperialism, whose evil is that it imposes a foreign regime upon peoples and subjugates the true indigenous spirit of those peoples, I put it to you that the oppression of the Martians has likewise yoked the spirit of the human race."

The crowd broke into spontaneous applause and cheering, and when the noise abated the military attaché said, "You speak of spiritual oppression, and yet we are at pains not to trample upon your beliefs, your religions…"

Holmes turned to me and whispered, "So much sententious claptrap, Watson. So many meaningless lies. We know the truth, and what is frustrating is that we cannot speak it!"

The debate went on, the Martian's spurious claims rebutted by Shaw and Chesterton's counter-arguments. The audience grew restive, and more vocal, with the occasional shout greeting the military attaché's claims, and as the hour wore on and the debate grew more and more heated, I genuinely feared that the meeting might erupt into violence.

I consulted my watch. It was approaching nine o'clock – high time the event was drawing to a close.

"We need to be moving, Holmes," I said. "If they go on any longer…"

Chesterton rose to his feet and cleared his throat. "Now, it is all very well for the attaché to claim his kind came in the spirit of peace, bearing gifts for the natives, gaudy beads and gewgaws as it were. But can we take these clamorous claims of peace at face value, my friends? Do the rumours of villainous violence, even murder, stand upon a foundation of fact?"

The audience was on its feet by now, shouting and launching screwed-up pamphlets at the Martian, who said into the microphone, "Murder? Violence? Who speaks of such…?"

He was shouted down. At the back of the hall, the Martian who had accompanied the military attaché turned and departed the chamber. A member of the audience stood and hurled a seat cushion at the attaché, only narrowly missing him. Shaw was on his feet, waving and calling for calm. The bowler-hatted official spoke into the microphone, "Please, if everyone would be so good as to…" but was shouted down by the angry crowd.

Amid the mayhem, Holmes rushed onto the stage and grabbed Chesterton by the arm, dragging him into the wings by main force. Shaw followed, with the Martian shuffling in his wake.

I took Shaw's arm as he stumbled. The auditorium was in chaos, with cushions and other projectiles, among them bottles, raining down on the stage.

As I hurried with Shaw and Chesterton along the corridor, the military attaché caught up with Holmes and took his arm with a tentacle. The Martian spoke, and my friend replied and shrugged him off.

"What did he want?" I asked as we left the attaché in our wake and emerged into the evening twilight.

"He is cognisant of the ambassador's plan, Watson, and asked if we had matters in hand. To wit, the drugging of…" He nodded to where Chesterton and Shaw were standing on the pavement, hailing a cab. "I assured him that all was well. Would that it were, Watson!"

We hurried to join the writers as a taxi pulled in to the kerb.

Shaw and Chesterton climbed into the rear of the cab, followed by Holmes and myself.

"The Cheshire Cheese, my good man," wheezed Chesterton, but Holmes leaned forward and in a tone that brooked no argument said, "Make that Baker Street, driver, 221B Baker Street."

# Chapter Twenty-Eight

*Confrontation at Baker Street*

"The infernal cheek of it, sir!" Chesterton protested. "Calumny to the person who keeps an honest man from his beer! Driver—"

"Driver," said Holmes, "221B Baker Street, and I will hear no more on the matter."

I twisted in my seat and was in time to see the military attaché emerge from the side door and stare up and down the street. As we turned the corner, the second Martian was clambering into a cab on the High Street. I was confident that neither was aware of our getaway, though I feared that they might send their people to Baker Street before the appointed hour.

"I think we should hear what Holmes has to say, G.K.," Shaw said in an undertone, so as not to be heard by the cabbie. "You mentioned earlier that our lives were in imminent danger, Holmes. Might I ask for amplification?"

"You are to be drugged and transported to the Martian Institute at Woking," Holmes murmured. "What would then follow would be unbelievable even to me, had Watson and I not had experience of the procedure on two occasions."

"Procedure?" Chesterton harrumphed like a bad-tempered walrus coming up for air.

"I will demonstrate the truth of our claims when we reach our rooms," said Holmes.

"But if the Martians had us killed," Shaw said, "then that would be playing into the hands of the opposition movement. Why, surely the Martians wouldn't be so stupid."

"Oh, the Martians are far from stupid, my friend. In fact they're diabolically clever. You see, they would have you murdered – as they have so cold-bloodedly murdered hundreds, even thousands of humans already – and then replaced with mechanical copies."

A sudden silence reigned within the confines of the cab, and then Chesterton spluttered, "Mechanical copies? Have you taken leave of your senses, man? Why, I've never heard such hogwash. Mechanical copies indeed!"

Shaw looked at Holmes with a glinting eye. "Elucidate, my friend," said he.

"I know this to be a fact from first-hand experience," Holmes said, "and Watson will corroborate. A fortnight ago, on Mars itself, Watson and I were copied."

He outlined our imprisonment by the Martians, and our subsequent escape from Mars aboard a Korshanan interplanetary ship. He went on to outline our travails since returning to Earth, the destruction of our own simulacra, and our ensuing adventures at the Martian Institute in Woking.

Chesterton and Shaw sat in silence, the former for once lost for words.

"And you say that the Martians have already murdered and

replaced countless prominent humans?" Shaw said in hushed tones.

"That is so," Holmes replied. "And just yesterday the ambassador handed us a list of over fifty opponents to their regime, with instructions to abduct them and have them delivered to Woking for the duplication process. And your names were at the top of the list."

"It's a tall tale," Chesterton said. "And, to be frank, I'm not sure I believe a dashed word."

"Perhaps," Shaw put in, "we should maintain an open mind until we have received the evidence that Holmes promised?"

"Which I shall be happy to carry out in a matter of minutes," Holmes said as the cab turned the corner and pulled up outside 221B.

I paid the driver and followed the others up the steps, but not before glancing up and down the length of the street to ensure that we had not been followed. To my immense relief, there were no other vehicles in evidence save the horse and cart of a rag-and-bone man.

Once safe within our rooms, Holmes waved our guests to the armchairs before the hearth and disappeared into the adjoining bedroom. I poured three brandies and a cordial and soda for Shaw.

Holmes entered the room bearing a sorry, sagging simulacrum integument in each hand. They hung like human hides that had been deboned and flensed. Their faces were particularly gruesome, with sucked-in cheeks and staring eye-holes.

"Good God, man!" Chesterton exclaimed.

Shaw took the simulacrum that had so recently parodied myself, turning the floppy integument over and over and exclaiming as he did so.

"And on the workbench," Holmes said, pointing across the room, "you will observe the mechanical innards that gave these automata the semblance of life."

I moved to the table, fetched a handful of circuitry, and offered it to Shaw, who stared at the tangled mass and then passed it to Chesterton.

"As I live and breathe," said the latter. He looked up at Holmes, suddenly sober. "And you say that many a prominent worthy has been murdered and replaced?"

"The most prominent of which is our prime minister, Asquith, as well as Lloyd George and Balfour, to name but three."

"They began the systematic slaughter and replacement of our people by luring them to Mars," I said. "There they were duplicated and then killed, with the simulacra returning to Earth in their place. Just recently the Martians have begun duplicating humans at Woking, and no doubt at locations in other countries around the world."

"But..." Shaw began, shaking his head. "But just last year Henry James was invited on a lecture tour of the red planet, to which he acceded."

"And in all likelihood succumbed to the depredations of the Arkana," Holmes said quietly.

"I wondered why he has fallen silent on the matter of the Martians – he was a vocal opponent, as you probably know."

Holmes tossed his own simulacrum skin into a corner of the room. "Our main concern now is to ensure your continued safety. To that end I will summon a cab."

He crossed to the telephone and spoke briefly into the mouthpiece.

"They will send a car within minutes," he reported.

"That's all very well, Holmes," Chesterton said, "but where the blazes will we go? Why, if the Martians want us dead – or rather, if they want to abduct us in order to carry out their infernal duplication – then we can hardly return to our homes. Why, what the deuce will I tell Frances?"

"If you give me your home telephone number," Holmes said, "I will arrange for a member of the Resistance to contact Frances and have her join you. For the time being we'll stay at a safe house in Barnes. You'll be in good hands. The Resistance will keep you safe, along with others on the Martian death list."

I heard the purr of an electrical engine outside and moved to the window. A cab beetled in to the side of the road and halted.

"Our cab," I said, and consulted my watch. "And not a moment too soon. It's a quarter to ten – the Martians said they'd send a car for you at ten. With luck we'll give them the slip and miss them by minutes."

Holmes hurried us from our rooms.

Twilight was falling as we stepped into the street, and from Regent's Park came the haunting double-note of the Martian tripod, "Ulla, ulla, ulla, ulla…" I cursed the noise, recalling the time, not that long ago, when I had been beguiled by the plangent melancholy of the otherworldly sound.

The nearby tripod ceased its threnody, and it was taken up by another further to the west, and then another and another.

"Look sharp, Watson!" Holmes cried, grabbing my arm. "Quickly," he called to Chesterton and Shaw. "Into the cab! No. 22 Willow Avenue, Barnes."

The pair needed no second telling. They crossed the pavement as fast as they were able, Shaw almost pushing Chesterton into the back of the vehicle.

We were about to join them when the crackle of an electrical gun sounded loud in the air, and Holmes pushed me to the ground. A car had drawn up in the middle of the road not ten yards away.

As I watched, transfixed, three Martians tumbled out and one of their number fired again.

We scrambled towards the cover of a pillar box, and Holmes called out, "Go!"

Shaw slammed the cab door after him and the vehicle jerked into motion.

A cry came from the Martians, followed by another shot. A bolt of electricity flashed over the departing cab. I drew my Webley and fired at the leading Martian, ducking back behind the pillar box as I did so. The Martian dodged and returned fire, the jagged charge missing my head by inches. Beside me, Holmes had drawn his electrical gun and was firing at the alien.

"Good shot!" I cried as the Martian squealed in pain and hit the ground.

I looked up, alerted by a sound, and stared along the street in horror. Beyond the Martian pair, standing tall a hundred yards away, was the menacing figure of a tripod.

"This way," Holmes said, almost dragging me along the pavement from the pillar box and into the more substantial cover of a council dustcart.

I peered along the street in the direction of the departing cab just as a second tripod appeared before the vehicle, two of its stanchion legs planted in the road. To the eternal credit of the driver, he avoided almost certain collision by swerving first right and then left in quick succession, careering around the pillars and turning the corner at speed. I almost cheered with relief, then turned my attention to the two remaining Martians.

They had taken cover behind a dustbin, perhaps ten yards further along the moonlit street. I fired off a shot from time to time, curbing their enthusiasm but only temporarily halting their advance: they darted from the dustbin and pressed themselves into a concealing doorway.

"It's only a matter of time before they are joined by others," Holmes said, and even as he spoke I heard the unmistakable sound of a tripod's elevator plate. I turned towards the tripod at our backs, and my stomach lurched sickeningly as I apprehended what was on the platform: two Martians armed with large firearms.

"You spoke too soon, Holmes," I said. "What do we do now?"

The tripod to the east was likewise disgorging its complement of Martians and they, too, were armed.

"We appear, Watson, to be trapped in a pretty pincer movement," said he. "But all is not lost."

"It isn't? Then I wish you'd tell me just how the blazes you hope to get us out of this one," I said as I fired again.

Little by little, half a dozen Martians were now advancing along the street from the east, the closest two pinned down by our fire. They now cowered behind a vehicle just ten feet away. I took the opportunity to reload the Webley.

"I'll keep these fellows busy," Holmes said, "while I suggest you turn about and halt the progress of those behind us."

Crouching, my knee joints protesting, I drew the electrical gun and, with it in my left hand and the Webley in my right, I fired off a volley of bullets and volts at the advancing Martians perhaps thirty feet away. They skittered on their multiple limbs and disappeared down a flight of basement steps.

With Martians advancing along the street from both ends, it would be only a matter of time before we succumbed.

"You said all is not lost," I reminded my friend. "Do you still maintain such optimism?"

"Indubitably, Watson. On the count of three, we lay down a

barrage of fire, fore and aft, lasting for five seconds – and then we run."

"Run?" I asked. "Run where?"

"Where else? Back up the steps, through the house, and exit through Mrs Hudson's rear window. You never know, Watson, the Martians might not have the back street covered."

I readied myself, gripping a weapon in each hand.

"One," said Holmes, "two, three!"

Together we lay down a pattern of fire, east and west, fit to stop an advancing army. I counted five seconds, then followed Holmes as he charged from the cover of the postbox and raced up the stairs.

As plans go, it was commendable in theory but somewhat lacking in practice. It possessed the singular disadvantage of placing us out in the open for the duration of perhaps three seconds, during which we were sitting ducks.

Ahead of me, Holmes arched in pain and fell to the ground, and then I felt the bolt of an electrical charge slam into the small of my back. I stumbled head-first against the stone steps and rolled, groaning in pain.

There I lay, cursing the Martians and staring up at a most wonderful full moon sailing through the clouds high above.

My very last thought, before consciousness slipped away, was that at least Chesterton and Shaw had managed to escape.

*Part Three*

*The Deeds of Professor Moriarty*

# Chapter Twenty-Nine

*En Route to Pentonville*

If truth be told, I had no expectations of surviving the Martian attack. As I lay staring up at the moon, I assumed it would be the very last thing I would ever see. As ultimate visions went, I thought, it could be a lot worse: there was something majestic and eternal about the full globe staring down on planet Earth, as it had since time immemorial. I was filled with a serene sense of peace, which gradually replaced the resentment I felt towards my killers.

Only then did it come to me that I was no longer lying on the steps of 221B, nor staring up at the full moon. Instead, I was imprisoned in the back of some moving vehicle, looking up at the weak illumination of a covered light bulb.

I was alive. They had not killed me, but rather were transporting me from Baker Street. The vehicle was rattling through the city at a fair clip, the sound of its engine loud in my ears.

"Holmes," I said, struggling into a sitting position despite the pain in my back. I was cheered to see that my friend appeared unaffected by the Martians' attack, and was sitting opposite me with his knees drawn up to his chest.

I pulled the shirt from my waistband and touched the small of my back experimentally. The flesh was tender, but I was relieved to find that I had suffered no burns. My vision seemed unaffected, though I did have a pounding headache.

"Where were you hit?" I asked.

He lifted his right arm and indicated his ribcage. "It is sore, but not burned. I think the padding of my waistcoat and topcoat prevented that."

"How's your vision?"

"No worse than it was," he reported, swaying from side to side with the motion of the vehicle.

I rubbed the circulation back into my tingling limbs and took a few deep breaths.

A quick inspection of my pockets told me that the Martians had taken my Webley, the electrical gun and the battery.

"I must admit, Watson, that I'm surprised to find ourselves in the land of the living."

"The very same thought crossed my mind," I replied.

"I suspect the Martians spared us from death only to exact greater depredations. We are more valuable to them alive, for the time being."

"They wish to learn how we passed ourselves off as simulacra," I said.

"They will have discovered our secret already, Watson, when they found the batteries," he said. "They will no doubt wish to learn the whereabouts of Chesterton, Shaw and our contacts in the Resistance."

"And knowing the Martians as we do, Holmes, I suspect they will not go about the business in a civilised manner over a cup of tea."

His lean visage looked grim. "Agreed. There is always the

possibility that they might resort to torture."

He was lost in thought for a while, then said, "When they do question us, the best course of action will be to play the innocent. Claim ignorance of any knowledge of the Resistance. When they ask us where Chesterton and Shaw are, we tell them that the last we saw of the pair, they were leaving Baker Street in a taxi, bound for we know not where. I have no doubt the Martians will see through our lies, but it might buy us time."

"For what, Holmes?"

"For the opportunity to work out a means of escape," he said. "We must remain vigilant."

I agreed, and pointed to his bare head. "I see the Martians have taken your deerstalker."

"And they are welcome to the wretched thing–"

A hatch between the rear of the vehicle and the cab slid open, and the ugly visage of a Martian stared through the bars at us.

The Martian spoke in English – for my benefit, presumably.

"Gentlemen, you are to be commended on your resourcefulness. I assumed that you had perished on Mars, even though my compatriots failed to find your bodies."

"Assumptions are often dangerous things, ambassador," said Holmes. "One should never place much credence in them."

Until then I had not been aware of the Martian's identity – one Arkana looked very much like any other, as far as I was concerned. I wondered whether I should read anything into the fact – to our advantage or not – that Grulvax-Xenxa-Goran had seen fit to accompany us to wherever we were to be imprisoned.

The ambassador waved a tentacle. "Imagine my surprise when I was informed that two of my simulacra were assisting our opponents. It was something of a shock, I must admit, when we discovered that you were indeed the original Holmes and Watson. Now, I would like to know how you escaped from Mars – who assisted you, and who your contacts were when you made landfall on Earth. Also, the writers you assisted yesterday evening: their whereabouts, please?"

I looked at Holmes. He regarded the opposite wall and remained obdurately silent. I felt the urge to curse the ambassador and spout indignant platitudes, but likewise held my tongue.

"You will soon have plenty of time in which to think about the benefits of cooperating," the Martian said, "which are these: give me the information I require, and you will be released under house arrest."

"And if we do not cooperate?" Holmes said.

Grulvax-Xenxa-Goran hesitated, and then his V-shaped mouth flipped open. "Then when we reach Pentonville we will take Dr Watson and remove his limbs one by one, until he agrees to be more amenable. When he is reduced to just a torso, Mr Holmes, we shall repeat the process on you. If both of you are still of a mind to remain silent, then the real torture will begin."

I almost flung myself at the bars, but Holmes gripped my arm and hissed, "That would gain us nothing, Watson."

To the Martian, he said, "You might threaten us with torture, ambassador, but never will we accede to your wishes."

I stared into the Martian's oily eyes, hoping that he might feel irked by my friend's defiance, but the alien's inscrutable physiognomy gave away nothing.

He muttered something in his own language and slid the hatch shut.

"So there we have it, Watson. Betray our friends and live under house arrest – though, of course, I would not trust the Martians to keep their word. They would happily execute us just as soon as they have the information they require—"

He was brought up short by a screech of brakes, quickly followed by a jarring impact as the wagon hit something with a resounding crunch. We were flung from our crouching positions and slammed against the bulkhead.

"Watson?"

"I'm all right," I said, rubbing my shoulder in the flickering light of the malfunctioning bulb.

Cries sounded in the night – both Martian and English – followed by the crack of multiple gunshots.

I gripped my friend's arm. "Do you think…?"

I was silenced by a sound from the wagon's doors behind us. A gunshot ricocheted off the metalwork, and a second later the door swung open.

We staggered to our feet and stared out in disbelief at the woman who stood in the darkened street.

"Quickly!" said Miss Fairfield, and disappeared down a narrow alleyway.

I gripped Holmes's arm in jubilation and lost no time in jumping from the back of the vehicle and taking to my heels. I chanced a quick glance over my shoulder: the wagon had slewed sidewise across the street, its front end buckled from the impact with the vehicle which had brought about the accident. I saw one Martian sprawled dead in the moonlight, and two others staggering from the crumpled wreckage of the cab. Hardly able to believe our good fortune, I dashed down the alley after Holmes's hurrying form, my heart thumping dangerously. It was a measure of my giddy relief that I even laughed at the horrible irony that I might drop dead of a heart attack as we fled.

"Halt!" came the cry from behind us, followed by the sound of gunfire.

"The ambassador," said Holmes. "Duck!"

I did so, panting for breath as we sprinted after the distant figure of Miss Fairfield.

The cry came again for us to halt, and I looked over my shoulder. The ambassador had been joined by two others, one of them armed with a rifle of alien design. The next second I heard the deafening report of its discharge. The projectile smashed into the wall a mere foot above my head and peppered us with a spray of pulverised bricks and mortar.

"This way!" Holmes cried, taking my arm and dragging me into a narrow defile to our right.

I ran on, relieved that at least now we were out of sight of our pursuers.

For the next few minutes we turned this way and that down a series of narrow alleys and ginnels, the Martian cries and gunshots sounding ever fainter as we fled.

At last we emerged into a wider alleyway, where an electrical car was waiting.

Miss Fairfield opened the rear door and we needed no encouragement to dive inside. She hurried around the car and climbed into the passenger seat, and then we were careering at breakneck speed down the canyon between buildings.

I leaned forward, eager to congratulate the driver.

The blood ran cold in my veins, and I felt Holmes's grip on my arm.

The driver's bulbous head was horribly familiar, even when seen from the rear. He turned, briefly, and smiled at us.

"Moriarty!" Holmes declared.

Miss Fairfield – or rather her simulacrum – twisted in her seat and raised what I initially thought was a bottle of perfume, then pumped the rubber bulb first at Holmes, and then at myself.

I was overcome with the familiar, sickly-sweet stench of chloroform, and for the second time in twelve hours I slipped into oblivion.

# Chapter Thirty

*France... or beyond?*

"Out of the frying pan," said Holmes, "and into the fire."

I surfaced through a sickly sea of nausea, only dimly aware of my friend's words, though sufficiently compos mentis to register relief at his presence. I was lying on my back, staring up at a low metal ceiling, which was divided into rectangles by a reticulation of girders. A dim bulb provided meagre illumination. The floor beneath me was likewise of metal, and ice cold. I struggled into a sitting position, still woozy from the chloroform, and winced at the pounding pain in my head.

Holmes was on his feet and inspecting the door of our cell, a rectangle of metal about five feet high, its threshold a raised lip of some six inches after the fashion of a doorway found aboard a steamship.

I had the sudden notion that Moriarty was taking us out to sea and dumping us there, but then reason took a grip and I asked myself why he would go to such lengths to effect our demise when a simple bullet would achieve the same end.

Moriarty had spent many years out of the country, and he must have established a base somewhere on the Continent. Perhaps he was taking us thither, for his own devious ends.

Holmes moved back to where I sat, lowered himself to the floor, and leaned back against the bulkhead.

"Where the blazes is he taking us, Holmes?"

"I could guess, but you know how averse I am to guesswork," said he. "The question I would rather ask is this: why has he elected to rescue us from the ambassador's custody?"

At that second we heard a sound from without: the shuffle of tentacles on metal, followed by the report of bolts being shot. The heavy metal door swung ponderously outwards to reveal two squat Martians on the threshold, both of them armed with electrical guns.

One spoke, and Holmes said to me, "We are to follow him, Watson."

We climbed to our feet and stepped from the cell, emerging into a dimly lit corridor of the same rolled metal floor and walls as our erstwhile prison. It came to me that we were not aboard a ship at all, but confined beneath the sea in a submarine.

We followed the first Martian, the second bringing up the rear and covering our backs with his weapon.

I put my submarine theory to Holmes as we went, to which he replied, "I agree that it does not seem to be a conventional ship, Watson. Observe the lack of portholes, for one thing. I have a theory—"

He was prevented from expounding upon it by a guttural grunt from the second alien. Holmes murmured, "He takes exception to the sound of our voices, and says that he will gladly shoot us dead if we continue the conversation. A threat that I rather think, all things considered, to be so much hot air."

He then lapsed into Martian, and a rapid back-and-forth between my friend and the alien ensued. "I put it to him," Holmes said a little later, "that whoever is in control here may take exception to our deaths, and he soon retreated into abject silence."

"Well done, Holmes," I enjoined, taking comfort from such a scant victory.

The leading Martian came to a bulkhead and an inset metal door. He pulled it open to reveal a roomy chamber equipped with rugs and floor cushions – which Martians used in lieu of furniture like armchairs and settees. Tapestry hangings depicting various Martian scenes hung about the walls.

Only then did I see the room's only inhabitant, standing with his back to us and staring through a long rectangular viewscreen. It was dark beyond the glass, and I made out distant lights and nothing else. Were we underwater, I wondered, and were the distant lights those of some luminescent marine fauna?

Professor Moriarty turned and lifted his thin, bloodless lips in what might have been a smile. The Martians took up positions to either side of the door.

"Can I provide you with refreshment, gentlemen?"

"You can provide us with an explanation," Holmes said. "Are you the original Moriarty – or his simulacrum? And where are you taking us?"

"All in good time, my friend. A drink?"

"Nothing for me," Holmes said.

"Nor me," said I.

Moriarty shrugged his sloping shoulders, then gestured towards the piled cushions in the centre of the room, saying, "Please, be seated."

"We'd rather stand," Holmes said.

Moriarty snapped something to the Martians in their own

tongue, and the next I knew the aliens were forcing us down onto the cushions. I arranged myself with as much dignity as I could muster, while Moriarty seated himself on an upright chair, regarding us with his hooded, deep-set eyes.

"Enough of the games," Holmes said. "State your business—"

"Such demands!" Moriarty chuckled. "And not a word of thanks for saving you from the ambassador's clutches."

"As if we are in any better a situation in *your* custody," Holmes said. "I repeat: where are you taking us?"

"Where else," Moriarty said, "but to the great man himself."

"So you *are* his simulacrum," I said.

"And what," Holmes said, "might the 'great man' want with us?"

The simulacrum was silent for a moment, and then by way of a reply, he said, "Recall 1891, Holmes? Switzerland, and the Reichenbach Falls?"

"How could I ever forget?"

"I, or rather my original, lured you to what I hoped would be your demise—"

"And failed!" I put in.

"Granted… But this time," the simulacrum said, "we will not fail." He leaned back in his seat and smiled across at my friend.

Holmes matched the smile. "So it comes down to that: simple, atavistic revenge? Revenge born of… what? Let me surmise… Insecurity? Jealousy? In a one-to-one contest, between the original Moriarty and myself, he could never best me. He failed to kill me at the Falls, and I subsequently succeeded in putting an end to his evil empire – even if he did survive. He has harboured an abiding grudge ever since, and unable to defeat me by himself, he crawled cap in hand to the Martians, and only with their aid could he succeed in capturing me… Oh, the once proud professor with all before him, reduced to throwing in his lot with a race as merciless as the Martians!" Holmes leaned forward, peering at the simulacrum. "But then, perhaps," he went on in almost a whisper, "you have found your match in the extraterrestrials, beings equally as evil as your original."

The simulacrum, to his credit, failed to rise to the bait. He heard Holmes out with an infuriating smile on his wan visage. "Your eloquence is scant disguise for your essential impotence, Holmes. Your impassioned rhetoric means nothing to me. You will be taken to Moriarty and he will humble you, and then put you to death as you should have been put to death more than twenty years ago." He gestured. "My only regret is that *I* will not be around to witness your end, but then it is almost enough to know that it will come to pass, and that I have been instrumental in bringing it about. Reichenbach will not be repeated."

"Where are you taking us?" I asked.

"Where else?" came the reply. "Where else but where my original now resides."

As if events had been orchestrated to illustrate his words, I became aware of a low rumbling sound – a sound that was almost a vibration at first, but which then mounted little by little to an audible roar. The room vibrated and shook to such an extent that my vision blurred.

And then it came to me: we were not aboard a submarine at all.

"Where else but Mars, my friends?" the simulacrum said.

In due course we were taken to a room containing two metallic tanks identical to the ones I recalled from my first trip to the red planet, tanks which looked so much like coffins. While one Martian stood in the corridor and covered us with his weapon, the other barked an order.

"We are to undress and then climb into the pods for the duration of the journey," said Holmes.

The Martian passed us two small vials containing the fluid that would render us unconscious, then withdrew from the chamber and slammed and locked the door.

"We would gain nothing by disobeying," Holmes said. "I for one do not relish the prospect of spending seven days confined in here, fully conscious throughout."

We undressed back-to-back and climbed into the pods, draining the sedative in one gulp. I sat back and laid my head against the wooden rest, and as the strange, warm gel flooded the pod and climbed the length of my body, I considered our return to Mars and what might await us there.

# Chapter Thirty-One

❦

*Towards Hakoah-Malan*

I t seemed that no time at all had elapsed between my draining the sedative and my awakening at journey's end. The sensation was similar to that of having undergone an operation – the time spent under the knife seeming an impossibly brief duration – though without the post-operative feeling of wooziness and confusion. Indeed, I felt fresh and invigorated – but then I recalled Moriarty's words and I was beset by apprehension.

Holmes was already dressed, his head cocked as he listened to the diminuendo of the interplanetary ship's engines. "From the turbulence we experienced a few minutes ago," he said, "I surmise that we have entered the Martian atmosphere and are approaching the port at Glench-Arkana."

I crossed to the metal door and attempted to turn the handle, but of course found it locked.

"Did you expect to find Moriarty living on Mars?" I asked, finding my clothes and dressing quickly.

"I had given the possibility some thought, Watson. Where better a place to hide than Mars itself? I expect we'll find him living in the lap of luxury, sunning himself on the clement uplands of the equator and enjoying all the ill-gotten gains that a collaborator can expect to find lavished upon him."

"The idea fair makes my blood boil, Holmes. And to think..."

"Go on."

"No, I can't bring myself to give voice to my thoughts."

Holmes regarded me shrewdly. "You were about to say, 'And to think, he will have the last laugh when he executes his wish to see us dead,' or some such." He shook his head. "The game is not yet over, Watson. As long as there is life in our bodies, and breath in our lungs, we are not defeated. We have faced many a peril between us, my friend, and this is but one more."

"I can't say I'm much looking forward to meeting the original Moriarty," I admitted.

"It will be interesting to see how the years have treated him. Whether experience has tempered the brash certitude of his self-regard, or whether age has bequeathed him a modicum of modesty, though I doubt it."

"As do I!"

"A man of Moriarty's single-minded megalomania can only be encouraged by the success he has achieved in siding with the Martians. I assume he will be even more insufferable than of old – and the thought makes me more determined that he shall not get his way."

I smiled. I wished I could be as confident as my friend about surviving our imminent encounter with Moriarty, but of one thing I was certain: I would not succumb without a fight.

We heard a key turning in the lock. The door swung open, and I turned to face a Martian on the threshold. He was one of three, and

I noticed immediately that not one of them was armed.

It occurred to me that we could always sprint from the room and take our chances at freedom, limited though they were aboard a Martian ship about to land on the soil of our enemy.

One of the aliens spoke, and then all three backed off to allow us to step into the corridor. Holmes said, "They have invited us to the observation lounge. After you, my friend."

As I stepped into the corridor and followed the leading Martian, I murmured over my shoulder, "Have you noticed that they're not armed, Holmes? D'you think they're the same guards as earlier?"

"The guards of earlier were members of an infantry battalion – that much I gleaned from insignia on their bandoliers. These characters, it seems to me, are civilians: not only are they not armed, but they bear no military sigils or the like."

"Rum," I said. "What's going on?"

"That I have yet to work out, Watson. Also, I detect in their tone of voice none of the resentment or hostility that was present in the brief words of the previous guards."

I grunted. "Perhaps they know of the fate that lies in store for us," I said, "and pity us."

"I think not, my friend." He spoke in Martian to the pair bringing up the rear, and they responded in kind. The exchange lasted for a minute, during which time we turned along another corridor, and then all five of us took our places on an elevator plate and descended.

"It would appear," Holmes said at last, as we stepped from the plate and followed the leading Martian along a short corridor to the observation deck, "that we are no longer under the jurisdiction of the militia, and are welcome guests of the Arkana governing council."

"Softening us up for the kill," I muttered to myself.

A great oval viewscreen occupied one end of the chamber, which was strewn with rugs and piles of cushions on which a dozen Martians disported themselves. Straps hung from the ceiling beside the viewscreen, and Holmes and I gripped these and stared out as we descended.

We were sailing over the equatorial desert towards the metropolis of Glench-Arkana. Far ahead lay the city itself, a grey smudge in the red, sandy wastes, and from it radiated a multitude of spokes, these being the system of transportation links I recalled observing on our first voyage here: arrow-straight canals and the more tenuous vectors of the monorails that spread to all points of the compass.

Despite the fact that the metropolis, and all that we could see, was the work of our mortal enemies, I could not help but be impressed: the sight of such technological wonders triggered in me a primal excitement, as if I were a little boy again, dazzled by his first sight of mighty steam locomotives.

Holmes touched my sleeve and murmured, "Observe, Watson. There, to the north."

I followed the direction of his gaze and saw, on the shimmering desert horizon, several plumes of bilious black smoke. I raised an enquiring eyebrow.

"I wonder if the Korshana assault on Glench-Arkana has begun already," he whispered, "and these are the preliminary skirmishes?"

"You never know, Holmes, they might provide the diversion we need to make good our escape."

"We can live in hope," said he.

I judged that the city was still some ten miles distant, and below us was the curious grey metal dome that Grulvax-Xenxa-Goran had described as the nerve centre of the planet, Hakoah-Malan. I pointed this out to Holmes, adding, "With luck, the Korshana forces might make that their target and disable all Glench-Arkana!"

"Your optimism knows no bounds, Watson."

To the north, the roiling columns of smoke thickened and billowed skywards. I imagined opposing ironclads joined in terrible battle, the Korshana desperate to avenge the depredations visited on their northern cities by the Arkana during the last planetary conflict.

A Martian joined us and reached for a strap, swaying with the motion of the vessel. Holmes pointed out the rising smoke and spoke in Martian.

The alien blinked its huge saucer-like optics at the far horizon, then replied.

Smiling, Holmes relayed what he had said: "Apparently the smoke is the burn-off from oil refineries – which I know to be nonsense, as the Martian oilfields are situated at the southern pole of the planet."

Holmes spoke again, and said in a murmured aside to me, "I asked where we were being taken."

The alien clacked its V-shaped beak, its reply gurgled. I was more than a little curious as to its response.

"Well?" I asked Holmes when the alien had at last fallen silent.

"Curious and curiouser," Holmes replied. "The fellow said that we are to be taken to Hakoah-Malan."

"Well I never," said I. "And did he say why we were being taken there?"

"He did not, and he was evasive about the reason. But I can only assume that Hakoah-Malan is where Professor Moriarty might be found."

"And not in the sunny equatorial uplands?" I jested.

The alien spoke again, and indicated something through the

viewscreen with a tentacle. Below, the outer suburbs of Glench-Arkana hove into view, and within a minute we were decelerating towards the very centre of the city and the docking station.

We hung on, swaying, as the great ship turned about and came down on a docking ring.

The ship made landfall with a clanging din of metal on metal, and the sound of the engines slowly died away. Soon all was silence save for the ticking of the vessel around us as its superstructure cooled in the aftermath of the landing.

The Martian bade us follow him and, along with the others, we mounted the elevator plate and descended once again. We entered the hold, a cavernous chamber of girdered arches, and a great door rolled open to admit the dazzling Martian sunlight.

A reception committee awaited us.

"I did wonder," Holmes commented as he took in the waiting Martians, "how long our convivial reception might last."

The Martians before us numbered a dozen. They all wore the bandoliers of the military and were armed with electrical guns and rifles. Their commander spoke with our guide, and Holmes relayed the gist of their exchange.

"The military are taking us into custody. Our guides are welcome to accompany us. It would seem, Watson, that security will be somewhat more stringent from now on."

One of our guides gestured for us to proceed, and as we stepped onto the ramp and walked from the hold, the dozen military personnel escorted us from the ship. We were marched at speed into a deserted underground precinct and then towards a shining monorail from which depended a bullet-like carriage. This we boarded with our escort of fifteen Martians, and no sooner had Holmes and I taken our seats than the vehicle slid off without a sound, shot from the underground station, and emerged into daylight.

I looked out at the passing streets of the capital city, at the bustling multitude of Martians that thronged every boulevard and thoroughfare, and recalled the last occasion I had been abroad on these very streets, when I had seen Miss Freya Hamilton-Bell – or rather, her simulacrum – succumb to a Martian assault.

That thought plunged me into a mood of melancholy as I considered our situation and the fact that soon we would be face to face with none other than Professor James Moriarty.

I was cheered, slightly, when it came to me that Miss Hamilton-Bell was in this very city, arranging for the transportation of the ancient alien menhir – and along with it the electromagnetic pulse generator. Then the unbidden notion that she might not succeed pressed like a terrible weight on my mind. In this manner, my thoughts veered from sanguine to despair in short order.

Ahead, the silver thread of the monorail left the outer environs of the city and curved across the dazzling desert. The carriage leaned into the bend, and we all tipped with the motion as the train gained speed and shot towards our destination.

"Observe," said Holmes, pointing.

Ahead, Hakoah-Malan came into view.

# Chapter Thirty-Two

*An Audience with Professor Moriarty*

Imagine if you can a great grey, low-slung dome like the glass of a pocket watch straddling the red sands of the horizon, a mile from end to end, and you will have some notion of how Hakoah-Malan appeared to us. The construct grew ever larger as we approached, so that when our train drew into the plinth surrounding the structure, the dome rose above us and fully occluded a third of the sky.

Our guide indicated that we should alight, and flanked by the armed guards we did so, staring up at the great curving parabola of the dome with the wind of the desert blowing in our faces. A moving staircase rose to the wall of the structure, and six guards scurried ahead, followed by Holmes and myself and our three guides, with the remaining six guards bringing up the rear. We rose steadily, drawing ever closer to an arched portal in the curve of the dome. It is strange to relate that my feelings were mixed at this point: while I naturally feared what might lie ahead, regarding Moriarty's expressed intentions towards us, yet I was taken with wonder not only at the architectural magnificence of the nerve centre but also at the thought of the technological marvels we would no doubt find within.

We stepped from the moving staircase and paused before the arched portal. One of the guards spoke into a grille, and presently the door slid open. At a gesture from the same officer, Holmes and I entered the dome, surrounded by the guards.

Here we boarded yet another elevator, and rose for a long minute until we came to a gallery which curved away dizzyingly around the inner curve of the dome on either side. From this gallery stretched a narrow rising ramp, at the end of which was yet another arched portal, this one silver and three times the height of the first. Through this portal I made out a structure like a ball, a great silver sphere suspended beneath the apex of the dome in a nexus of filigree silver girders.

Holmes touched my sleeve and nodded ahead minimally, and I saw what had caught his attention. Before the arched portal, far ahead, stood a dark figure.

I took this to be Moriarty at first, until my vision adjusted to the distance and I saw that it was not a human figure at all, but a Martian.

Again an officer led the way, and we followed him along a walkway.

When we arrived at the rearing silver arch, it was clear that the waiting figure was a sorry specimen of Martianhood indeed. He seemed unsteady on his many limbs; his brown integument was faded in patches almost to ochre, and his huge eyes were filled with viscous fluid so that they resembled bowls of mushroom soup. I was to learn later that he was of great age – almost two hundred Terran years old, in fact.

He spoke in whispery tones to the military leader, and then to the head guide.

The military leader interrupted, addressing the old Martian at length while truculently waving a tentacle. The elder replied in a hushed voice. His response drew a reaction from the armed Martians: they took a step towards the old Martian, lifting their weapons...

Holmes spoke to me in a whispered aside. "There seems to be some uncertainty as to who is allowed through the portal. The old fellow claims that only he, and his 'guests', can have admittance: the military and our guides are excluded."

The elder spoke again, and the military leader barked his reply.

The atmosphere was charged. I noticed that one or two of the guards had lifted their weapons and were aiming them at the ancient Martian's head-torso.

The altercation rose in volume – interrupted, suddenly, by a booming voice issuing from a speaker above the portal.

Martian words rang around the gallery, and had the effect of silencing the argument. The guards backed away from the elder and lowered their weapons.

Holmes had his head cocked to one side, frowning as he listened.

"What does it mean, Holmes?" I asked.

"The voice proclaims that only the venerable Martian and ourselves are allowed access to the inner sanctum."

The booming voice fell silent, and I cast an eye around the cowed guards.

Our guide whispered, "The Great One has spoken."

The upshot of this was that the guards, and our erstwhile guides, moved back along the ramp, leaving only Holmes and myself standing before the elder Martian.

He regarded us with his great glaucous eyes, then said in creaking English, "It is an honour indeed to meet you, at last. Professor Moriarty has told me much about you, Mr Holmes.

Please, if you would care to come this way."

The Martian led us through the open arch, and a door slid shut behind us.

"Welcome to the inner sanctum of Hakoah-Malan," he said. "I am Keeper Karan-Arana-Lall."

I stared about me in wonder. We were in a huge dome – the upper hemisphere of the central hanging sphere, no less – surrounded by banks of humming machinery like silver vials and retorts made gargantuan, and all illuminated brightly from within like outsize electric lights. Before us stretched another ramp, and I saw that Holmes's attention was on this – or rather, on what stood at the distant terminus of the inclined approach. I tried to discern the expression on my friend's face: an admixture of wonder, bafflement and, I think, pity.

For at the far end of the long ramp, reduced to the size of a penny piece, was a circular apparatus of chromium bars and struts, and pinioned in place at the centre of this nexus was a human figure for all the world resembling a spider at the centre of its web. Though perhaps the analogy was erroneous, for a spider in its web is in control, and the distinct impression I received on seeing the figure caught within this mesh of bars and spars was that he was not so much in control as... *controlled.*

Karan-Arana-Lall gestured with a palsied tentacle. The ramp was wide enough for us to proceed three abreast, and like this, with Holmes in the middle, we made our way towards the human figure suspended in the chromium web.

At last we paused before the great circular apparatus and stared up in wonder at what Professor Moriarty had become.

How to describe the figure that hung before us, so at odds with the authoritarian edict that had boomed out just minutes earlier?

His limbs had become withered and atrophied through lack of use; he hung, splayed like an etiolated caricature of Da Vinci's Vitruvian Man, his flesh maggot white, his arms and legs mere dangling, useless stalks. The great bulging dome of his skull emphasised the shrunken state of his limbs and emaciated torso, and the passage of time had etched lines and wrinkles in the flesh of his face and swollen brow. Attached to his head, like a tiara or a crown of thorns, was a metal belt connected by wires to the chromium outer struts of the circular apparatus that contained him. Other leads were plugged into his body by way of catheters, one jacked straight into his jugular, while another was plumbed into his flank beneath his jutting ribcage.

At the sight of him, my erstwhile fear at my probable fate was suddenly overtaken by revulsion.

I glanced at Holmes. His face was a graven image of shock and wonderment.

Karan-Arana-Lall sank to the floor as if in reverence.

Moriarty regarded us with his sunken eyes. His lips moved, minimally, yet his words reached us.

"Behold the man," he croaked.

At last, Holmes found his voice. He reached out, gesturing to Moriarty. "What happened?" he asked in barely a whisper.

"What happened?" Moriarty repeated, a note of humour in his tone. "What happened is that I was rewarded for my work, for my loyalty."

"But," said my friend, almost lost for words as he gestured at the chromium frame and the vast array of machinery crowding around, "all this...?"

"All this," Moriarty said, "is processing my thoughts, distilling my wisdom – taking everything I have ever known and experienced in my long and eventful lifetime and using it to come to some understanding of what it is to be... Man. It is the Martians' way of learning everything about those they wish to crush."

"And you colluded in this?" Holmes said with barely suppressed rage.

"Colluded?" Moriarty repeated. "You could say that. It was in 1894 that I formed an alliance with the Martians – and in so doing sealed not only my own fate, but that too of the human race."

Holmes appeared uncharacteristically mystified. "But how could this be? In 1894 the first wave perished in little under a month, slain by terrestrial pathogens–"

"But not before I contacted them, Holmes, and offered to assist these terrible beings that had achieved what mankind had not and could not – the conquest of space and travel to another world!"

"Insane!" I said.

Moriarty's tiny, sunken eyes swivelled to regard me as if I were no more than an insect. "Insane? Yes, Doctor, you might say that." He switched his attention back to Holmes. "But look at it from my perspective, if you can. The year is 1894, and I have retreated to a fastness far from civilisation. I had only ever failed at one endeavour in my existence until then, and that was to rid the world of you, Holmes. Imagine my rage when I discovered that you, like me, had survived the plunge that fateful afternoon! And not only that, but you had succeeded, while I crawled from the gorge and retreated so that my broken body might mend itself, in dismantling the very web of crime I had spun across the length and breadth of Europe, causing the arrest of my associates and minions."

"It was," said Holmes, "more than a little satisfying, along with the knowledge that you were dead and no longer able to torment the civilised world. Little did I know, Moriarty!"

"So I retreated," the professor went on, "licking my wounds, you might say. I lodged myself in a remote Austrian village, slowly regained my strength, and plotted my revenge. Oh, how I dreamed of one day carrying through what I had signally failed to achieve at the Falls – the death of Sherlock Holmes! And then the Martians came."

"And while all humanity cowered under their merciless jackboots," Holmes said, "when every civilised man and woman would have opposed the invaders had they possessed the wherewithal to do so, you saw not tragedy in what had occurred, but an opportunity to further your own ends."

"You state the truth with admirable pithiness, my friend. Why mourn the inevitable, why cry at the fate of pitiful mankind at the hands of those stronger, and fitter, and more intellectually able? I looked upon the defeat of my kind and laughed – and schemed to make myself invaluable to the mighty invaders."

"You sicken me, Moriarty!" I said.

The professor ignored my outburst. "A Martian cylinder had come to Earth a few miles from the schloss where I then resided. While the residents of the nearby village fled for their lives, having heard of how England had been ravaged and its citizens put to death, I approached the pilots of the cylinder. The first wave of invaders were equipped, if you recall, with translation devices, and thus I claimed that I could assist their cause."

"And yet this was when you had seen the terror, the death and destruction, they had wrought on our planet?" Holmes said. "You knew of their evil deeds, and yet you were happy to assist them – but for what reward, Moriarty?"

The professor was silent for a time, contemplating his next words – thinking back, perhaps, to that terrible time almost twenty years ago. At last he went on, "What reward, Holmes? What reward? Why, think about it! I have only ever wanted one thing, my friend: knowledge. Knowledge, and the power that that affords over one's fellow man. Manifest in the Martians' presence on our planet was the fact that they possessed wisdom in every field, and I wanted to partake of this cornucopia!"

He twitched his lips in another unsuccessful smile. "So I approached them with my offer of assistance, and they imprisoned me – and then one of their number fell ill, and another... I convinced their commander that I might be able to treat his comrades."

"You?" I scoffed. "I was unaware that you were a doctor of medicine–"

"But the Martians did not know that," said Moriarty. "When word came in from other Martians all across the globe that they were falling victim to earthly pathogens, I suggested a retreat – a return to Mars to better study the bacteria and viruses of Earth, so that a second, and better equipped and resourced, invasion might take place. In this, I said, I would be more than willing to lend assistance."

"You fiend!" I began.

"They saw the wisdom in my words and prepared to return – building an interplanetary ship with their incredible Handling-Machines. We returned to Mars in due course, and while my erstwhile Martian travelling companions were quarantined and duly died, I made contacts amongst the Martian hierarchy. I state in all modesty that some amongst the Martians recognised my genius, and were convinced that my knowledge of the human race would be more than useful, and so I began the work of plotting the second Martian invasion."

"You!" I said. "If not for you..." I spluttered into silence, words beyond me.

Holmes closed his eyes for a time, his expression one of despair.

"You assisted the Martians," he said at last, "you colluded in what you hoped would be the massacre of mankind."

"I came to sympathise with the mighty Martians, Holmes. You see, for all their genius, for all their scientific and technological prowess, they are a dying race – or rather, their planet is slowly dying as it moves gradually away from the primary and its breathable atmosphere dissipates into space. Nothing they do can prolong their existence on Mars beyond a few centuries – a millennium at most – but across the gulf of space is a pristine planet ripe for the taking. Only ill-fortune had prevented the success of their initial invasion."

"And you were determined to ensure that their second invasion succeeded," I said.

Moriarty scowled. "Don't assume such high-minded virtue, Doctor! But for my intervention, a second wave of Martians would have overrun our planet and immediately killed every last man, woman and child! It was I, Professor James Moriarty, who suggested to their military leaders another, more efficient way. Why kill the human race, I reasoned, when it might prove useful to the Martians' aims? The invaders would need workers to assist in the building of our new cities and infrastructure. I suggested what came to pass – the story that the first invasion was a race of inferior, bellicose Martians, and that the second wave was more compassionate, and could work in harmony with the human race... Until such time as the Martians came to use them for their own ends."

"So you quite willingly betrayed mankind for the price of your own self-aggrandisement?" I said.

"Not so much self-aggrandisement, Doctor, as knowledge and power. I asked the Martians for a dwelling in equatorial Mars, with a laboratory equipped with the latest apparatus so that I might extend my studies of their sciences. Also, I requested that when the rout of Earth was complete and the populace quelled, and culled, the Martian military leaders should spare the finest human minds so that they might form a small country of their own, a technocracy that would devote itself wholly to the pursuit of knowledge."

"Let me guess, Moriarty," Holmes put in at this point. "You would appoint yourself as their ruler – am I correct?"

"You know me well, Holmes. But then who else might have been in a better position to lead them? Who amongst the human race knew the Martians better than I did? I alone was supremely positioned to pass on the fruits of the Martians' knowledge to our finest minds. I foresaw a sizeable domain – one of the larger Mediterranean islands, perhaps – populated by brilliant minds with myself as their overseer. I would divide my time between Earth and Mars, lauded by the few remaining humans and respected by the Martians."

Holmes stared up at the shrivelled, shrunken homunculus hanging before us, and asked, "But you did not gain that, Moriarty. The Martians did not grant you the knowledge and power you so craved."

The professor was silent for a time, and then stunned me by saying, "No, Holmes. No, they did not. The Martians betrayed me."

# Chapter Thirty-Three

*A Deal with the Devil*

"Shortly after my arrival on Mars in '94," Moriarty went on before we had time to react, "I was installed in a dwelling on the outskirts of Glench-Arkana, and one day I was approached by a Martian technician who told me about the science of the simulacra and the equally arcane field of cognitive duplication. Their scientists had recently made great headway on both fronts, and now the time had come to roll out the process for the benefit of Martiankind. As I was proving myself so useful in their understanding of all things human, my contact said, they would do me the signal honour of selecting me to be the first subject of the duplication process." Moriarty paused, his expression reflective. "I must admit that my vanity was flattered. My mind and body would be duplicated, once, twice, thrice... many times! But then I began to think through the ramifications of the process, and I asked the technician for a little time in which to consider his kind offer."

"Your vanity might have been flattered," said Holmes, "but it was that very vanity which gave you second thoughts. As things stood, you were unique – what might be the consequences to your ego of having to contend with more than one Moriarty on the planet?"

Moriarty laughed, though the sound more resembled a cackle. "I admit that this might have been one consideration, Holmes – but the other was of a more practical nature: the Martians relied on me as the sole font of knowledge concerning many aspects of Earth. By agreeing to duplicate myself, might I not be diluting the strength of the power I possessed? After a long day of deliberation, I contacted the technician and thanked him, but declined to undergo the process."

"And then?" I asked.

"Can't you guess? A week later, a delegation of Martians arrived at my dwelling in the capital city. I thought it merely the regular committee that met with me from time to time to discuss matters concerning Earth and the second invasion – but this time they were accompanied by members of the militia. I was arrested and imprisoned. The following day I was transported across the desert, and not one of the militia deigned to answer my questions. Why was I being held? Where were they taking me? Did the ruling Martians know what was happening? I was brought here, the great edifice that was the nerve centre of the planet, and while in a cell in the bowels of the dome I was drugged...

"When I came to my senses, I found myself shackled to this infernal frame, manacled by hand and foot, my head braced in the apparatus of the duplication process, with tubes inserted into my body... I was told that already a dozen copies of me had been made and would in time be despatched to Earth to serve the Martian invasion. In the days and weeks and months that followed, ever more duplicates were made. These possessed my intelligence, but there was one very significant difference between myself – the original – and the simulacra. The latter did not possess true autonomy, they could be controlled by Martian programmers. This was the final indignity: to know that there were brilliant copies of me out there which were no more than obedient puppets dancing to their masters' whims."

"And this was eighteen years ago?" Holmes said.

"For that long I have been imprisoned here, kept alive by nutrient fluids, my body wasting away while my mind is as active as ever…"

Holmes was nodding to himself, and finally reflected, "An impartial observer, Moriarty, might opine that you had reaped the just reward for your perfidy: you elected to throw in your lot with a merciless regime, and in turn they were… merciless."

"Perhaps I should have anticipated their treachery," Moriarty conceded, "but, you see, I considered myself indispensable. What irony – I *was* indispensable, so they made copies of me!"

"And you were powerless to resist," I said, and despite my better judgement felt the first stirrings of pity for the man hanging before us.

Moriarty regarded me. "Oh, I was far from powerless, Doctor. I had the means at my disposal to resist, and resist well!"

I was about to comment that his current predicament, imprisoned here like a helpless animal, suggested that his resistance had been futile – but Holmes said, "And the form of that resistance, Moriarty?"

The professor was silent for a time, staring down on us as he considered his words. "The Martians had thwarted my plans," he said quietly. "The only agency in the past that had been of sufficient wit to successfully oppose me, Holmes, had been your good self – and for this I reviled you more than any other man on Earth. But now… now an even more worthy candidate for my hatred had supplanted you. The Martians, after promising me so much, had given me nothing – even worse, they have made my life a living hell, lashed impotently to this frame year after year. But I used the time, and my considerable intellect, to plot and scheme and plan my revenge. I would play the execrable creatures at their own game, and defeat them!"

I shook my head. "But how? I mean, what could you do, imprisoned here like this?"

Moriarty's gaze shifted from Holmes and myself and settled on the Martian, Karan-Arana-Lall, huddled to one side, his great eyes closed. "I was given a Keeper," Moriarty said quietly, "the loyal Karan-Arana-Lall, old when he began the job of monitoring me and keeping me alive, and even older now."

At that point, Moriarty spoke in Martian to Karan-Arana-Lall, who rose to his full height and moved off down the ramp. When I next looked, the Martian had settled before the arched portal a hundred yards away, staring back at us with his eldritch eyes.

Moriarty went on, "I came to know Karan-Arana-Lall well, over the years, and came to understand that he was a creature of great wisdom and compassion. He was a doctor who had given his life to serving others and saving lives, not taking them. And I saw my chance. Little by little I made him aware of what his people were doing to my race; that, although the Earth was big enough to contain humans and Martians side by side, the latter had embarked on a course of incremental genocide that would end in the extinction of the human race.

"My influencing of Karan-Arana-Lall was a slow, gradual process of propaganda, but I knew that I was on the road to success when one day he came to me and said that he had met certain Martians in Glench-Arkana, both Arkana and Korshana, who were opposed to what their fellows were doing on Earth. Little by little, through him, I built up a network of contacts among the Martians, and then spread these contacts to Earth, so that in time members of my own people came to realise the true motives and aims of their Martian overlords."

At this point, Holmes interrupted. "All," he said, "brought about not by any late-blooming realisation that what the Martians were doing was morally wrong, but as a means of revenging what they had done to you! You amaze me, Moriarty – never have I come upon such a base and twisted rationale for doing what is right!"

Moriarty smiled. "There is an old phrase, Holmes: the end justifies the means. And certainly in this case it is true."

My heart had set up a laboured pounding as I considered his motives in bringing us to Mars. "Aboard the interplanetary vessel," I said, "one of your simulacra said that you planned to kill us."

Moriarty laughed at this, and said almost aggressively, "Look at me! Do you see a weapon about my person? Do you think I can climb down from this hellish contraption and strike you dead? It is all I can do to frighten the guards when I speak through the microphone!"

"Then you will instruct Karan-Arana-Lall to do the deed," I said.

Moriarty licked his bloodless lips and said, almost tiredly, "No, Dr Watson, I will not. In a short while, though, Karan-Arana-Lall will do my bidding. He will leave here in a covered vehicle and drive directly to Glench-Arkana. There he will halt at the Museum of Natural History where he will rendezvous with your acquaintance, Miss Hamilton-Bell, and pick up the menhir. In his vehicle he will have stowed the electromagnetic pulse generator–"

"You know of the plan!" I cried.

Moriarty smiled. "My dear Dr Watson," said he, "it was *I* who was instrumental in its inception. It was *I* who contacted

Korshanan scientists, via Karan-Arana-Lall, and helped them develop the generator. It was *I* who set up the scheme to have it delivered with the menhir, and it was *I* who suggested to the Korshanan people that they should attack Glench-Arkana on this day. Also," he went on, "I had sympathetic technicians make simulacra of me which were beholden to me and to me only, not to the Arkana. The copy who effected your rescue in London and brought you here was one such."

"Your actions might save mankind," Holmes said, "but this is of no concern to you, is it? You act merely to gain revenge and see the Martians defeated and driven from Earth."

A lengthy silence greeted his words, and at last Moriarty replied.

"I have had a long time to do nothing over the years but *think*, to think and dwell upon existence and its meaning, and in this time I have come to one overriding and abiding conclusion, and it is this: existence is ultimately meaningless. The only thing that invests life with any meaning at all is the diktat of one's own egotistical will. That is all, nothing more. A selfish stratagem, I agree. I care nothing at all about the human race and its survival or destruction. I do care, however, about what the Martians have done to me – destroyed my life, used me, and left me a pathetic, powerless shell of my former self. Or *almost* powerless. I shall have my revenge when the Arkana are destroyed, and I will have the ultimate satisfaction of their knowing that it was I who brought them to their knees."

"And how will they learn of that?" I asked.

"Because with Karan-Arana-Lall's assistance I have drafted a missive, informing the authorities of my actions."

"And then you will have Karan-Arana-Lall help you escape from here?" Holmes asked. "But surely he could have gained your freedom before now?"

A terrible light burned in Moriarty's eyes as he stared down at my friend. "Oh, there is no escape for me, Holmes. I have become so weakened over the years that I rely upon this infernal contraption to sustain me…"

"Then…?"

Moriarty licked his thin lips, clearly relishing what he was about to say. "Why do you think you and Watson survived the copying process in the museum? Why do you think the Arkana did not simply kill you then, and have your simulacra take your place?"

"I must admit that that question has tasked me for some time," said Holmes.

Moriarty cackled. "Or perhaps the correct question is: *who* do you think was responsible for your salvation?"

Holmes stared at the professor, shock informing his aquiline features. "You…?" he said.

Moriarty nodded in satisfaction. "Me!" he cried. "I had sympathetic Arkana infiltrate the museum and transport you to the desert, knowing full well that the resourceful Miss Hamilton-Bell would effect your rescue."

"You saved our lives…" Holmes said, a light of terrible understanding dawning in his eyes.

"So that, eventually, you would stand here before me and we could do a deal…"

"I begin to see…" Holmes said.

"I can effect your escape from here," said Moriarty. "Karan-Arana-Lall will take you, via an elevator, to an underground chamber where his vehicle is waiting. In one hour you will be in Glench-Arkana. There you will rendezvous with Miss Hamilton-Bell, who will be at the museum taking receipt of the Keld-Chenki menhir. You will then proceed to the spaceport and leave the planet. Soon after that, the first Korshana bombs will rain down on the city."

"And in return for our freedom, I must...?"

A silence filled the chamber then, and I was aware of my pounding pulse.

"Kill me," Moriarty said.

# Chapter Thirty-Four

## The Death of Professor Moriarty

I stood transfixed, stunned by the enormity of Moriarty's words. That he was granting us our freedom was hard enough to take in, as I had reconciled myself to the prospect of certain death; but that he was in effect begging Sherlock Holmes to end his life was almost too much to believe. Even now, at the eleventh hour, I suspected some trick or subterfuge from the villain.

"I have informed Karan-Arana-Lall of my desire," Moriarty said, "and though he understands, he cannot bring himself to be complicit in my death, nor to kill me himself. He has served me well for almost twenty years, after all."

"But the bombs that the Korshana will unleash on the city," Holmes said. "Why did you not arrange for them to fall on Hakoah-Malan, too?"

"For one thing, Holmes, the Arkana built this dome to be bombproof – and for another…" He hesitated.

"And for another," Holmes said, "you wish *me* to be the agency of your demise."

"Of all the human beings against whom I have pitched myself," said Moriarty, "only you do I deem a worthy opponent. Only you have thwarted my efforts to rule supreme, and while in the past I have cursed your name and reviled your soul, yet I must acknowledge you as... as my equal."

Holmes's lips quirked at this. "An accolade indeed," he murmured with heavy sarcasm.

"I am at the end of my tether," Moriarty went on. "If I were to survive, my future would be bleak, kept alive artificially with all the time in the world to dwell on what might have been, to regret past decisions and failures. You cannot begin to imagine the hell of my situation thus far... It gives me immense satisfaction to know that with my death I will be defying the Arkana – and that, thanks to my scheming, they might even be defeated and driven from Earth." He hesitated. "Well, Holmes?"

My friend was silent for a time, his gaze distant even as he stared at the shackled apology for a human being hanging before us.

"I have never knowingly taken a human life in all my time," he said.

"But you tried," Moriarty interrupted, "at Reichenbach."

"No," said Holmes. "There I was fighting for my very life. But now..."

"Yes?" Moriarty's eagerness was almost pathetic.

"Now, Moriarty, you leave me with little choice. But let me say – I am doing this for myself and for Watson, not through any misplaced sympathy for you or your predicament."

An expression of relief swept over Moriarty's features. "There is little to it – merely disconnect the catheter in my jugular and I will be dead within a minute. Earlier I informed the guards that my audience with you will last two hours. You will have sufficient time to flee before they become suspicious."

"And alarms will not be triggered?" Holmes asked.

"I prevailed upon Karan-Arana-Lall to disable all the fail-safes and alarms that monitor my well-being," Moriarty said. "Now, time is of the essence. Please, Holmes, step up."

My friend hesitated, and I gripped his arm and murmured, "Holmes, if you're in doubt – then I will gladly do as he bids."

"No, Watson, I could not let you…" He paused, then went on in a whisper, "To take any life, even one so vile as Moriarty's, is a burden."

He stepped forward. Moriarty's eyes stared with a dark intensity absent until this moment. I looked on, aware that I was witnessing a historic event – both in the grander scheme of things, in that it was part of the larger fight against the Arkana, and in the more personal arena of the long-running contest between two men on the opposite sides of good and evil.

"Do it!" Moriarty cried in almost orgasmic glee.

Holmes reached up and gripped the tube penetrating the professor's jugular – and hesitated. He leaned close to his enemy then, and murmured something to him – quite what, I never did learn, for despite my entreaties in the months that followed Holmes kept his silence.

Moriarty's eyes widened fractionally – and then Holmes tugged on the jugular catheter, and blood syphoned out and spurted across his emaciated frame, and the light in his eyes dimmed and he slumped, rapidly dying.

Holmes turned away, his expression unfathomable.


We hurried down the ramp where Karan-Arana-Lall was waiting, his eyes averted from what had taken place.

"It is done?" the Martian enquired in English.

"It is done," Holmes replied.

"This way, then," said the alien.

We hurried along the circular gallery. For my part, I expected the arched portal to slide open at any second and the guards to spill through, shouting orders for us to halt and drawing weapons.

We came to an elevator plate and stepped onto it after the Martian. We descended at speed, through the floor of the gallery and into the bowels of the dome, passing banks of buzzing and flashing machinery, miles of pipework and a confusion of cables. I looked up and saw a circle of light high above us where the sunlight penetrated the skin of the dome. Of pursuing Martians there was no sign. Was it too much to hope, I wondered, that we might escape Hakoah-Malan, and eventually Mars, with our lives?

We came to an underground chamber where a number of empty vehicles waited in line. Karan-Arana-Lall crossed to a black, beetle-shaped pantechnicon, slid open a hatch in the rear of the vehicle, and gestured us within.

We crouched in the darkness as the door slid shut, and the alien climbed into the cab and activated the electrical motor. We started with a jolt, and I clutched my friend's arm in the gloom.

In due course the vehicle emerged into the light of the desert. A glass partition separated the cab from the cargo area where we crouched. Through it I could see the hunched figure of the Martian, pushing and pulling a series of levers.

Ahead, a wide road curved through the paprika sands of Mars, with the metropolis of Glench-Arkana a grey blemish on the horizon. Perhaps a mile to our right was the monorail that had carried us to Hakoah-Malan, which this road paralleled for the length of its journey.

We seemed to be moving at walking pace, though our actual speed was difficult to determine as the featureless desert to either side offered no landmarks with which to judge our progress. Also, my impatience was exacerbated by the notion that one of the guards might casually glance from the dome and question the presence of a vehicle making its way from Hakoah-Malan. I was beset by a hundred such fears and doubts as we headed towards the city. It was almost too fantastical to assume that, within an hour or so, we would be in the presence of Miss Hamilton-Bell. I smiled as I anticipated the expression of bewilderment, and hopefully delight, on her face at the sight of us.

The Martian spoke, and his words came to us through a grille in the partition. "We will drive immediately into the delivery bay of the museum, and there we will collect the sacred stone from Miss Hamilton-Bell."

"And the pulse generator?" Holmes asked.

"It is stowed in a secret compartment beneath your feet," said the Martian. "When Miss Hamilton-Bell has secreted the pulse generator within the stone's crate, you will take the generator's place in the secret compartment. Do not worry – it is sufficiently large enough to accommodate you both. Then we will drive to the spaceport, through the security checks, and into the hold of the *Xenarian*, bound for Earth."

"You make the process sound simple," Holmes observed.

"With luck it will be."

Holmes fell silent, and I stared through the windscreen at the road ahead.

The desert rolled away endlessly on either side, wind-sculpted into a series of rills and scooped hollows. There was a severe majesty, even beauty, in the immense landscape that in any other situation I might have been able to appreciate: as it was, I was too preoccupied with what might lie ahead. Any number of pitfalls awaited us, not least that the security check at the spaceport might uncover our ruse, while I lived in fear of Moriarty's death being discovered and all the hounds of hell – or their Martian equivalents – being unleashed.

Less than one hour later we came to the outer environs of Glench-Arkana, a built-up area of domes and the leaning, dagger-like edifices. At the sight of these signs of habitation, I breathed somewhat easier.

At that point Karan-Arana-Lall shattered my complacency with a casual observation. "I do not wish to alarm you, my friends, but it appears we are being followed."

Instinctively I turned and stared – but of course, I saw nothing more than the inner panel of the rear hatch.

With admirable calm, Holmes said, "More details, please, Karan-Arana-Lall."

"A security carriage, of the type used by the Arkana militia, has been tracking us for the past ten minutes."

"Could this be mere coincidence?"

"I fear not," the Martian replied.

"Can you take evasive action?"

The alien hesitated, then replied, "It is fortunate indeed that we are entering Glench-Arkana. I might be able to lose our pursuers in the crowded streets. However..."

"Go on," Holmes urged.

"Now that, in all likelihood, the militia have the details of this vehicle, I would be unwise to use it to collect the sacred stone."

"Then what's to be done?" I asked in desperation.

The Martian considered my words before replying. "There is only one course of action. To your right you will observe a circular tentacle-hole in the metal deck. Slide the panel aside and take out the case containing the pulse generator."

Holmes slid open the panel and hauled out a large black valise, straining with the effort.

We were moving at speed along a busy thoroughfare, our driver dodging other speeding vehicles with but inches to spare. Holmes and I tipped over as we suddenly turned a corner. The valise remained where it was, anchored to the deck by the considerable weight of the pulse generator.

We accelerated along a relatively quiet street, fruit stalls and open shopfronts flashing by on either side. We turned left, then right, and proceeded down a wide tree-flanked avenue, then turned suddenly down a narrow street.

"I think," the alien said at last, "I have succeeded in losing the militia. I will take you within walking distance of the museum, where I will drop you. Take the case, Mr Holmes, and head for the museum, and present yourself to Miss Hamilton-Bell. Inform her of the situation, and instruct her to arrange alternative transportation for the sacred stone and the pulse generator."

Holmes nodded, grim-faced. "There remains the small question," he murmured to me, "of how we might effect our escape from Mars."

A bolus of fear had lodged itself in the pit of my stomach. We might have evaded the militia, but I quailed at the thought of being stranded on Mars.

Holmes leaned forward. "And you?" he asked our driver.

"I will go to ground and make my way north to the stronghold of the Korshana," said Karan-Arana-Lall. "And now we approach the alley where I must leave you. If you head down the alleyway, then turn right, you will see the ziggurat of the museum immediately ahead."

The vehicle came to a sedate halt, and we climbed out into dazzling sunlight, Holmes hauling the valise after him. Our sudden emergence into the street occasioned a small crowd of Martians to stop and gawp.

"Good luck," Karan-Arana-Lall called after us, and we watched as the vehicle beetled away along the crowded street, turned a corner, and was lost to sight.

"This way, Watson," Holmes said, and I hurried after him down the narrow alley.

# Chapter Thirty-Five

*At the Museum*

We emerged onto a boulevard busy with pedestrians and wheeled vehicles. Our presence as we turned the corner and hurried towards the museum caused much comment among the Martians, with citizens stopping to stare as we passed. I felt as conspicuous as a butterfly in a beehive, and feared that it would only be a matter of time before we were apprehended by the security services.

The weight of the valise impeded our progress; we took it in turns to share the burden.

"Almost there, Holmes," I panted, staring along the busy street at the stepped form of the ziggurat. I gripped the bag as if my life depended on it, its weight forcing me to adopt an ungainly limp. In my paranoid state I half expected to be stopped at any second and forced to reveal the nature of my burden.

We came at last to the museum, and Holmes led the way into its shadowed atrium and crossed to a reception desk, our arrival attracting curious stares and comments from museumgoers and staff alike.

Holmes addressed the Martian at reception, who heard him out and then spoke a few words over a loudspeaker. In due course another Martian approached, and Holmes repeated his story. I had taken the opportunity to deposit the valise on the floor, but no sooner had I done so than the second Martian ushered us from the foyer and along a corridor, and I picked up the bag and followed, groaning under its weight.

We entered an elevator and descended into the basement of the ziggurat, then stepped out into a corridor of grey roughcast and followed the alien down a veritable warren of tunnels. At last we paused before a double door, beside which was a grille into which the Martian spoke.

My heart was thudding, and not just with the effort of hauling the valise. I looked ahead to meeting Miss Hamilton-Bell, and to her reaction to our unexpected arrival.

The door, remotely activated, swung open and the Martian gestured us inside.

The first thing I noticed within the long, low room was a packing crate the size of a grand piano laid upon a trolley in the centre of the floor; the second was the three Martians standing around it; and the third was the fact that there was no sign of Miss Hamilton-Bell.

Holmes crossed to the aliens while I remained beside the door. He spoke to them hurriedly. I had no inkling as to whether these Martians were friend or foe, and I was ready to turn and flee at a word from Holmes.

I saw movement at the far end of the chamber. A door had opened, and a human figure stepped from it and stopped in her tracks, staring at us.

Far from exhibiting delight at our presence, Miss Hamilton-Bell appeared shocked. She reached into her jacket pocket and withdrew what at first I thought to be a weapon – then I noticed a simulacrum detection device in her hand. She directed it at Holmes, pressed the stud, then stared at the light. It glowed red, and an expression of relief flooded her features as she hurried across to us.

"But... Mr Holmes? Dr Watson?" she began. "How...?" She drew us to one side, murmuring, "How on earth...?"

Holmes interrupted, nodding discreetly in the direction of the Martian trio. "Are they to be trusted?"

"Implicitly, Mr Holmes. They are sympathetic to our cause; indeed, they were instrumental in planning the delivery of the pulse generator." She shook her head and gave a brief laugh. "But your presence here? And how timely! We're awaiting the arrival of the delivery wagon containing the–"

Holmes cut her short. "How we came to be here – it's a long story, the details of which I will be happy to explain later. The delivery wagon driven by Karan-Arana-Lall was followed by the security forces, and he thought it wise to make himself scarce. More importantly, we have the pulse generator. There remains the small matter of concealing the valise in the crate with the menhir, and then arranging alternative transportation to the spaceport. And then," he went on, "the not inconsiderable problem of how Watson and I might escape from the planet."

"One moment, gentlemen," she said, and hurried across to the staring Martians. She spoke hurriedly to them, then returned to us.

"I've given instructions for one of my colleagues to summon another haulier," she said. "That should not take long. As to how to effect your escape..." She pressed a finger to her carmine lips.

"There is only one thing for it, gentlemen," she said at last.

We crossed to the packing crate, and the Martians lifted its lid to reveal a long, grey stone nestling in what I took to be straw packing, before realising that it was the desiccated stalks of the red weed.

Miss Hamilton-Bell assisted me with the valise. We lifted it onto the side of the crate and thence into the tangle of stalks at the foot of the Keld-Chenki menhir. Meanwhile, two Martians created a space in the nest of stalks on either side of the sacred stone.

I looked at Miss Hamilton-Bell. "Are you suggesting what I fear?" I ventured.

"It is the only means by which I can guarantee your safe passage, gentlemen. It will be a tight squeeze" – she regarded my girth, briefly – "but it will be only for an hour or two at most. Once we are aboard the interplanetary vessel, you will be released."

"And the vessel…?" Holmes began.

"Do not fear – it is crewed by Arkana sympathetic to our cause. Now…" She gestured towards the hollowed nests in the red stalks, and Holmes and I clambered into the crate and lowered ourselves on either side of the menhir. I turned this way and that until I found a relatively comfortable position amid the stalks, my stomach pressing up against the cold stone.

No sooner were we settled than she gave instructions for the lid to be replaced, and we were plunged into darkness.

As the lid was screwed into position, I managed to arrange a bundle of stalks to create a passable pillow beneath my head. It was hot within the crate, and our breath made it even warmer. Our heads faced each other over the top of the stone, and so we were able to converse in whispers.

"Are you aware, Watson, that the dried stalk of the *Hedera helix rubrum Martiannica* contains a form of opiate which, when ingested, has a soporific effect?"

"Another fact gleaned from the *Encyclopaedia Martiannica*, Holmes?"

"That is correct, and I also made my own investigations with a sample of the plant many years ago. A small amount induces a not unpleasant sense of lethargy."

"A seven per cent solution, perchance?"

"It is pleasing to note that even in these somewhat pressing conditions, Watson, your sense of humour has not failed you."

"Do you intend to indulge now?"

Holmes considered the question. "In the circumstance, no. We must keep our wits about us in case all does not go to plan."

We heard a prompt knocking upon the timbers of the crate, followed by Miss Hamilton-Bell's peremptory, "Quiet in there, gentlemen, if you please."

Thus admonished, we fell silent.

Then we were moving, the crate rolling smoothly across the floor on the trolley. The journey lasted some three or four minutes, then ceased. I could discern, through a hairline gap in the timber at the end of the crate, a splinter of sunlight. Evidently we had come to a halt on some kind of loading bay. I fell to wondering, as we waited, how strict the security checks might be at the spaceport. While the militia might have discovered Holmes's mercy killing of Professor Moriarty, there hopefully would be nothing to link the death to the transportation of the menhir to Earth.

Unless, of course – my overactive brain reasoned – there was a traitor among the ranks of Arkana sympathisers.

I heard the sound of an engine, followed by Martian voices, and then we were moving once again, bumping and banging amid shouted instructions as the crate was loaded onto the delivery wagon.

I made out the sound of a door sliding shut, and the sliver of sunlight suddenly vanished. The wagon started up and trundled off, its motor purring.

A little later came the sound of a welcome voice. "All well in there, gentlemen?" asked Miss Hamilton-Bell.

"As well as can be expected," I replied.

"I can tolerate the discomfort," Holmes said, "in preference to the alternative: having to negotiate our own egress from the planet."

"You will be feted, in time, as heroes of the Resistance," she said.

"And you," he replied, "as a heroine."

There was a lapse of some seconds before she said, "Let us hope that all goes as well as it has so far, gentlemen. We are almost at the spaceport. Silence from now on, I think."

The wagon stopped, then started again, then stopped – like this, for the next fifteen minutes or so, we progressed in fits and starts. I suspected we were in a queue for customs, with security checks being carried out on the vehicles ahead of us. Already I was feverishly hot, and wished I'd had the foresight to bring along a flask of water.

Miss Hamilton-Bell whispered, "Quiet, gentlemen. We are approaching a security cordon."

The wagon started up again and we trundled forward, then halted.

I heard the rear hatch slide open, then footsteps and the sound of Martian voices. Miss Hamilton-Bell spoke, and a security guard replied.

I raised my head to the slit between the planks and squinted out. I could see nothing other than Miss Hamilton-Bell's shoulder, and beyond her a Martian security official. They seemed to be engaged in some protracted debate. It came to me that our very lives depended on Miss Hamilton-Bell's ability to see us through the security check.

All it would take for us to be discovered, I thought, was for a customs official to insist on inspecting the contents of the crate...

She moved from my narrow field of vision to reveal the Martian who stood facing the open wagon. For a terrifying second, it seemed that his vast dark eyes were staring straight through the crack at me. Then, to my relief, he turned and moved away, and Miss Hamilton-Bell climbed in beside the crate and slid the door shut.

The vehicle started up again, and I let out a relieved breath.

I was about to express my relief to Holmes when a deafening explosion rent the air, and the wagon rocked on its wheels. I heard Miss Hamilton-Bell exclaim aloud. The wagon accelerated. Another explosion sounded close by. I wondered if it was the security guards, firing upon us.

We were bumping along at speed now. I heard cries and screams in Martian from far away. I wanted to call out, ask Miss Hamilton-Bell what the blazes was going on, but I was being rattled so violently from side to side that I could scarcely gather my thoughts.

Then the wagon halted and I heard the doors open. The crate shook as it was unloaded and trolleyed, presumably, towards the interplanetary ship. We were tipped suddenly at an angle – we were evidently moving up the ramp into the cargo hold of the ship. I heard more cries in the alien tongue, echoing in the cavernous hold. The sliver of daylight winked out and I assumed the ship's cargo doors were being closed preparatory to departure. I heard another explosion, much muffled, and guessed then that the Korshana attack on Glench-Arkana had begun ahead of time.

I heard the sound of feet rushing hither and thither, and then more cries. Explosions came one after the other, and I thought what tragic ill-fortune it would be if the ship were to be struck now, just as we were about to escape.

It was infernally hot within the crate and I was finding it hard to breathe. On top of this, I was taken with an attack of claustrophobia. I wanted to get out, to stretch my limbs and run about like a fool. I took a grip on myself, closed my eyes, and sought to control my breathing.

All was silence for a space. I heard no cries, nor footfalls. Even the crump of explosions from without had ceased.

Then the crate was rattled like a toy in the hands of an infant, and the loudest explosion yet caused my ears to ring, and I knew for certain that the ship had suffered a direct hit. I screwed my eyes shut, waiting for the crate to be crushed by falling girders.

"We're hit!" I cried, unable to maintain my silence.

But Holmes was laughing. "I think not, my friend! Though, I admit, for a second I thought so, too. No, we have taken off. Listen…"

Oh, the calming effect of my friend's reassurance as I heard the low, constant thrum of the interplanetary ship's blasting engine as we powered away from the surface of Mars. Such was my relief that I almost wept with joy.

I wanted to be released immediately. The crate was like a coffin, and I felt a resurgence of claustrophobic panic. I wanted to look upon the comely visage of Miss Hamilton-Bell, and congratulate her, and stare out at the planet as it grew ever smaller in our wake.

The seconds ticked by; minutes elapsed. Fifteen minutes, and then thirty. I was sure that an hour had gone by, and then I was gripped by the conviction that we had been forgotten, to asphyxiate within the crate – what a way to meet one's end!

I was about to cry out, a little later, when I heard footsteps ringing along the deck of the cargo hold, and then voices. Presently came the welcome sound of tools at work on the fixings of the crate, and the lid was dislodged and electric light flooded in.

Miss Hamilton-Bell stared down at me, concern etched on her features. "Why, Dr Watson… you look all in!"

She helped me out, and then rushed around to do the same for Holmes. A Martian advanced and held out a cannister of water – bless him! – and I drank my fill and passed the cannister to Holmes. I must have presented a sorry sight to Miss Hamilton-Bell and the three Martians, beet-red of face and saturated in the juices of my own perspiration, but Miss Hamilton-Bell had more pressing matters to concern her.

"Gentlemen, the attack on the city has begun early. We were forced to take-off against regulations, and the security forces have therefore deemed this an enemy vessel and brought their cannons to bear on us. With luck they will not find our range."

She led us to an elevator plate, and we rose to an observation deck and stared out through the viewscreen.

I exclaimed in wonder.

We were high above the city of Glench-Arkana now, and we looked down on a scene of devastation. Buildings were blazing, while others were partially wrecked or demolished entirely. A hundred vehicles shuttled this way and that alongside fleeing citizens, and still bombs rained down on the city and sent up great geysers of fire and debris.

A puff of smoke appeared from nowhere in the sky to our right, followed a split second later by a great detonation and a concussion: the ship rocked in the blast wave of the near-miss, and we held on to the straps and swayed this way and that.

"They have found our range," I said. "Surely the next missile will account for us!"

"But we're outstripping their guns!" Miss Hamilton-Bell exclaimed.

I beheld another puffball of black smoke away to our right and a little below our tail fins, and then another – but she was right, the guns might have found our range, but we had powered on beyond and were making good our escape.

I stared down at the devastated city, and wondered if this might be the beginning of the end. How long might the conflict continue before the forces of Arkana were brought to their knees – and how long might the fight on Earth continue once we had joined battle with our conquerors?

The ship moved ever further away from the face of Mars, and now I could make out Glench-Arkana surrounded by swathes of crimson desert – and there, far to the west, connected by the silver filigree monorail, was the great grey disc of Hakoah-Malan. I considered the corpse within the chromium frame, and the hell Moriarty had endured for year upon year, and I thought of all the evil that the man had committed.

I glanced at Holmes. He too was staring down at the disc, and his expression was as if graven from stone and unreadable.

Presently Miss Hamilton-Bell escorted us to our cabins, where she thanked us and left us to undress. I did so wearily, and climbed into the suspension pod in anticipation of the oblivion I would enjoy for the duration of the voyage home.

# Chapter Thirty-Six

*Finale in London*

Once we had landed at Battersea docking station, our exit from the ship was effected in the same manner as we had entered: we were concealed in the packing crate and in due course processed through customs – though not without a hitch. According to Miss Hamilton-Bell, the station's security forces, alerted by word from Mars, had questioned the ship's captain long and hard as to his precipitate departure. His claim that he had been saving his ship and crew from the rebels' bombs convinced the security forces, and in due course he was allowed to unload his cargo.

After a bumpy ride across the capital, the crate was opened and we found ourselves in a basement room in the Natural History Museum. Miss Hamilton-Bell greeted us, then lifted out the valise and passed it to a young man who hurried off without a word.

She took us to her office high in the west wing of the museum and, over a welcome cup of Earl Grey, outlined the course of action the Resistance would take over the next few days. This was dependent, of course, on the success of the electromagnetic pulse generator. At eleven the next morning, an accomplice of the young man who had collected the valise would take the device aboard an air balloon and, high above London, activate the generator. Then every member of the Resistance, and the military personnel and politicians on our side, would hold their collective breath and pray that its activation had the desired effect: that every tripod and simulacrum across greater London would be disabled. Then the fightback would begin in earnest. Military leaders would send their infantrymen and fusiliers up against the Martians; the Institute at Woking would be sacked, along with the tripod manufactory and every other Martian factory and stronghold up and down the land. All across the face of the Earth, the other pulse generators that had been ferried from the red planet would be activated, in cities as widespread as New York and Sydney, Moscow and Johannesburg, and human armies would rise against the tyranny of the invaders.

"But that will only be the start," she went on. "Then will begin the long, arduous job of rebuilding, of wresting back control of what the Martians have taken from us. We are under no illusion as to the long haul we face, but the fact is that we will be masters of our own destiny once again, no longer corralled like sheep. We will be free!"

"Well said," I declared. "And if there is any way in which we can further assist the cause..."

She smiled. "You have been instrumental in our success so far, gentlemen. I suggest that after your exertions you rest for the next few days, and watch events unfold."

She thought it prudent that we did not return to our rooms in Baker Street, and suggested instead that we lodge for the time being at the safe house at Willow Avenue.

Towards six that evening we took our leave and caught a cab to Barnes, first stopping off at Baker Street to pack overnight bags and replace our timepieces taken by the Martians while we had languished in Pentonville.

At Willow Avenue we discovered that Mr Wells and Miss Fairfield had moved to another address in London, and that only Miss Lenton was in residence. Over dinner we recounted our adventures on the red planet, and after a nightcap of brandy retired to bed. Sleep that night was a long time coming. I lay awake well into the early hours, staring at the half-moon through the bedroom window, aware that we were on the eve of a momentous day in the history of the planet.

After a late breakfast the following morning, Holmes suggested that we stroll across Hampstead Heath and from Parliament Hill watch events unfold across the capital. Miss Lenton had business in Chiswick, supervising a first-aid post set up in anticipation of casualties in the forthcoming conflict, and she set off soon after breakfast. At ten we took a cab to Highgate and from there walked across the heath.

It was a perfect autumn day. The sun was warm, the sky cloudless, with just the merest hint of a breeze to offset the heat. The heath was quiet on this working day, with just a few nannies and their charges enjoying the weather, along with the odd dog-walker and the occasional old couple strolling along arm in arm.

We passed a tripod, silent and monumental, as it stood silhouetted against the sky. It was one of the multitude that were stationed around the capital, remaining *in situ* to relay their monotonous eventide refrain, "Ulla, ulla, ulla, ulla..." I considered the Martian ensconced within the cowl as he looked down upon the capital. Little did he realise what this auspicious day would bring!

We hurried past this symbol of Martian domination, and I for one gave an involuntary shiver.

We climbed the hill and settled ourselves on a bench with all London spread out before us. We saw distant, ambulatory tripods marching back and forth on patrol, and a dozen or more air-cars buzzing through the air for all the world like faraway bees. The streets of the capital were busy with pedestrians – they, like the unsuspecting tripod pilot, oblivious of the events about to take place – and trilobite cars rushed hither and thither.

At one point Holmes touched my arm and murmured, "There..."

He indicated a group of workmen in the shadow of the tripod – surely more than might be required to dig a short drainage ditch next to the path.

"And there, Watson."

An army wagon idled along Highgate Road and came to a halt beside another tripod. As we watched, several infantrymen climbed out, lit cigarettes, and stood around in groups of two or three, chatting casually.

I checked my watch. It was ten to eleven.

"I don't know about you, Holmes, but I'm dashed nervous."

"I will admit to increased cardiac activity," he said. "I wish my head could overrule my physiology. I know that all is likely to go to plan, with perhaps one or two hiccups along the way, but that irrational part of me cannot help but fear..."

"Fear what, specifically, Holmes?"

"Oh, that the Resistance has informers in its midst, and that the Martians know all about its plans."

I shook my head. "But surely they would have been cognisant of the pulse generator before now," I objected, "and apprehended us yesterday? And they would have rounded up members of the

Resistance worldwide, and we would have heard about it by now."

"I know. You are right. But so much rests on the success of the next few hours and days…"

I had not seen my friend in such a state of tension for quite a number of years, and I sought to soothe our nerves by producing my hipflask and offering him a tot. He partook, and passed the flask back to me. I smiled to myself as I thought that we might be taken as a pair of retired old codgers, whiling away the day with reminiscences and brandy.

Holmes regarded his watch. "One minute to eleven."

I counted down the seconds in my head. Beside the tripod, a workman was scrutinising his pocket watch and another was staring into the skies. The soldiers on Highgate Road had flicked their cigarette butts into the gutter and were fingering their rifles. I scanned the heavens, but could not discern the air balloon carrying the pulse generator.

Ten seconds, nine…

A tripod strode across the heath perhaps half a mile below us as the seconds counted down, and I found that I was holding my breath in anticipation.

"Two, one…" Holmes said, and gripped my forearm. "This is it!"

Nothing happened. I wondered if both our timepieces had been fast. I felt as if my heart had stopped, and I was clutched by sudden despair.

And then…

"Look!" Holmes cried.

The tripod taking great strides half a mile away seemed to hesitate all of a sudden. Its central leg, reaching forward, vibrated like the questing antennae of an insect. It failed to find a foothold and slowly, balancing precariously on two legs, it succumbed to gravity and toppled forward, its cowl striking a high wall and splitting asunder like a ripe fruit.

"And there!" I cried, pointing to where the workmen had sprung into action. One of their number was scaling the foremost leg of the stationary tripod, and when he reached the cowl he inserted some small device into an orifice and shinned back down with inordinate haste. The rest of his fellows retreated into the cover of nearby bushes and a second later the bomb exploded. The tripod toppled, crashing through trees and bushes, and the workmen fell upon the Martian struggling from the wreckage and beat it to death with pickaxes and sledgehammers.

The air was rent on every side with more explosions than I could count. The soldiers in Hampstead had set up a mortar and launched a missile at the nearby tripod, scoring a direct hit. The cowl blazed and its hapless pilot squealed his death agonies as the tripod slowly toppled.

All across the heath, men and women were running to and fro, quite startled by the violence. It must have seemed, to the ignorant citizen, as if all hell had broken loose. We sat on our bench, leaning forward and taking in the spectacle before us; we had, as it were, a ringside view, voyeurs to an orgy of violence that saw our Martian overlords opposed by those they thought quite cowed. Not that they did not fight back, however. As we watched, we saw several tripods firing their heat-rays upon innocent crowds even as they swayed out of control; we saw men and women die in flames, these victims little comforted that, soon after, their persecutors fell to earth to be set upon by angry, vengeful mobs. Some tripods ran amok, demolishing buildings in their path, and crowds took to the streets in a bid to escape.

We learned later that the effects of the pulse generator had reached as far as Staines in the west and the Isle of Sheppey to the east, as far north as Brentford and south to Guildford. In other cities up and down the land, Resistance members had fought the Martians, bringing down tripods and Martian air-cars with rockets and mortars, though these brave souls had suffered many casualties, and the Martians had taken much longer to defeat. Indeed, in Glasgow the fight was still going on one week later, with scattered cells of fighters scurrying like rats in the ruins of their city and striking the Martians with well-planned hit-and-run attacks.

Across the world, bands of rebels attacked the Martians in cities as far-flung as Delhi and Tokyo, Cairo and Buenos Aires – with the aid of the pulse generators and without. Great gains were made in the days that followed, with a hundred thousand Martians slaughtered and just as many taken prisoner. Not that the rout was universal, however. We learned from special editions of *The Times*, put out by presses no longer under the censorship of the Martians, that the aliens had fought back successfully in Toronto and Rabat, though military assistance was being rushed in to these benighted cities from New York and Tunis respectively.

At three o'clock, with the city still and smoking before us, Holmes suggested that we make our way back to Barnes.

A strange atmosphere prevailed all across London: few citizens were venturing out, and still fewer cars – and no cabs – were abroad. From time to time we came across people who had come to stare at the scene of devastation, the burned-out buildings and the broken mains where tripods had fought back, the shattered pipes sending geysers fifty feet into the air. Here and there we happened upon knots of first-aiders giving succour to the hurt and lame, and I stopped and gave assistance where I could. Everywhere we came upon toppled tripods like swatted insects with their iron limbs sprawling. In every instance the Martian pilots within the cowls had died on impact or been summarily put to death by Resistance fighters, and their noisome cadavers hung from the wreckage of their machines or lay in the streets, their flesh picked at by scavenging crows and magpies.

On Chelsea embankment we happened upon the first simulacrum casualty we had seen that day. On the pathway of a Georgian townhouse I saw the prostrate figure of a well-dressed gentlemen, his entire body twitching in what I thought at the time to be some kind of fit. Holmes and I rushed to his side. He lay on this back, staring into the sky with open eyes, the muscles of his face pulled by a hundred ghastly spasms and his limbs jumping inhumanly. He was evidently still alive and yet, when I felt for his pulse, I found none.

Holmes laid a hand on my arm and murmured what I had belatedly come to realise, "A simulacrum, Watson."

He reached into the fellow's frock coat and, after a moment's search, found a wallet and within it a card.

"He is – or rather was – Sir Humphrey Grenville."

As I stared down at the simulacrum's twitching visage, I mourned the passing of the original Sir Humphrey, who knows how long ago.

We later learned that, worldwide, the pulse generators had accounted for the deaths – or rather, the deactivation – of over a hundred thousand simulacra. In Great Britain alone ten thousand perished that day, and we heard many a sad story of distraught spouses and family members discovering palsied simulacra, only to learn much later that their loved ones had died at the hands of the Martians months, and sometimes years, previously.

We left the simulacrum of Sir Humphrey Grenville in its

death throes and continued on our way.

It was almost five when we finally arrived at Willow Avenue, thoroughly exhausted by the long walk and by all we had beheld. Miss Lenton returned a little later, a bloodied bandage spanning her forehead. Ministering to others at the first-aid station at Chiswick, she and another nurse had been struck by shrapnel from a tripod exploding nearby. Despite her injuries, however, she was elated with how the fight had gone. I gave her a thorough examination, finding her wounds superficial and gratified that she was not concussed, and ordered her to bed with a sedative.

At six, just as we were finishing a roast beef sandwich and were about to leave the house in order to lend our help at the nearest first-aid station, the telephone bell shrilled.

Holmes picked up the receiver and spoke briefly to the caller, then replaced it and turned to me.

"That was Miss Hamilton-Bell," he said. "She is at the Martian Embassy."

"The embassy?" I said in surprise.

"She wishes to see us," he went on. "Or, rather, the ambassador would like to speak to us."

"Upon my word," I exclaimed. "Whatever can the devil want?"

"We shall find out presently, Watson. She is sending a car to pick us up."

It was almost seven o'clock by the time a cab arrived at Barnes, collected Holmes and myself, and made its slow way back through the shattered streets of central London. Already, I was cheered to see, citizens were at work clearing the debris and making right the damage. Firefighters were putting out the last of the blazes, and a public house, its windows shattered, had a chalked sign outside proclaiming: *Business as Usual.*

We arrived at the embassy to find a toppled tripod blocking the drive, its cowl shattered like a gourd, and we were forced to step over its extended limbs and proceed on foot.

A cordon of police surrounded the building, keeping a curious though silent crowd of onlookers at bay. We gave our names to a sergeant and were duly escorted inside.

Miss Hamilton-Bell was pacing the foyer, and smiled when we approached. "Mr Holmes, Dr Watson." She was beaming. "All is well. Indeed, events have proceeded beyond my wildest expectations. The Martians have almost capitulated – well, here in Britain, that is. The fight still goes on abroad, but the news that is coming in is good."

"You mentioned that the ambassador wishes to speak with us," Holmes said.

"Just so. He is upstairs in his office, under armed guard."

"Do you know what the deuce he wants?" I asked as we hurried up the curving staircase.

"I am afraid not, Doctor," she said. "He refused to say."

I was a little apprehensive as we crossed to the double doors, outside which a constable stood to attention. He saluted and opened the door to allow us entry.

The Martian ambassador stood before the window, his back to us. Three armed soldiers, their weapons drawn, occupied the room beside himself.

Miss Hamilton-Bell cleared her throat. "Ambassador," she said. "Mr Holmes and Dr Watson…"

The alien turned, or rather shuffled around to face us. Gone was the braggadocio with which he had last confronted us, in the wagon to Pentonville Gaol. Now he seemed to sag, and his vast dark eyes were lacklustre. He moved slowly towards the desk, steadied himself with a tentacle against its side, and stared at us.

"Mr Holmes, Dr Watson," he said at last, in barely a croak. "We meet in somewhat altered circumstances."

"You wished to see us," Holmes said brusquely. "I suggest you state your reason."

"Just to... to..." For a second, it seemed that his command of our language had failed him. He cast about for the words with which to express himself, then went on, "Just to say that Professor Moriarty was correct in all he had to say about you, Mr Holmes."

I glanced at my friend. Holmes maintained his aloofness as he asked, "And what, pray, was that?"

"I made a point of meeting Moriarty when I returned to Mars in the early years," the ambassador said, "and we had long and interesting conversations. Your name often came up. He held ambivalent emotions towards you, Mr Holmes. While he reviled you, he admitted to a grudging respect. Indeed, he told me that you, and only you, among the many teeming millions of your planet, were his equal; that only you possessed the qualities of intelligence and rationality required to rival his own." At this point the ambassador made an odd grating sound in his V-shaped mouth, and I wondered if it were a rueful chuckle.

"It is a great pity," he went on, "that we did not suborn you to our cause, Mr Holmes – though I suppose we did attempt to, somewhat belatedly, in duplicating you with the simulacrum."

"Which, I am glad to say," Holmes put in, "failed signally."

"I should have heeded Moriarty's words and realised that you would be a foe amongst foes. But the fact is that I underestimated you, and paid the price. I am given to understand that the professor is dead, killed by your own hands."

Holmes stared at the alien, and it was some time before he

inclined his head. "That is so, yes," he said.

"I often received the impression," the ambassador went on, "that Moriarty wanted me to end his suffering, but was too proud to beg."

"And you, knowing this full well, in your cruelty elected to prolong the hell of his existence."

"He was valuable to us…" the ambassador said.

At this, Holmes sneered. "No, ambassador. You had his simulacra – you could well have ended his suffering, but in your sadism you elected not to. And to think," he went on, shaking his head, "that your downfall might have been averted if only you had granted Moriarty his wishes all those years ago: territory of his own on Earth, and a chosen few over which to rule. But no, in your lust for power you denied him this, imprisoned him and copied him and cruelly used his knowledge. And in so doing, ambassador, you turned him against you. In the end, he had only one option left to him – to help bring about the end of your tyranny on Earth."

The Martian swayed. "He?" he said, confused. "*He* brought about…?"

"He liaised with the Resistance movement here on Earth, and worked with the Korshanan people to develop the pulse generator, and had Watson and myself deliver it–"

"No!" the ambassador cried, leaning against the desk for support.

Holmes made for the door, and there turned and addressed the Martian for the very last time. "I wish you a long life, ambassador. A long life in which to reflect upon the fact that your personal cruelty was the root cause of your ultimate defeat. Good day to you."

Whereupon Holmes swept from the room, leaving the Martian ambassador calling after him feebly in his own ugly tongue.

\* \* \*

Two days later I invited a few friends to our rooms in Baker Street.

Miss Freya Hamilton-Bell was present, exhausted from her never-ending duties with the Resistance, but exultant at how the course of events was playing out. Chesterton and Shaw had come out of hiding to celebrate with us, and I remembered to buy beer for Chesterton and carrot juice for Shaw. I located Mr Wells and Miss Fairfield at her apartment in Chelsea, tired but elated after taking part in the rebellion two days earlier. Miss Lenton hurried over from her nursing duties at Chiswick, her head wound now almost healed. Mrs Hudson had laid on a cold spread, and a warm autumn breeze blew in through the open windows of our sitting room as we sat about drinking and discussing the events of the past few days.

Miss Hamilton-Bell relayed the news from Resistance cells around the world: the Martians were virtually defeated in America and Russia, though in China and South America the fight continued. All around the globe, the countries which had succeeded in banishing the Martian scourge were lending arms and munitions to those still at war with the invaders.

"As well as repelling the Martians," she reported, "the war has achieved the not inconsiderable benefit of bringing nations together which might before have been at loggerheads, and so creating a commonwealth of people with like-minded aims and ambitions to build upon in future."

Chesterton hoisted his pint glass and drank to that.

"And those Martians who survived the fight, like the ambassador," I asked, "what of these?"

"They are being rounded up as we speak, Doctor, and shipped

back to their own planet, where they will find themselves in Korshanan custody."

"And the fight on Mars?" Miss Fairfield asked.

Miss Hamilton-Bell smiled. "I am happy to report good news on that front, too. Word has reached the Martian Embassy, via the sub-space communicator: due to the fact that Arkanan resources were stretched to their limits in making fast their grip on Earth, they were complacent in defending their equatorial territories. The Korshana have made great gains, capturing the major cities of Glench-Arkana and Lavat-Lantana. Even as we speak, peace treaties are being drawn up between their races, and I look forward to the day when we can welcome Korshanan delegates to our planet in the spirit of peace."

"Well said," Shaw called out.

Holmes, in a mood of abstraction, had moved to the window and was staring out at the small red point of Mars rising through the twilit sky.

"A penny for them, Holmes?" I said.

He turned like an actor upon a stage and addressed the gathering. "Who would have believed, my friends, that in the closing years of the nineteenth century this world was being watched so closely by intelligences greater than our own, and yet just as mortal? Who would have guessed that, as we went about our business, we were being scrutinised and studied like specimens under a microscope? And who would have thought, given all the terror that has befallen our benighted land, that it would end as it has?"

Wells raised his glass to this. "Do you know, Holmes, I've been thinking of penning an account of all this horrendous business, the war between our worlds. And if I might borrow from your soliloquy...?"

Holmes smiled. "Feel free," he said.

I recharged our glasses and Holmes proposed a toast.

"To victory, and to peace," he said.

We raised our glasses.

"To victory," we said, "and to peace!"

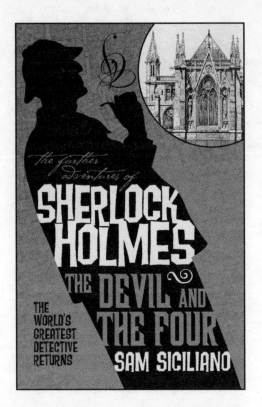

## THE FURTHER ADVENTURES
## OF SHERLOCK HOLMES

# THE DEVIL AND THE FOUR

*Sam Siciliano*

Sherlock Holmes's latest case takes him to the heart of Paris, in pursuit of Marguerite Hardy, a mysterious Frenchwoman who fled her English home when she received a strange letter. Desperate for her safe return, her husband begs for Holmes's help. But Holmes's investigations will take him and his cousin, Henry Vernier, into a world of theft, seduction and betrayal – and uncover a secret that has been buried for twenty years.

ISBN: 9781785657023

# AVAILABLE NOW!

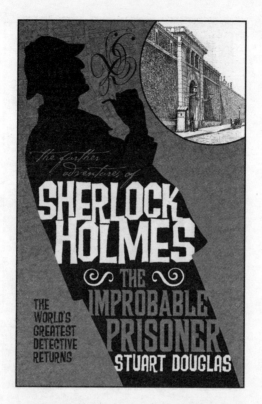

THE FURTHER ADVENTURES
OF SHERLOCK HOLMES

# THE IMPROBABLE PRISONER

*Stuart Douglas*

Following a summons to a fictional patient, Dr Watson finds himself
arrested for the horrific murder of an elderly woman. Imprisoned and
with the evidence against him, Watson's only hope is that Sherlock
Holmes can discover the identity of the real killer. But when a
mysterious letter appears to link Watson to blackmail and a notorious
street gang, Holmes must use all his powers of reasoning to save his
friend from the hangman's noose.

ISBN: 9781785656293

## AVAILABLE NOW!

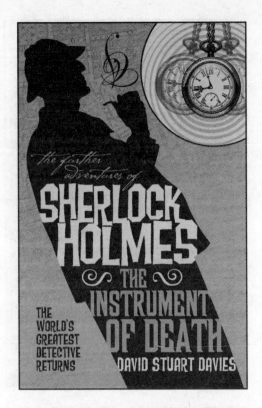

THE FURTHER ADVENTURES
OF SHERLOCK HOLMES

# THE INSTRUMENT OF DEATH

*David Stuart Davies*

A society lady staged the theft of a priceless ruby and tried to frame
her husband – but just as Holmes reveals the truth, she is found
murdered. Holmes deduces that this is no crime of passion, but the
work of a ruthless killer with no connection to the jewel. With reports
of a man in a strange, trance-like state, Holmes finds himself entangled
in a dangerous game of cat and mouse with the sinister Dr Caligari...

ISBN: 9781785658488

# AVAILABLE NOW!

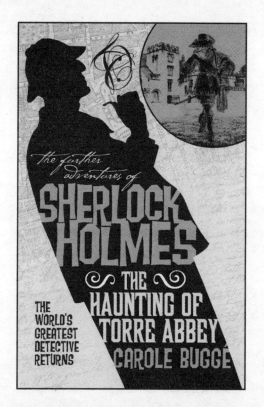

## THE FURTHER ADVENTURES
## OF SHERLOCK HOLMES

# THE HAUNTING OF TORRE ABBEY

*Carole Buggé*

Sherlock Holmes receives a request for aid from Lord Cary, whose
family home, Torre Abbey, is seemingly haunted. While sceptical,
Holmes believes that the Carys are in danger, a belief that proves
horrifyingly accurate when a household member dies mysteriously.
Holmes and Watson must uncover the secrets of the abbey if they are
to have any hope of protecting the living and avenging the dead.

ISBN: 9781785655821

# AVAILABLE NOW!

For more fantastic fiction, author events, competitions,
limited editions and more

VISIT OUR WEBSITE
**titanbooks.com**

LIKE US ON FACEBOOK
**facebook.com/titanbooks**

FOLLOW US ON TWITTER
**@TitanBooks**

EMAIL US
**readerfeedback@titanemail.com**